"I want to do something." She leaned into him and heard his indrawn breath.

Then he shut his eyes. "Victoria. I know you mean well. When I first met you, I doubted you could even polish a fork. I can see you care for the children, but caring isn't enough." He paused and opened his eyes again. "Even love isn't enough. Ranching is a tough life. It's not meant for families."

His voice hitched as he continued, "Please leave, Victoria. I don't want the children hurt. I don't want to be—" He cut off his hoarse words.

She reached out and touched his chest. The cotton was rough, durable, the muscles beneath firm. It was as if she could trust this man with her life. He seemed so salt-of-the-earth dependable. Hardworking stock. She had to shut her eyes for a moment, for surely he was stealing her focus. "I can help. I can learn to do—"

He took her wrist and pushed her hand down. "No, you can't help. Now leave before I do something stupid."

She leaned closer. "Like letting me try?"

He shook his head. "No, like kissing you."

Barbara Phinney was born in England and raised in Canada. After she retired from the Canadian Armed Forces, Barbara turned her hand to romance writing. The thrill of adventure and her love of happy endings, coupled with a too-active imagination, have merged to help her create this and other wonderful stories. Barbara spends her days writing, building her dream home with her husband and enjoying their fast-growing children.

Books by Barbara Phinney

Love Inspired Historical

Bound to the Warrior
Protected by the Warrior
Sheltered by the Warrior
The Nanny Solution

Love Inspired Suspense

Desperate Rescue
Keeping Her Safe
Deadly Homecoming
Fatal Secrets
Silent Protector

Visit the Author Profile page at Harlequin.com for more titles.

BARBARA PHINNEY

The Nanny Solution

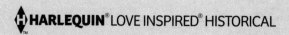
HARLEQUIN® LOVE INSPIRED® HISTORICAL

Recycling programs
for this product may
not exist in your area.

LOVE INSPIRED BOOKS

ISBN-13: 978-0-373-28368-2

The Nanny Solution

www.Harlequin.com

Printed in U.S.A.

When pride cometh, then cometh shame:
but with the lowly is wisdom.
—*Proverbs* 11:2

Dedicated to Kate Kelly,
a great author and even better friend.
You will be sadly missed.

Chapter One

Boston, 1882

Victoria Templeton sank into the Queen Anne chair. Her mouth fell open in a most unfeminine manner as she gaped up at her pacing, overwrought mother. "What do you mean, 'we're broke'?"

Abigail Templeton-Smith continued to pace, all the while wringing her black handkerchief. When the maid entered the front room with afternoon tea, the older woman flicked the small black square, essentially shooing away both the girl and the refreshments.

Victoria's attention then settled on her mother's gown. The mourning outfit was terribly outdated, its black bombazine dull in the barely lit room with the window curtains drawn tight. Where was the tasteful mourning suit Mother had worn just yesterday? The last time this old thing saw any use was when they'd buried Victoria's father, ten years past. "Mother? What's really going on?"

"Must I repeat it? We're broke!" Abigail dropped onto the settee and plucked at the skirt of her outfit. "I had to dig this old thing out because I gave all but one of my mourning clothes to Bess."

Her mother's maid? "Why?"

"She found a buyer over on Tremont Street. An actress from Chickering Hall, in fact, who approached me last week, saying my mourning outfits would add to an upcoming play. Can you imagine the cheek of that woman? I brushed her off at the time, but after I saw Mr. Lacewood, well, I sent Bess to see her…"

Victoria struggled to follow her mother's words. Mr. Lacewood had been her stepfather's solicitor, but what did he have to do with her mother's mourning outfits?

"…and she was able to get a pretty penny for them. Naturally, I retained this old thing for when I'm at home and one good one for—"

"Why on earth did you sell your mourning clothes?" Victoria interrupted, all the while trying to refrain from gaping unbecomingly at her mother.

"Do not interrupt. It's terribly ill-mannered." Abigail blinked before finishing her tale. "As for why, well, I did it for a train ticket!"

"Where are we going?"

Her mother looked away. "Not we, Victoria. Me. I'm going down to the Carolinas to stay with your aunt Eugenia until this dreadful mess blows over."

Victoria wanted to remind her mother that the "dreadful mess" was her second husband's recent suicide. But since the marriage hadn't been a happy union, what else would her mother call it?

Still, something else was terribly wrong. Her mother had never been a loving woman who'd defend her only child to the death, but would she really abandon her own daughter? Would she plan her departure even before

Charles was cold in the ground? Yes, Boston was talking about his suicide, and yes, Victoria had yet to shed a tear for the oily character, but his death was hardly a "dreadful mess."

Victoria moved to sit down beside her mother, her back straight, thanks to her corset, and her expression as firm as the bustle that she'd pulled up behind her. "I want the truth, Mother. You've just told me we're broke and that you're leaving. I know you met with Mr. Lacewood this morning about Charles's affairs. And this?" She flicked at her mother's skirt, receiving in return a sharp glare. "I can't believe you still have this, let alone have it on. Now, Mother, it's time for the whole truth. Every last detail."

Though Victoria was only twenty, she had inherited her father's sensibilities instead of her mother's shallow neediness. She loved her mother but couldn't deny that the woman who'd given birth to her was not known for her warmth and compassion.

Her mother edged away. "Charles had some heavy gambling debts. Ones that must be paid."

"Gambling debts! Why must they be paid if Charles commit—" She cut off her own words. No need to constantly repeat the words that were the unfortunate reality.

Abigail's voice fell to a whisper. "I gave him control over your estate. I'd given him everything. It isn't good form for a woman to deal with finances and we both know that Charles proved me wrong whenever I made a suggestion about money."

Victoria wanted to interject that apparently Charles was the one who was proved wrong in the end, but the bitter comment lodged in her throat. There was no good reason to point out the obvious, and Mother was shamed enough.

"Charles said that profit could be made with the right investments." Abigail's voice hitched as she continued, "A month ago, he promised me we would see changes in the investments. Only then did I suspect what type of 'investments' they really were."

Victoria gasped. "What were they?"

"He was gambling. Heavily, I'm afraid." Abigail's chin wrinkled, her cheeks flamed. "Mr. Lacewood said, considering how he'd spent more than we owned, the best thing would be to liquidate the estate."

"Whose estate?"

Her mother said nothing.

Victoria smacked the settee beside her, causing the older woman to jump. "Mine! Given to me by my father for my future! Wasted because you think it unseemly for a woman to handle her own finances! Mother, how could you?"

"I had no idea he was gambling!"

With an unfeminine snort, Victoria stormed to the window and shoved open the curtains to let in the weakening October sun. While in mourning, one kept the draperies closed, but Victoria couldn't stand the dimness.

Then remembering that a good deal of the fine local population strolled past at this time of the day, she hastily yanked the drapes back together. Best not to appear unseemly. The black wreath on the front door of their Federal-style town house had limited their visitors. And thankfully, her mother had insisted on a small funeral. Just as well, considering the cause of death. Suddenly the white crepe at the neck of Victoria's black dress all but choked her. Oh, she couldn't wait to be free of this thing! Surely six months of mourning a thief was overdone.

A thief! She spun and pushed her hands against her hips. "Now we have nothing?"

Abigail sniffed. "I was as shocked as you are."

"So shocked he stole from us that you came home and sold all of your mourning outfits for a train ticket south."

"Not all of them and don't make it sound so horrible, please. I saved one good outfit for when I travel."

"First class, I assume."

At the acid tone, Abigail bit her lip, but didn't look up. "I can't be seen traveling second class out of Boston. Please don't make a fuss, Victoria. This house and the summer home in Portland will be put up for sale immediately." Abigail finally looked up with a hollow expression. "And please don't solicit your friends for money. Allow me to leave Boston gracefully. I need to be gone before the ad is published."

"What about Francis? He could help, surely?"

Abigail shook her head. "No. You two weren't engaged yet. Charles had promised he would make the arrangements, but he didn't and I dare not ask now. Francis's father doesn't tolerate this kind of disgrace. He's a Brahmin, after all." She let out a shaky sigh. "We'll never be able to secure a decent marriage for you here."

Victoria blinked. It had been her hope to marry into Boston's highest class. Surely Francis would help; after all, their families had been considering a marriage between them. But even as she thought that, she knew the truth. Dutiful Francis would want nothing except to maintain propriety. He'd told Victoria decency and honor were values on which the United States were built. To discard them would be discarding all patriotism.

"What am I to do, Mother?" Victoria asked quietly. "Have you given any thought to me?"

Abigail's expression softened and she leaned forward, all the while patting the space beside her on the settee. Victoria refused to comply. "My dear, if I could take you, I would. But Eugenia is trying to find good matches for your unruly cousins. Each is bent on having a career first, then after that, choosing their own husband."

"That's not a new idea, Mother."

"At least you were going to allow us to arrange your marriage."

Of course. Why wouldn't she? The men in the circles Victoria frequented were wealthy, Brahmin men with long, drawling accents and Old World charm. Who wouldn't want to marry into that lifestyle? Victoria knew little of her cousins, but she could read the writing on the wall here. Aunt Eugenia was afraid of competition. And her mother would never risk her invitation by arriving with Victoria.

She swallowed. *Dear Lord in heaven, what am I to do?* Then she asked her mother in a quiet, wobbly voice, "When do you leave?"

Abigail stood. "This coming Saturday."

Three days hence, for it was Wednesday today. "And me, Mother? If the house is to be sold, where am I to go? Have you considered me in any of this?"

Abigail bit her lip. "I have thought of you, Victoria. I really have. Last week, after I received Walter's condolences, I wired him. I received his telegram this morning."

Victoria had met her mother's older brother once, at her mother's second wedding, but barely remembered him. He lived in some western frontier town. Mother claimed he was making his fortune there.

"Your uncle says he'll take you in."

She immediately bristled. "Like an old maid?"

"I'm so sorry for all of this." Abigail found her black handkerchief and dabbed her eyes. "It was a mistake to allow Charles to handle the finances. I see that now."

Victoria hesitated. For all her faults, Abigail was still her mother. She hated to see her own flesh and blood on the verge of tears. "I'll need some money for the train fare."

Abigail walked to the sideboard and opened her purse. "Walter wired to say that he can send you money. I didn't want to ask for myself, but for you…"

Victoria stiffened. "I won't take charity, least of all from a relative I don't know."

"He's your uncle!" Abigail tossed a swift look at Victoria. "He thinks it will work out well."

Victoria stilled. She knew her mother. Something else was amiss. "Why would he think that? He hasn't had any contact with us. What's going on?"

Abigail held out the telegram. "Walter suggested you may take a liking to his business partner, who is a widower. It would keep the business in the family. Your uncle says he will send some money so you can travel in comfort. You'll need to look your best when you arrive and first class has very nice Pullman cars."

Snatching the telegram, Victoria flicked it open. "So I can be purchased for the price of a first-class ticket?"

Abigail stiffened. "You're not going to find anyone here who will take you in for the long term. That's just the way it is."

Victoria sagged. Her mother was right, at least about

accepting her Uncle Walter's offer of accommodation. "Fine. I'll go. But I'll ask Mr. Lacewood for a loan. Once I'm out West, I'll find a way to repay him."

"Borrowing from our solicitor? We already owe him! He's settling Charles's affairs discreetly."

Within Victoria, irritation swelled again. Her mother had allowed Charles to ruin them, but *she* wasn't allowed to borrow train fare from their solicitor? "I'll be sure to thank him for his discretion." She swept from the front room.

Her mother hurried behind her. "You mustn't ask him for money. That's too embarrassing!"

Bent on ignoring her, Victoria scooped up her small purse and threw open the front door. But her exit was blocked.

A tall man stood at the door, his knuckles raised to knock on the wood above the wreath. And down the few steps behind him were four children of varying heights, all staring at her.

Mitch MacLeod dropped his hand. The slender, black-garbed woman who'd flung open the door glared at him. Perhaps rightly so. He was a disgrace. His suit needed ironing, and he hadn't had the time today to even shave. He was only thirty, but this afternoon he probably looked fifty. He cleared his throat as he removed his Stetson. "Miss Victoria Templeton?"

An older woman hurried up behind the young woman. For a few stalled seconds, he stood there, waiting for the younger to answer.

"I am she." Those words sounded more like a challenge than a confirmation. "And you are...?"

"My name is Mitchell MacLeod. I need the services

of a woman—" He cleared his throat again. "I mean, I would like to employ a young woman to assist my family as we travel west. My solicitor, Robert Lacewood, suggested you, since you were planning a trip out West, anyway."

The woman, Victoria, swung her glare over her shoulder. Just by looking at the pair, Mitch could tell they were mother and daughter, with the younger one's fine, dark blond hair a shinier version of her mother's. But Victoria's expression was hardly respectful.

The older woman, the recently widowed Mrs. Abigail Templeton-Smith, he presumed, cringed as she spoke to her daughter. "I may have let that slip this morning, but Mr. Lacewood would have guessed your, ahem, need."

"Say it, Mother. My need for money. Well, let's hope Mr. Lacewood's discretion lasts through the sale of the house."

Mitch looked up the front facade. He would have never considered searching for a nanny in one of these fancy brownstones, but he trusted Lacewood. The man had been honest yet prudent with his wife's affairs, he thought, remembering the squalling infant he'd left in a nurse's care for the afternoon.

His gut clenched. His own children now stood obediently behind him. The marriage between the children's parents had been a convenient arrangement, but neither he nor Agnes had put their hearts into it. Still, Agnes had trained their children well. Would she have done the same for the infant, had she not died in childbirth?

Focusing back on the women in front of him, Mitch decided to explain the immediate need. His time was short. "Miss Templeton, Mr. Lacewood thought you were planning a trip out to Proud Bend, Colorado. It's close to my ranch. I have need of a woman who can assist me, and in return, I'll pay for her fare."

He tried a hopeful, earnest expression. "Perhaps we can discuss this inside?" He knew little of this class, but he presumed socialites never chatted at the front door. He'd realized as he'd climbed the steps that he was taking a huge chance that this Victoria Templeton would accept employment, but Lacewood had seemed optimistic. Mitch glanced around as Victoria stepped back from the door to allow him entrance. They owned this house yet needed money? Could they be spendthrifts? Perhaps. Who was he to know this sex?

No one, he thought, bitter pride blossoming on his tongue. He was a rancher, after all. Ranchers focused on their herd, not on figuring out fickle women.

Victoria led him, with his children in tow, into the front room. She marched straight to a small bell, which she rang. A woman in a uniform appeared, and refreshments were ordered. The mother stopped at the parlor entrance and looked down at his brood, as if noticing an appalling sample of vermin for the first time. Then, with a short sigh, she strode to the settee and sat down.

"Have a seat, Mr. MacLeod." Victoria offered him a fussy chair while she chose to sit beside her mother. "Do you drink tea?"

"I can." Mitch hadn't come to fiddle with dainty teacups and tiny biscuits, but if it was needed to secure help, so be it. He glanced over at his children, who hovered at the door to this fancy room, lost little souls that they were. With a short nod, he indicated for them to enter and sit, although Matthew, his oldest, remained standing, as if on guard. Mary shared a nearby armless chair with her brother, John, while the youngest in tow, Ralph, sat cross-legged on the floor in front of them, his dark brown curls bouncing as he looked around. Their eyes widened to saucers when the tea and biscuits arrived. But when the older woman offered them nothing, they thankfully stayed silent.

Following his gaze, Victoria looked over at the children. Mitch knew she'd caught the very small shake of his head that warned them not to beg. Her attention darted back to her mother, who, ignoring all else, supervised her maid as she filled each cup.

Clicking her tongue, Victoria snatched the tiered silver tray of sweets and marched over to the children. "Your hands."

They gaped at her. "Hold out your hands," she revised.

They all obeyed. Mitch shut his eyes. Ralph's grubby paws would need a good scouring. The boy could find dirt in heaven, he was sure. But, ignoring the state of the children's hands, Victoria dropped two biscuits into each outstretched palm.

In turn, each child whispered a polite thank-you.

"Miss Templeton, I need help," Mitch said when Victoria returned the tray to the table between them and sat down again. "I have to return to my ranch, and as good as my children are, they need a woman while traveling out there, especially considering two of the five are girls."

Victoria glanced again at the children. Even her mother, who'd been busy looking down her nose at the whole situation, also turned. It was Victoria who spoke. "You have four children, and only one of them is a girl."

"The baby, Emily, is in the care of a nurse right now."

"And your wife, Mr. MacLeod? Where is she? Is she still in her confinement?"

Mitch's jaw tightened. "She died in childbirth a month

ago. September 4, to be exact. I'm hoping to take the children to our ranch, the one I've been building for my family."

It was all he would say on the subject. For, no matter what, he would not reveal the truth about Emily's unknown paternity.

Your pride will be your downfall, Mitch. Don't go thinking it will serve you well. When pride cometh, then cometh shame.

The pastor of the church in Proud Bend, the town closest to his ranch, had spoken the warning before Mitch had left for Boston to collect his family, now that his new ranch was ready. Mitch had also boasted that he would pay off his mortgage within two years, and that he would then have the finest beef cattle within view of Castle Rock. What awaited him here—his wife's death, the unexpected child—had brought the pastor's words into sharp focus.

He pushed aside the memory. It would serve no good purpose to dwell on things that brought shame.

"No mother?" Her eyes widening, Victoria interrupted his thoughts. "Poor things." Her brows then knitted together as she looked over at him. "My condolences."

"Thank you. Yes, it has been difficult on them." *And me, in a way you'll never know.* Mitch tightened his jaw, holding himself back from saying something that might reveal the betrayal still coursing through him. "Lacewood is seeing to my late wife's final affairs, for I need to return to my ranch. And I can't do so without a woman to assist me. Are you going out West, Miss Templeton? I can pay for your fare and a small stipend in return for your assistance."

It sounded a foolish thing to say, but Lacewood had

suggested those exact words. "The trip is broken up by switching engines and lines, but it's remarkably fast, only three days, two nights," Mitch added, hoping the solicitor's optimism hadn't been misplaced.

Victoria's mother shook her head. "I'm sorry, Mr. MacLeod, but my daughter's fare is already taken care of."

"I'll take it."

Both her mother and Mitch looked to Victoria. She folded her arms. "My fare *hasn't* been purchased yet."

The older woman looked aghast. "But you need to travel first class, Victoria. You need to look your best when you arrive. You won't get any rest helping this man."

Knowing he was being ignored, Mitch spoke up. "I can't afford first class, but I'm told you'll get your rest. It's a second-class car, but it's a Pullman sleeper one."

He couldn't guarantee rest. He just said that because dropping the fancy Pullman name might help his cause, although that company no longer made those second-class sleepers, he'd been told. They would travel in an older model.

The mother gasped. "Second class! That will never do!"

Victoria, however, smiled sweetly at him. Too sweetly. "I said I'll take the job. When do we leave?"

Chapter Two

The young porter hefted Victoria's bags off the damp platform. The early morning's cold drizzle reflected the mood of the day. Victoria looked sidelong at the four children staring at her from under the cover of the train depot's narrow overhang, each clutching one small bag. She cringed. Her maid had managed to pare her luggage down to four pieces, but they seemed huge compared to everyone else's. Yet she needed it all, and she hadn't even packed a mourning dress.

And why should she? She refused the convention of grieving the man who'd ruined her life. What she wore today was conservative in style and color and quite expensive. It was more than suitable.

Her mother had taken six bags with her. Her departure yesterday had been surprisingly difficult for Victoria, despite the discontent between them and the fact that Mother had come and gone in Victoria's life several times. With her need for the cool air of Portland in August or the warmth of the Carolinas in February, she was always leaving Victoria in the care of a nanny, but this time their parting was different. Their home must be sold. Discreetly, of course, the assets liquidated as per Mr. Lacewood's instructions, after consultation with an investor. The staff would be let go, each with a glowing letter of recommendation.

Victoria took one lamenting look down the platform, wondering if she'd see any friends. She recognized no one. A blessing, really, she told herself, all the while fighting disappointment. Mother had asked that this dreadful affair be completed as quickly and quietly as possible and such meant no one must know they were slipping out of town in disgrace.

Once she was settled in Colorado, she would write to the few women she called friends and explain everything. Perhaps by then, time might have softened the emotions roiling through her.

And Francis? Would he call before the harvest soiree that his mother was to host? Shouldn't she write to him, too? Abigail had not invited his family to Charles's funeral. Victoria clenched her jaw. Honestly, a funeral shouldn't require invitations as though it were some exclusive fete. All she could do now was hope that Francis would not call to an empty house.

Oh, who was she trying to convince? She and Francis had shared only a trio of engagements. Not one word in their conversations had ever suggested that he'd been interested enough to come calling. They owed each other nothing.

Which was what Victoria had right now, apart from a few small coins in her purse. Once the young porter had finished stowing all her bags save the one she'd asked to be made readily available, she dropped one coin into his palm as she thanked him. He nodded.

With an edgy exhalation, Victoria watched the porter

disappear. What was she going to do when her money was gone? She had good secretarial skills, because of her education, but Walter was expecting her to trade his charity for a marriage to his partner. Mother had married Charles out of convenience. What had that done for her? It had turned her into a poor relation. Victoria firmed her shoulders. Marriage to a stranger? No. As soon as she arrived in Proud Bend, she'd start looking for clerical work.

Her heart lurched at the bitter humiliation.

A sturdy breeze rolled down the platform, bringing with it the foul, oily smoke from the locomotive and forcing Victoria closer to the children to prevent her lovely traveling outfit from catching the soot.

It was a dark green skirt suit in a quiet style suitable for the day. The bustle was small and the tailored waistcoat with its unobtrusive buttons could fit both mourning and traveling. She battled the filthy breeze that seemed determined to lift her skirt.

Victoria searched the platform again. It would soon be time to board. Mr. MacLeod had asked her to be here at 7:45 a.m. sharp, a good half hour before the train was to leave this Sunday morning. Indeed, his children were here, standing dutifully against the wall, staring at her as if expecting her to vanish in a puff of smoke.

"Miss Templeton?"

She turned and found Matthew holding out her small change purse. He was nearly as tall as she was. "You dropped this."

She patted down the small hidden pocket in her skirt and found it empty. Then, accepting the coin purse, she smiled. "Thank you. I wouldn't want to lose this. It's all I have."

The young boy's bland expression didn't change.

Poor mites. Their mother had entered a hospital and had not returned. Victoria couldn't blame them for expecting her to disappear, as well. She peered once more up and down the platform. Had their father decided that he couldn't handle the stress of caring for all these children? He hadn't struck her as that type when they'd met at the brownstone, but what did she know about men? They could all have a bit of that slick behavior her stepfather had shown.

"Where is your father?" she asked Matthew.

"He's gone to get the baby."

"Oh." She consulted the large clock that hung from the rafters. "The train leaves in fifteen minutes. Do you have the tickets?"

Matthew shook his head. Gripping her purse tighter, Victoria bit back uncertainty, torn between pulling those frightened little children into her arms and marching into the depot's office to ask for copies of the purchased tickets. Finally she said, "We may as well board and get you all settled in. Do you have any more bags?"

"No, ma'am."

"Why do you have so many?" Mary piped up.

Feeling her cheeks color slightly, Victoria peered down at the little girl. How old was she? About seven? "A lady needs a lot of things."

"Papa says I'm a lady, and all I have is this." She hoisted a small drawstring bag. "One nightgown, a fresh pinafore and stockings. Why do you need more?"

Glancing around, Victoria drew the children toward the train. "The things a lady wears underneath are bigger, that's all. And some of them can't be crushed. Besides, I'm bringing soap, and all of you will need a good scrubbing. Now let's hurry. I don't want your father to have to deal with us should he be late himself."

As they climbed aboard, the conductor asked for their tickets. Victoria felt the heat rise once more into her cheeks. She had no idea the conductor would demand the tickets so early. She'd taken the train when they'd traveled up to Portland last summer, but Charles had seen to those details. "I'm sorry. They haven't arrived yet. Are we assigned seats?"

"Yes, ma'am, but I have a list of the passengers. What is the name?"

"MacLeod. Mitchell MacLeod," a deep voice behind her answered.

Victoria turned to find Mitchell climbing up with great ease despite the baby he held. Swathed in a simple white layette and a brown blanket, she nuzzled her cap, which had managed to cover half of her face. Her attitude was clearly deteriorating.

"She's hungry," he said bluntly.

Victoria swallowed. "Do you have any milk for her?"

"Yes, but let's get settled first. Here, take her." Supporting the baby's head, he shoved her into Victoria's arms. In that brief moment, panic swept through her. Until now, Victoria had yet to hold a baby. Ever.

Oh, dear, what was the child's name? Mitchell had told her, but she'd forgotten it in her haste to accept his offer. *Oh, yes, Emily.*

For fear she might drop Emily, Victoria drew her close as Mitchell surrendered the tickets. Glass clinked in the cotton drawstring bag he held. She half expected the bottom of the bag to start leaking milk, but it didn't.

Hoping that Mitchell knew how to bottle feed the infant, Victoria smiled bravely at the rest of his children. They did not return it.

Goodness, she thought. This was going to be a long trip out West.

A porter led them to their seats, speaking as he walked. "I can show you where you can warm the milk, ma'am."

Ma'am? Did he think that she was married? Regardless, Victoria thanked him before turning to Mitchell. "Am I expected to feed Emily? We didn't discuss the finer details of my employment."

Mitchell removed his tall, wide-brimmed hat and slipped it into the compartment above them. Was it one of those Stetsons she'd read about in stories of the Wild West? He chose then to peer down at her, his thick, chestnut hair springing free into enviable curls. Her dark blond hair had only a light wave to it. Although slimly built, Mitchell had broad shoulders and arms that strained his jacket's sleeves. He was obviously a man used to hard work. "Have you ever fed a baby before?" he asked.

Reddening, Victoria glanced around. By now, the car was nearly full. A young woman carrying her own infant squeezed past, her wide, slightly dated skirt sweeping away everything in its path. She settled in a seat across from them. When Victoria returned her gaze to Mitchell, she shook her head. "Until this moment, I hadn't even held a child. I have no siblings nor friends with children. Mother thought they were messy and felt it unbecoming of a lady to fawn over them." Her smile felt watery. "Do you know how? I presume we should warm the milk, and I can only hope that bag has everything we need."

Mitch frowned at her. What on earth kind of woman had he hired? When he'd met Victoria a few days ago, she was genteel and seemed full of common sense, unlike that fretful mother of hers.

He'd assumed she would know about babies. Didn't all women? Grimacing, he realized that he should have asked that question when they'd first met. But by then, he'd been in Boston for a fortnight and at the time still reeling from his wife's passing two weeks before that—and of course from Emily's arrival. The hospital hadn't even contacted him about Agnes's death, he recalled grimly. They'd simply arranged for her church to bury her.

Mitch was thankful for their compassion. But by the time he'd terminated the rental agreement of her home and figured out how to set aside his anger at the situation she'd created, another week had passed. Only by the charity of the nurse who'd attended Agnes during her final hours did the baby get the care she deserved. The nurse had then instructed him to either find a nursing mother or purchase the bottles and baby's milk needed. The doctor had suggested the latter also.

By then, time had become even more precious. He'd needed to hire a woman to help him during the train ride out. Not just any woman, but a trustworthy one. Mitch had heard tales about women willing to care for babies, but once payment was given, the children often died mysteriously.

Mitch looked down at Emily, her nuzzling and fussiness escalating. A good screaming bout would soon begin and his heart wrenched. She may always represent the worst betrayal in his life, but he could not abandon her. He'd never be able to live with himself if he did.

He rubbed his forehead. "I'll show you what to do."

He turned to his oldest son. "Matthew, mind the young ones. We'll be back in a moment."

He strode to the front of the sleeper car. He could only assume Victoria followed, because he couldn't hear a thing over the train whistle and the din in the car. The train lurched ahead and immediately, he spun, fully prepared to catch Miss Templeton and the baby. But all was fine. Miss Templeton's grip might have been a bit tight, but she'd kept herself steady.

The older porter tending the fire in the small stove of the train kitchen looked up when they approached. Victoria watched Mitchell thrust the cotton bag at him. "We need some baby's milk warmed, please."

Still holding the baby, Victoria slipped in beside Mitchell, determined not to miss a thing. She had better learn all she could as quickly as possible.

The porter took the cotton bag and loosened its drawstring to peer inside. He nodded and told them he would deliver the warmed milk to their seats.

As they made their way back, Mitchell said to Victoria over his shoulder, "You do this each time. I'll see to the man's gratuity when we reach Denver. That's when we change lines."

"Where will we store the milk between the feedings? It's already quite warm in here."

"I expect the kitchen has an icebox, but each time we stop, I'll purchase more if need be, plus food for us." He slowed. "I won't waste money on the food made at train depots, though. It's inedible and the children will only refuse to eat it."

By the time they'd reached their seats, Emily's whimpering had become full-out wailing. Automatically, Victoria bounced her lightly. She wasn't looking forward to feeding her. Why, she hadn't even peered inside that cotton bag. What on earth did a baby's bottle look like?

"Would you like the window seat?"

She quickly shook her head. "I don't think so. If you expect me to feed and change the baby, I'll have to sit closest to the aisle." She cringed. Oh, dear—change the baby? Another task of which she knew nothing.

Nodding, Mitchell slipped in ahead of her, stepping over the basket that he must have had delivered. Victoria took her seat beside him, glancing over at the young woman across the aisle. The baby in *her* arms rested comfortably, no doubt well fed.

The woman eyed her up and down, her interest far too blatant. Uncomfortable at her nerve, Victoria looked away, realizing she probably looked foolish, still with her gloves on, as though a child was something to avoid touching. She wasn't. The child was beautiful. Victoria suppressed a smile as she looked down at Emily. At least now she could see the baby's face, since she'd removed her small bonnet. She'd removed her own hat as well and slipped them both in beside Mitchell's Stetson before they'd strode up to see about warming the milk.

A few minutes later, after far too many screams from Emily, the old porter arrived with the bottle.

It was shaped like a flattened lemon, made of clear glass with a rubber nipple sticking up at one end. Victoria thanked the man, and after fitting the small blanket over her waistcoat to protect it, she eased the bottle down to Emily's mouth.

At least the baby knew what to do. Being careful not to tip up the bottle too much, Victoria awkwardly began to feed her.

It worked well for a bit, but before long, Emily began to squirm. "You need to burp her," Mitchell advised. "Bottles let in too much air. That bothers them."

"Are you sure it's not the milk?" Victoria asked, wondering how one burped an infant. Around Beacon Hill, nannies cared for infants. Victoria had seen them strolling the streets in the latest large-wheeled perambulators that came over from Europe. But she'd never seen an infant burped.

"No, it isn't the milk. The doctors now say that mother's milk is not good enough, and that this formulation is better." With a frown, Mitchell took one of the blankets in her basket, tossed it over his shoulder and held out his arms. "Here, let me show you how to burp her."

Taking the baby, he met Victoria's blue eyes with his brown ones. His were a lovely color, she decided, as rich and dark as the wood that made up her mother's highly polished secretary.

Those lovely eyes were also guarded and wary. Why? Blinking, she watched him gently support Emily's head as he took her. Resting her against his broad chest, he began to rub and tap her back. The simple action was almost hypnotic. She'd never seen a man so gentle.

"Why did you accept my offer of a job if you have no experience?" he asked.

She snapped out of her foolish reverie. "Why did you hire me without asking about it?"

"I was in need." He did not hold her gaze again, she noted, but rather studied the child. "Why did you answer my question with one of your own?"

She flushed and swallowed. "You already knew that I was going to Colorado. I assumed Lacewood had told you everything else about me." That was all she would say on the matter. The reason she was leaving Boston was no one's business but hers. It was bad enough that Mitchell probably knew that her home needed to be sold, her mother having already fled to the Carolinas. He didn't need to know anything more.

Heat filled her cheeks and she looked everywhere but at Mitchell. She was headed west to live as a poor relative, someone the family was hoping would marry one of her uncle's cronies and be gone from their house. "I may as well earn a small wage for traveling there."

"Your income will be very small, you know that. I'm deducting the cost of the fare from it."

Victoria swung her attention back to him. "I know. But I don't need much." She had absolutely no idea *what* she would need, but surely it couldn't be too much.

Well, she was going to have to say it out loud sooner or later. Victoria lifted her chin. "I plan to find some employment there."

Mitch raised his brows as he carefully shifted Emily. He was drawing the stares of nearly everyone on the train car with his behavior, but frankly, until Miss Templeton—*Victoria*—learned this simple task, he needed to burp the baby. The nurse at the hospital had shown him everything he needed to know about feeding Emily, but the rest, such as this burping, he'd done before with his other children.

He finally gave Victoria his full attention. "What kind of work are you seeking?" She didn't look the employable type.

"Well." She cleared her throat. "I have some secretarial skills. I can read, write and have a decent grasp of mathematics."

"So you haven't actually searched yet? Or sent any letters? Proud Bend is a rather small place."

She blinked without answering.

Victoria was indeed an oddity. Like him, considering he was caring for a baby while the woman beside him watched like a studious pupil. Mitch knew little of her save the fact that Lacewood could vouch for her character...and that there had been a death in her family, but he knew that only from the black wreath on her front door. There seemed to be a problem with money, judging by the need for train fare.

Why? Her brownstone was worth at least three of his ranches. Yet she was heading west to meet a man who had been willing to send her money for a first-class train ticket.

Was he her beau? Mitch frowned. She certainly didn't act as though she was going to meet the love of her life. Or was Victoria a mail-order bride who'd naively decided she'd rather work as a spinster instead of marrying? He'd already gathered that her family's situation had turned dire. What had precipitated her new decision?

No. He would not pry, not even about her vague plans for employment. He didn't want Victoria, or anybody in Proud Bend, to know his business, so he ought to stay out of other people's. Ranching was lonely work, something best left to bachelors who weren't encumbered by fickle women who acted too much on emotion, needy things that they were. And he wasn't seeing anything in Victoria that changed his mind. She was most likely a socialite in financial disgrace, forced to Colorado to marry a man who wanted something cultured on his arm. Mitch would leave her to her naivety as soon as they stepped off the train at Proud Bend. That would be best for everyone. No point in the children expecting she'd be a fixture in their already battered lives.

Proud Bend was a small town southwest of Denver, but it was up-and-coming with its own church, bank and three stores, not to mention the blacksmith and the school and a few establishments Mitch chose not to frequent. The train depot had taken on the post office's duties, something that seemed odd at the time, but the townsfolk preferred it that way. Beside the smithy sat the sheriff's office and behind it, a small jail. The boom of the gold rush and the offer a few years back of cheap land for ranching along with Colorado joining the union had all worked in Proud Bend's favor. The town was thriving and healthy.

A few years ago, when he'd first arrived, he'd been so impressed that he'd named his ranch Proud Ranch, after the town. He'd spent that first winter carving the sign above the entrance to his land. He had been building a home for the family he'd left out east.

Then the honeymoon ended. That spring someone in town commented that they were surprised Mitch could even write. Mitch had held his tongue. Two things he'd learned from being the son of a retired schoolmarm. Know your letters and keep your mouth shut.

Thinking of letters, he still had an unread one from Lacewood in his breast pocket. The man had written a long explanation when Mitch had told him that he couldn't keep his last appointment due to this train trip. If there were still questions, Mitch could write him. First, though, he needed to read the letter while there was still daylight.

He handed a calmer Emily back to Victoria.

"Her milk doesn't seem to sit well with her," she commented.

"She'll have to get used to it. There is no substitute."

Lips pursed, Victoria began a slight rocking, something that accentuated the insistent clacking of the wheels on the rails. Before long, the baby was asleep. Mitch glanced at his children. As expected, they took the rear-facing seats, but Ralph and Mary weren't impressed with the arrangement, craning their necks to peer out the window at what was coming.

His gaze wandered. Some other passengers still looked his way with open curiosity, except the new mother across the aisle. She was taking an extraordinary interest in Victoria.

And why not? Victoria's outfit was stunning, especially compared to the basic accommodations second class offered. The color of a forest at twilight with equally dark lace and plenty of pulled up layers tucked in spots to make the whole skirt look like a series of green waves, her outfit was sober but tasteful. It could almost count for a mourning suit. In fact, it seemed to respect both necessities—that is, mourning and traveling. She'd also abandoned her hat, he noticed, though he couldn't say when. She must have set it up in the compartment above them beside his Stetson. Did she know that whole compartment would become a berth in a few hours?

"Can we play a game?" Mary asked.

Mitch nodded. "Why don't you play I spy?"

Thankfully, Matthew started them off. Mitch's heart lurched. They'd lost their mother and yet they seemed to be handling it better than he was. It was a fact that Ralph had acted up yesterday, and Mary cried herself to sleep most nights, but overall they were adjusting. Mitch was grateful that a simple game could keep them occupied.

He'd been out West for so long, they hardly knew him. Matthew and John remembered him, and Ralph took his cues from his brothers and had warmed to him, but Mary had treated him with distrust. For the briefest instant, Mitch regretted his decision to ranch, but he stalled that thought. It put food on the table. He'd made the best decision he could for his family.

And Emily? His attention dropped to her as Victoria laid her gently in the wicker basket on the floor between their feet. Along with some sheets that the porter had tucked away, he'd had that basket delivered directly to the train.

The baby squirmed and Victoria placed a quietening hand on her. Mitch felt his jaw tighten. He had been gone so long that Agnes had turned to another man. Emily would never know either of her parents.

No. She would have him.

As Victoria straightened from her soothing pats, their gazes locked again. She had the most perfect features. Regal, yet not overly aristocratic. Despite being genteel, she was broke, he assumed, and therefore she would have had few decent marriage prospects in Boston. If she wasn't too fussy, her chances might be better out West.

Mitch tore his gaze away and glared out at the passing landscape. Forget it, he told himself. Compassion was the ruination of a man, especially a rancher who needed to focus on providing for his family.

Families need more than food and shelter.

He bristled. Where had that thought come from?

From your own common sense, fool. Haven't you already learned that? Providing for children took more than putting food on the table. It meant being there, supporting the mother of one's children.

A stab of pain radiated out from between his tightening shoulders. Well, he was a rancher. He couldn't spare the time. He'd do right by the children, but this just proved again that ranchers were better off staying single.

"I won!" Mary called out, interrupting his thoughts. "It's my turn now."

Remembering his letter, Mitch pulled it out and opened it. His reading skills were fine, but it was a struggle to understand Lacewood's long, flowing script.

After a short preamble, the solicitor began to explain that Agnes had made certain arrangements before she'd died. A chill ran through Mitch. Had she known she would not survive childbirth? Had it been a difficult pregnancy?

His heart sank as he read further. A few years back, Agnes had signed on to the ranch's mortgage just as he had, although the paperwork had taken many weeks and visits to the post office to complete. Agnes had considered that fact in her will.

Then he read Lacewood's summary. Not only did Mitch now have an extra mouth to feed, and to figure out how he would explain Emily's presence without getting tongues a-wagging, but he also had this to explain to the bank that held his mortgage—a month-old baby who wasn't even his blood now owned half of Proud Ranch.

Chapter Three

Mitch's fingers tightened around the fine vellum paper that carried Lacewood's letter. Agnes had left her estate to Emily, no doubt concerned that he would abandon the infant otherwise. She'd been mistaken but had left him in a difficult spot nonetheless. He needed to tell the bank at Proud Bend that Agnes had passed. The bank manager, a man who had as many scruples as Colorado had oceanfront homes, would expect Mitch to provide him with the proper papers to say he'd inherited her share, but all he had was proof that Emily was now half owner and Mitch was her guardian.

He could contest Agnes's will but, Lacewood had advised, the judge would ask the reasons. If Mitch was to answer that he wasn't the girl's father, the judge would not look favorably on him continuing guardianship and thus controlling the ranch, nor would he give Mitch full ownership and leave the infant with nothing, against her mother's wishes.

Mitch rubbed his forehead. He had no desire to see any harm done to Emily, nor did he want to smear his late wife's memory by revealing her indiscretion.

Not for the first time, Mitch wondered about the man who had fathered Emily. No one came forward with a name. No man owned up, either, and Mitch had been too stiff-necked to search for him. He'd had enough to do in Boston, and as far as he was concerned, if the man had abandoned Agnes, he didn't deserve Emily.

Regardless, he could not lie to any judge, should he contest the will. At his first meeting with Lacewood, the solicitor had pointed out that in the eyes of the law, any child born to a married couple was assumed to belong to the husband. It was only a legal assumption, yes, but it was also best for Mitch to continue with that thinking.

Except for the fact that in Proud Bend, he'd been seen at church every Sunday. When would he have found the week needed to travel east, father a child and return?

He would deal with any questions as they arose. First up, he needed to sell some yearlings to make his mortgage payment. And quickly, too, for last fall, he had seen the wily bank manager smear the reputation of Proud Bend's haberdasher, thus costing the man his once viable business. Two months later, the bank foreclosed on the store, then sold it for a tidy profit.

If Mitch didn't make his mortgage payment, that bank manager would do the same to him. Or, more specifically, force Mitch to sell his land's mineral rights for a song, because the man had already made an offer for them. Mitch felt his face heat and tension rise in him.

He would not be cheated out of what was rightfully his.

Shutting his eyes, Mitch tipped back his head until it hit the top of the seat back. Since he had absolutely no idea what to do, he was left with two options. Pray and wait to see what would happen.

He had already prayed, many times since returning to Boston.

But he was very bad at waiting.

"Are you a gentleman farmer?"

Mitch opened his eyes. Sitting primly beside him, Victoria waited with the calm expectation that he'd answer her promptly. "I beg your pardon?"

She repeated her question.

"No." He frowned. "Whatever gave you that idea?"

"A number of things, not the least of which is the way you speak. It's far more cultured than what I would expect from a farmer."

He folded his letter. Roughly. "It's a ranch, not a farm."

"What's the difference?"

Unceremoniously shoving the letter into its envelope, he answered, "A farm is usually smaller, and they raise crops like corn and wheat or various vegetables or fruit. A ranch is big, has strictly livestock, like cattle or sheep, or even horses. They are raised, bred and sometimes kept for years."

"What do you have?"

"Mostly cattle. Though I do have a few sheep closer to the house."

"Why?"

His head throbbed and he shut his eyes again. So many questions. "Sheep aren't as good at fending off predators like wolves," he answered. "Cattle are better at it." He paused. "I once saw two cows make mincemeat of a wolf. They charged and gouged him with their horns right before my eyes. If I put the sheep out with the cattle, the wolves would go after them."

He continued on, with more enthusiasm than he'd expected he would have. "Although, I am experimenting with a donkey in my herd."

Victoria looked mystified. Her eyes widened, her lips parted. For a moment, he forgot what they were discussing. "A donkey? Why?"

Mitch cleared his throat. "They guard the cattle. They may look like they don't care, but believe me, they hate dogs and wolves. And they have a powerful kick to them."

Victoria removed her gloves, tugging one delicate finger at a time. It was fussy little gesture, he thought. And yet, in Victoria's hand, it was slow and fascinating, a sheer, perfectly choreographed art form in itself. How could ladies possibly wear them for as long as they did? "How did you discover that?" she finally asked. "How long have you had your donkey?"

He blinked. Her questions were in strange contrast to his wandering thoughts. "When I first went West to take ownership of my land, I traveled with an old rancher who'd been on one of the original wagon trains. They used donkeys as pack animals and began to realize their potential as guards for their cattle. He suggested I get one. It wasn't easy to find a docile one. Most are cantankerous because they've been overworked in the mines, but I found one that wasn't so bad and took her out to the pasture. I haven't lost an animal to wolves since she's been there."

"Are there a lot of wolves?" She leaned closer.

"Some. The rancher who owns the land next to me claims a wolf sired his dog's pups."

"Is that possible?"

"Yes, but the resulting animal is unpredictable at best. Not to worry. My donkey keeps my herd safe."

John stood and tapped Mitch's knee. "Will we be able to ride her? Like Jesus did in the church play?"

Mitch was surprised at his son's knowledge of their faith. Agnes had taken the children to church? Apparently she'd been a good mother, after all. *But that was all.* Still, he shook his head. "No. She's not broken. I'd have to break her first."

"Why do you have to break her if she's not broken?" the boy asked.

Despite his insistent headache, Mitch smiled wryly. "That means you can't ride her."

Crestfallen, John sat back in his seat between Matthew and Ralph. Were tears forming in his eyes?

The reaction cut into Mitch's heart. He remembered when John was Emily's size. Agnes had struggled to keep the boy full; he was so hungry all the time. He'd learned to crawl early, too, and had developed an interest in dangerous things.

John had been seven when Mitch left to start the ranch, two years ago. Mitch leaned forward. "But I have some ponies, and I'll teach you how to ride them."

John's face lit up. Warmth spread quickly through Mitch, and as he glanced Victoria's way, he caught her own soft, approving smile. The warmth increased, stopping his breath for a moment. He sat back quickly, clearing his throat and scowling at her.

Abruptly, Victoria looked as crestfallen as John.

She recovered quickly and leaned close. "If you're not a gentleman farmer, how did you learn to read? I saw you reading that letter. The writing looked difficult to understand. And where did you live that you could learn to both read and to ranch?"

He offered a smile that tugged up one side of his

mouth. "My mother had been a schoolmarm for years before she married. She was thirty by that time and quite set in her expectations."

"Thirty! And she went on to have you?"

"Then my two brothers. And being set in her ways meant that not even my father could change her mind when she said she was going to teach us everything she knew."

"She would be very proud of you if she saw how well you read that letter."

Mitch shook his head. "I didn't read it that well. Lacewood's handwriting is difficult. He stretches out every letter."

"Then he needs your mother leaning over his shoulder as he writes." She smiled. "Where did you grow up? In Boston?"

He folded his arms. Was she saying that Boston was so big that the classes of people would never intermingle? Fighting sudden irritation, he answered, "No. I grew up near a small town on the shores of Lake Michigan."

"Michigan? I saw a map of our route at the depot. It won't be so far from us as we travel. Perhaps your family can come to visit you someday."

"Unlikely. My father has a large farm and is reluctant to leave it."

"And now you own ranch land." She turned pensive. "It's good to own land, I think. I should like to again, some day."

Again? So she was without money and desperate enough to take the first job offered her without asking about its details. She'd been as desperate as he'd been.

Fine pair. But that was the only thing they had in common. "Even better to own both the land and the minerals under it."

Mitch shut his mouth, inwardly reprimanding himself for allowing that to slip out.

A frown marred Victoria's perfect features. "I don't know what that means."

"No one has the right to mine my land. It was a provision allotted to a few ranchers at the beginning of the process of selling government land. It stopped after someone realized what exactly they were giving away."

"What were they giving away?"

"The right to own all the coal, fine stone and such. All the minerals that are underground. And the rights to do with them as you please."

"But the government is building the West. It doesn't seem fair to hoard it."

Mitchell frowned at her. "What do you think should be done?"

"The minerals under your land *should* be mined. I hear the gold rush has helped Proud Bend prosper. Shouldn't we do this to help our country?"

She couldn't be that naive about big business, could she? Was she really hinting that he should give away his rights for the good of the country?

"I mean," she amended, "you should at least look at what's there."

"A prospector already did a good assessment. I know exactly what's under my land." There was coal and silver as well as a small amount of gold and gemstones, the prospector had told him after surveying the sharp gully at the western edge of the north pasture.

"Then why aren't you mining?"

"I don't believe we should tear apart a land to extract

a few tons of whatever is under it. The beauty of God's creation should count for something. And the land above needs to feed cattle. I'm not hoarding anything. There are plenty of mines. I just want to have the right to do what I feel best for my land."

"Will you ever mine it?"

This was a subject he didn't want to deal with right now. "I'll probably lease out the rights for a short time, but I'll stipulate that they cannot destroy my grazing land, which will mean no one will want to touch it."

"But isn't it building the West?"

"So is ranching and farming. We need to eat more than we need iron or gemstones."

Her brows raised, she looked impressed. "That is true."

He sat back, surprised she didn't argue with him. It was difficult enough with that banker wanting those rights. On several occasions, Smith had told Mitch he wanted to purchase them. Each time, Mitch had refused, but the pressure mounted.

Feeling his head pound at the thought of the stubborn banker, he quickly changed the subject. "As I was saying before," he told Victoria, "when my mother married, she had to retire. But she still had that need to teach. My brothers and I didn't have a chance to be ignorant."

"And a good thing that was." She laughed, the merriment sparkling in her bright blue eyes.

Despite his headache, his mouth curled up into a smile, too. It must have been the rocking of the car. Or was it the sense of adventure now that the stress of the past week was gone? He could set aside the worry of dealing with the bank for at least the next few days. Whatever the reason, the warm coziness offered at that moment with Victoria, despite how she'd peppered him with questions, appealed to him. Without forethought, he leaned toward her again. "It would please my mother to know that you thought I spoke like a gentleman. I will have to include that in my Christmas letter to them."

Victoria felt her merry expression slide away. Mitchell wrote regularly to his mother? Should she do the same to hers? Although they'd parted amicably, mostly due to Victoria's determination to let go of any hard feelings, and partly because of her mother's awkward relief, Abigail's abandonment still stung her.

But she should write her. With Charles's death, the care and control of Victoria's inheritance should have fallen on Abigail, but since everything had been squandered, Mr. Lacewood had said that he would not bother Abigail with any more details. Victoria would turn twenty-one in a few months, probably before everything was finalized. If there was anything she didn't understand, Mr. Lacewood had added, she could seek out her Uncle Walter's advice. He'd even mentioned that they'd known each other in college years before. Walter would help Victoria.

But that wasn't Victoria's option of choice and she decided to say as little as possible on the matter. Soon enough, there would be no legal reason for Walter to assume control of her affairs. Besides, she wasn't her mother. She was quite willing to take on the administration of her finances, such as they now were.

An unchristian thought popped into Victoria's head. She could withhold any news from her mother. Keep her fully in the dark.

She tightened her jaw. It was a vindictive idea, though

it lingered for a mere second. Could she really be that cruel?

Mitchell caught her attention as he shoved the envelope into his jacket pocket. She'd been watching him as he read, as she'd said earlier, but she hadn't mentioned his deepening frown. Despite the cozy moment they'd just shared, something in that letter still bothered him.

What was it?

She sat back. It wasn't her business, nor did she want it to be. There was already too much shared knowledge between them. His quiet suspicion when she revealed her silly plan for employment proved that much. Victoria tightened her jaw. She knew she couldn't live off charity forever and knew she would never survive without a more substantial plan.

She had only one choice. She would settle in first and then ask around. Even a job as a store clerk would suffice, especially considering Uncle Walter's plan to have her marry his business partner. Victoria felt her face heat, and she glanced over at Mitchell. Thankfully, he didn't notice. She with her careful observation and he with his suspicion, they were proving to be quite a pair, reluctant bearers of each other's secrets. It would be better if they stopped learning so much of each other's business. It was quite unacceptable.

"Well, your ranch sounds very interesting," she said in a clipped tone, effectively ending the conversation as she deliberately turned her attention to anything but him.

The train wended its way around some rolling hills, the trees' lovely fall colors beginning to wane. The children grew bored of their game and their eyelids sank. Thankfully. She had no idea how to mind four children and a baby for three days.

Before long, Emily began to fuss again, her legs pulling up and her face scrunching into a pained expression. Victoria reached for her and to her horror realized the child needed changing.

In her haste to punish her mother, she'd leaped into a situation she hadn't fully appreciated. Lifting the baby up, she knew they needed to visit the washroom first. Victoria threw a slightly panicked look at Mitchell, but the late nights with the baby and caring for his other children had taken their toll on him. He was fast asleep.

The porter passed at that moment and she asked him for another bottle of warm milk. He nodded and continued forward. The woman across from her stood at the same time Victoria stood, her expression knowing as her nose wrinkled. "If you nursed your baby, that mess wouldn't smell so bad."

What a crass remark. Victoria battled the embarrassment she knew she shouldn't feel. "I'm not her mother. The baby's mother died giving birth." She lifted her chin and continued. "I've been employed to assist with the children." There, she'd said it again. She'd been employed.

Would it get any easier?

The woman's gaze softened as she looked down at the dozing children. "They're motherless! Poor things." Unexpectedly, the woman rolled her gaze up and down Victoria's outfit before allowing it to drift over to Mitchell. "A mighty fine father he is." She flicked her head to her husband, who sat with his chin to his chest, his eyes closed. "This one has yet to hold our baby."

The woman then narrowed her eyes. "So you're not his new bride, eh? Gives me hope if I ever get rid of this layabout."

Victoria's eyes widened. Good gracious, how was she to answer that? "I—I need to change the baby before the milk comes."

The woman stopped her passage, her raw-boned features tightening in an intense stare. "My doctor told me that my milk ain't no good and that new stuff they sell is better. But I can't see how God would give us something bad for our babies. Too bad you can't nurse her. I've always had plenty, I keep telling my husband."

Still horrified at the unrefined topic, Victoria looked down at the woman's baby as it rested comfortably in a basket tucked between the facing seats.

At a sharp turn, the car rattled back and forth, causing both women to grab each other. After the train returned to its usual rhythm, the young mother's fingers lingered on the smooth fabric of Victoria's smart outfit. "That's a lovely thing you're wearing. And a fine cut to it. Ooh, I'd do anything to own something like that."

A smile grew on Victoria's lips as the idea formed. "You don't say?"

Mitch awoke slowly, with great resistance, as if being pulled from a pit of thick mud. The car was warm, suppressing his desire to rouse. Though he eased open his eyes, he still kept them hooded. The train's rhythm made it easy to just sit there, his head rocking slightly as he leaned against the window. He felt as if he'd slept all night, but the setting sun blazed through the windows on the opposite side of the train. He'd slept for only a few hours, for the fall days were short.

Below, he could see Emily sleeping in her basket, a look of contentment on her face. And across from him, he noticed Matthew and John playing a game. Scratch cradle, by the looks of the taut string Matthew held. John was trying to maneuver his fingers inside to pull up on several lengths at once.

Beside him, Mitch noticed with his eyes still only half open, sat Victoria. She looked stunning in a warm, rose dress, the color practically glowing as the setting sun now cast gold and orange upon it. She had Ralph on her lap, and together they held the string of their own game of scratch cradle. Across from Ralph, perched on the opposite seat, was Mary, listening carefully to Victoria's soft instructions on which strings to pluck. Because of the heat, all the children had abandoned their coats and hats.

Wait. Opening his eyes more fully, Mitch frowned at Victoria. A warm, rose-colored gown? It was flattering on her, but that wasn't the gown she'd been wearing when he'd dropped off to sleep.

Did she think that afternoon dresses were necessary even on the train? Had she continued the old-fashioned habit of wearing certain attire depending on the time of day?

His frown deepened as his gaze expanded beyond her. The sun chose that moment to tuck itself behind a rolling hill, and he could see more easily the woman who'd been eclipsing the burnished rays of early evening.

That young mother across the aisle wore a dark green outfit. Even now, she sat preening herself, smoothing some imaginary wrinkle or untucking an errant line of lace.

He straightened. Was she wearing Victoria's fine clothes?

Chapter Four

Fully awake, Mitch stared. Not only was the woman wearing Victoria's dress, but she was also wearing her excessively fancy bonnet, too. What on earth was going on?

Mary chose that moment to pull up on some of the strings and the knots tightened around Ralph's fingers. They all laughed and Victoria cried, "You've made the soldier's bed! But where is the soldier?"

"He's shooting the bad men," Ralph yelled out.

Victoria laughed and hugged him. He looked up at her, his youthful eyes wide with innocent curiosity. "Miss Templeton, are you going to be our new mommy?"

Even the two older boys froze. Immediately, Victoria's gaze shot from Ralph to slam into Mitch's. She swallowed hard. Though he'd seen her horrified when she'd held Emily for the first time, this instance topped that occasion.

Her lips parted, and her cheeks flushed. She looked totally and quite attractively lost. Quickly composing herself, she cleared her throat. "Now, look what we've done. We've woken your father."

"No. I awoke a short time ago."

"Daddy, Miss Templeton—"

"Shush yah, Ralph," Victoria chided, and Mitch heard her Boston accent clearly in her words. "The train isn't the place to ask those questions."

Mitch unfolded his arms. "That's right, Ralph. We will discuss this when we get to the ranch. Now is the time for more important things." He rolled his gaze over to Victoria. "Like asking Miss Templeton about her new gown."

Automatically, Victoria shot a look across the aisle at the woman, who, satisfied her outfit was perfect, chose to watch the passing scenery. Victoria turned back to Mitch. He leaned forward. "And why is that young lady across the aisle wearing your old one?"

Her color deepened. "Please don't make a fuss. I can explain."

As he leaned back, Mitch loosened his tie. He must have been dog-tired to fall asleep with that thing strangling him. "You don't have to answer to me, Victoria. May I call you that? I didn't buy the gown for you. I was merely curious as to why you switched."

"We didn't switch. I gave my outfit to her," she said. "In a manner of speaking."

"Really? I'm interested in hearing the details."

"While you were sleeping, Emily fussed again. I think she had an upset stomach. I asked the porter to warm more milk for her, but she obviously needed something better."

"Yes, the milk makes her fussy. The doctor said it's because it's so rich and that she needs to get used to it."

Victoria looked dubious and lowered her voice. "The young mother told me that nursing is better. Then she said she'd do anything for an outfit like mine. By the way, it's an outfit, not a gown."

Mitch felt his eyes widen. "So you just gave it to her?"

"Allow me to finish." Victoria huffed. "I purchased the woman's services for the duration of this trip. She will nurse Emily and change her if I am unavailable. And I must say that since she took over those duties, the baby has slept like a…well, a baby!"

He couldn't believe his ears. "You sold your outfit for milk? I would say that she got the better end of that bargain."

"I don't believe so."

Mitch gaped at her. Was the simple task of caring for a child that distasteful?

Simple task? He halted his internal grumblings. Since returning to Boston and discovering that Agnes had died in childbirth, he'd been awake several times each and every night. The baby's reasons were obvious, but the children's crying had hurt more, especially that of Mary, who seemed prone to night terrors.

No. He would not call caring for children a simple task.

Nor was it one to trade off for a scrap of material.

He folded his arms. "Was your job that distasteful?"

"No, but I now have a child in my care who isn't fussy. And you don't have to purchase milk at every stop, thus saving you money."

Mitch leaned back. He hadn't thought of that. It was certainly a consideration. They had only about twenty minutes at each stop, and in that time, Mitch would have to find a store that sold both this new-fangled baby's milk, plus some food for four children and two adults.

Victoria lifted her brows knowingly. "And you won't have to tip that porter as much at the end of this trip."

After starting a new game with Mary holding the string and Ralph trying his skill, Victoria added, "I've saved you time, money and aggravation."

"But I certainly cannot pay to replace that outfit for you."

"You don't need to, Mitchell." She sniffed. "May I call you that?"

He nodded. He preferred Mitch, but Mitchell seemed more akin to Victoria's personality.

"You can give me the money you were going to spend on milk and the tips for warming it."

"It still won't cover the cost of that outfit."

"I have others." She leaned back against the padded backrest of the seat and sighed, her attention turning to the children.

The conversation was over. Annoyed for some reason, Mitch worked his jaw. While he was asleep, Victoria had transformed from a horrified socialite to a canny businesswoman, and yet, right now, she was leaning back as if she was sitting in luxury beyond measure, all the while doting on his children.

This proved once again that he was better off single. Women were too fickle. Who would consider these seats that pleasurable? Even the woman across the aisle didn't think so. The bustle of the green outfit prevented her from sitting back and she sat so rigidly, she could have been sealed in concrete. Victoria appeared not to be bothering any longer with her usual perfect posture.

Who could figure out women? Not he.

Victoria's mother would have died of pure horror if she'd known what her daughter was doing this very minute. Corset-less, she was slouching back in a seat in second class like a coquette in a canteen.

Victoria nearly gasped out loud. Had she actually thought those words?

Mitchell was still frowning at her. "Perhaps this situation is my fault. I should have asked you first if you liked children."

She straightened, opening her mouth as if to argue back. How could he ask that? Then she gasped. Was that really why she'd foisted little Emily onto the first nursing mother she'd spotted? Because she hated children?

No. "I don't think it's that at all," she replied. "I simply don't have any experience with children. And being cloistered in a train car with a baby whose milk makes her sick is not a good introduction. Not to mention how the poor child is in pain. I simply used some common sense." Realizing that she had some wisdom, and yes, some initiative, she lifted her chin. "I actually found teaching the other four scratch cradle to be rather enjoyable. Before you woke up, we'd had quite a laugh trying to figure out what shapes we'd produced. They got sillier the more we played." She blinked and turned away. "I'm sorry if you feel you've made a mistake in hiring me."

His answer was clipped. "I just find it irrational that you sold an expensive outfit to avoid work you'd been assigned."

Victoria was sure that wasn't his reason. His tight words told her there was more to it.

Though, what he said made sense. It was irrational to sell an expensive outfit on the spur of the moment. Mercy, was she as foolish as her mother, who'd sold her expensive mourning outfits for a train ticket that would have cost a quarter of what the clothes were worth?

Victoria bit her lip. She'd been hurt by her mother's departure from Boston without her. Abigail's decision to sell her clothes had then epitomized the strained situation. For the cost of a train ticket, her mother had destroyed Victoria's hope that they could work out their dire finances together.

She stole a look at Mitchell. And for the cost of a wet nurse, Victoria had destroyed Mitchell's belief in her. Her empty stomach flipped. Yes. She was as foolish as her mother. Someday, she might need him as a reference, especially if she was to seek employment in Proud Bend. What would Mitchell tell a potential employer? That she'd sold a fine outfit to avoid work?

Tears sprang into her eyes. Suddenly, she was an impoverished girl who'd probably never secure employment. Everything was falling apart.

"I'm hungry."

Which boy said it, Victoria couldn't guess. But when she turned her attention to the three children sitting on the bench seat in front of them, plus the one still on her lap, Victoria didn't need to know. They all stared hollowed-eyed at their father.

"At the next stop, I'll purchase some food for you," Mitchell growled.

His frown deepened, despite the children appearing satisfied at the promise. She leaned close to Mitchell. "Is there a problem?"

Mitchell consulted his pocket watch. It was a basic model, nothing like the elaborate one Charles had owned. Victoria's heart tripped up. Had her stepfather purchased his with some of her inheritance? She hadn't seen the watch for some time. Had he then sold it to finance his gambling?

"According to the schedule, we aren't expected to make another water stop until after dark."

"Water stop?" she asked.

"For the train. Steam is lost and they need to refill the boiler in the locomotive. I'm sure they'll replenish supplies in first class and take on more coal if necessary, but these stops are mostly for water. There aren't many track pans to scoop it up as we pass."

She had no idea what he was talking about. "So how is that a problem?"

"I'm afraid the general store won't be open then, which means I must rely on the local roadhouse. Except anything I buy will be wasted, for the children won't eat what those people pass off as food. And to purchase something here from the porter will cost a ridiculous amount, I'm afraid." He grimaced. "I saw to the baby's needs, and purchased the bedding we'll use, but I didn't have time to get any food."

Victoria sat back, then bolted forward, and not from her ingrained habit of sitting upright in a corset and bustle. Ralph clung to her as she cried, "Wait! I can help!"

She squeezed Ralph into the opposite seat between his siblings and stood. With a wave, she called the porter over. Several passengers, including the woman now wearing her beautiful outfit, peered up at her, obviously looking for any distraction from the boredom that was their trip. Victoria asked the young man to retrieve her portmanteau, the one she'd asked to have available.

"What are you doing?" Mitchell asked.

The porter returned and after opening her case on the seat, she began to rifle through it. It was an appallingly gauche act, one she would have never expected she'd do, but she was glad her housekeeper had the wisdom to pack what Victoria was now searching for.

Victoria hauled out a wicker box. "Found it!" She plunked it onto Mitchell's lap, and then closed the case. The porter took it away again. Victoria sat down and took back the box.

"Treats and sweets from my housekeeper," she declared.

Immediately the children clamored around her. Victoria couldn't help but smile. It was like Christmas morn to them, she was sure. With great fanfare, she removed the lid.

Her maid had hugged her one last time before Victoria had left for the depot, whispering in her ear that the housekeeper had tucked into her portmanteau some treats for the long journey.

"Whatever for?" Victoria had asked her.

"So those men Mr. Charles owed money to don't get all the good stuff in this house," her maid had hissed fiercely. "That's what Mrs. Handelson said. She said she won't have their filthy paws snatching up all the fine food she'd made and saved."

Victoria now blushed at the memory. Her mother would have never told the staff the reason for their predicament, but the walls had ears. Everyone in the household, from the housekeeper down to the errand boy, would have known. It had been an embarrassing moment for Victoria, to hug her maid goodbye and at the same time learn the staff knew all about their dire situation.

What else did they know? That her mother had sold expensive outfits for little more than a pittance? They would, for Abigail's maid had conducted the sale.

Shoving away the humiliation, Victoria smiled brightly at the children. "What do we have in here?"

She didn't know herself, but found a Jaffa orange, so big and bright and firm it surely must be the first of this year's harvest. Several mince tarts covered in sturdy, honey-glazed pastry sat beside it. Sugared almonds and a few boiled eggs were tucked all around them, along with multiple crisp-looking biscuits, although some had broken. Deep down was a wedge of old cheese wrapped in a fine linen napkin. Victoria lifted the tarts to discover two meat pastries underneath. She recognized Mrs. Handelson's signature decoration on the tops. She let out a silly squeak of delight, more for the children's sake, when she spied some bricks of precious chocolate in one corner.

"We have a feast here!" she whispered to the children, thankful for the provisions. "But what should be first?"

"To give thanks?" Matthew suggested.

Victoria smiled. The boy would make a fine gentleman someday. After they said grace, during which she was sure the children kept their eyes open for fear the food would vanish, she dug back into the box.

"Let's start with the two meat pastries." She pulled them out and carefully broke them, a half for each child. They were gone as fast as she handed them out. She gave them each a piece of cheese and as equal a portion of broken biscuit as possible before handing the orange to Mitchell.

"Perhaps you could peel this?"

Her face fell. His expression was anything but thankful.

Mitch begrudgingly began to peel the orange. "Where did you get an orange this time of year?"

"It's a Jaffa orange. They come from Palestine, but

usually just before Christmas. My mother has a fondness for them because they are so sweet."

Nothing about this woman made sense, Mitch thought. When had she planned to pull out this treat box? The other day, when they'd first met, she'd offered his children biscuits in open defiance of her mother's scathing look, giving him hope that she liked children, but she'd then pawned off Emily on that woman who sat across the aisle, who was also looking with great interest at the treat box.

Then Victoria had kept the children busy with scratch cradle, seeming to enjoy the experience. Mitch glanced down at Emily, who was beginning to stir again. She'd need to be fed and changed soon. Victoria would no doubt simply hand the child over to the other woman like the mistress of a mansion. Yet her actions right now were more of a child at Christmas than an overbred lady.

The children eased over to him, their eyes wide and focused on the orange he was absently peeling. He hadn't had one of these in years, not since some had been given to him as a wedding gift. The scent of fresh orange wafted up through the stuffy hot air into his nostrils, stirring his own stomach, for he had not eaten all day, either.

He was not hungry, he told himself. And he could feed his own children without Victoria's help. He'd hired her to mind them, but mostly to care for Emily. And she'd foisted that duty off pretty quickly.

Still irritated, Mitch divided the orange into segments, telling the children in a gruff tone to take only one each.

"You should eat, too," he told Victoria coolly. She took a segment.

"As should you."

Begrudgingly, Mitch took the final segment.

He could feel Victoria's curious gaze linger on him a moment, before it returned to the treat box. "Only one more thing tonight. Too many sweets will cause nightmares," she warned them. She divided up the mince tarts into tiny portions, and Mitch noticed with a frown that she saved the larger portions for them, and not the children.

"I don't need any more food," he snapped.

"Yes, you do. The children have already wolfed down the meat pies and would polish this whole box off if we let them. You and I won't do these children any good if we're hungry and grouchy. So eat."

Their gazes locked and he could see her pale eyes defiant beneath uplifted brows and a suddenly stubborn chin. He could argue that they shouldn't eat any more in order to save it, but it would look as though he couldn't afford to purchase food for them. And with most of the passengers around them far too curious, he'd rather not invite any more interested stares.

He should be grateful to God that her housekeeper had the forethought to provide this box.

Her housekeeper. Mitch knew she and her mother each had a personal maid, too. He'd seen them peeking out of the kitchen when he'd herded his children into the parlor. What had he been thinking, hiring Victoria as he'd done? She was going to make a fool of him the whole trip with her fancy airs.

His jaw set and his mouth pursed into what felt like a thin stubborn line, Mitch took the portion of mince tart and accepted a small chunk of cheese.

He waited until Victoria bit into her portion, her action more of a delicate nibble as she held her hand under her chin to catch any crumbs. What he did—shove the whole third of the tart into his mouth—felt clumsy and tactless.

The pastry was delicious, melt-in-your-mouth good, as was the cheese. With his last swallow, Mitch turned away.

Evening deepened, and while Victoria was seeing that Emily was prepared for the night, the porters set about making up the berths. Here in second class, passengers had to provide their own bedding. He'd purchased it and had it delivered to the train, knowing he'd need it at the ranch, anyway.

More purchases, more money borrowed from the bank, borrowed from Smith, the man who wanted his mineral rights so much his latest offer had borne an edge of a threat.

When Victoria returned with the baby, he gaped at the change. In the newly lit lamplight, she looked more like a schoolgirl than a young Boston socialite who seemed to have, for whatever reason he did not wish to learn, fallen on hard times. The porter had prepared all the bunks with plump mattresses, straw-filled and topped with wool, making up the beds with the sheets Mitch had purchased. Many of the passengers had already settled in theirs for the evening.

Now it was their turn.

Although Victoria had bartered away her corset and bustle, and had been wearing this dress with only a petticoat and chemise, she suddenly realized she wasn't dressed for bed yet. An awkward situation, with Mitchell so close. His sudden and rather penetrating stare didn't help.

"Don't worry," he muttered. "The boys and I will take

the upper berth. You and the girls will take the lower one."

She looked around. "What about our belongings?"

"The porter and the conductor will see that anything we can't take into the berths is secured."

Mary flung open the curtain below. "Look, Miss Templeton! Look at the big pillow!"

Victoria bent down and peered in as Mary pounded the pillow with two small fists. Mitchell had set the baby's basket and her treat box at one end, and Mary, although still dressed, was pressed against the bottom portion of the curtained window.

"If that is all, I'll say good-night." Mitchell then told the boys to move down to the end before he heaved himself up, completely ignoring the porter as he hurried down the aisle with a small step stool.

Victoria watched him disappear into his berth and yank closed the curtains. Well, he couldn't wait to be rid of her companionship, could he? With a surprisingly heavy heart, she slipped into the lower bunk and closed her curtains.

Mitch's sleep was deeper than he'd expected, he decided the next morning, considering he'd had a long nap and had shared the berth with three boys who took up the majority of the space. Finally, when he heard the porter gently awakening the passengers, Mitch opened his curtain and eased out. If at all possible, he'd let the boys sleep longer.

Victoria was already up, fixing Mary's pinafore. Emily was out of her basket and kicking about on the bunk. Before he could speak, the boys jumped down.

"The train is slowing, Papa," Ralph announced. "I can feel it."

"We're coming into a depot. The locomotive needs to take on more water."

"I'm hungry," Ralph said.

Mitch nodded, albeit gruffly. Yes, he needed to find some food. The children would want to dip into Victoria's wicker box of treats, no doubt, but it was his responsibility to feed them, not hers.

The train jerked and wheezed to a stop, causing Victoria to career into him. He caught her and held her steady. But she immediately pulled free and reached for the baby. Thankfully, Emily was still centered in the soft bedding.

Victoria smoothed the infant's clothes as she lifted her. "Go find a store," she told Mitch. "All we need is a bit of bread and cheese and maybe some fresh fruit. I'll take the children out for some air. We could all use a cold drink, so I will find a pump, but we won't leave the depot."

Mitch bristled at the authoritative tone. "I know what to buy. I have fed my children before." At the sound of the door at the end of the train car being opened, the boys tore off toward it, leaving Mitch to grit his teeth. Then, with a sweep of his hand, he indicated that Victoria should go first down the aisle. With Mary in front of her, and the baby secure in her arms, she walked ahead. Her fine purse dangled from her wrist. It matched the outfit she'd bartered away better than the one she now wore, but with her regal walk, Mitch doubted anyone would dare even consider the fashion *faux pas*, as his mother might have called it.

Cool, fresh air barreled into the car. It smelled as though the town had seen a good thunderstorm overnight. When he reached the door, Mitch spied Ralph already jumping in a nearby puddle.

They'd only just climbed down when Mitch called to his children, deciding to take Matthew for the extra pair of arms to carry back some food.

But that would leave Victoria with the four young ones. On an afterthought, he said, "John, you come with me. The rest of you stay with Miss Templeton, and mind what she says."

"Excuse me!"

Both Mitch and Victoria turned. The conductor climbed up the stairs and waved his hat to secure everyone's attention. "We have a delay, I'm sorry to tell you. A storm blew through here last night and a large number of trees fell onto the tracks. It will take at least a day to clear the debris."

A murmur of disappointment rolled through the crowd.

"As soon as possible, we'll let you know when we are able to get under way again. The train may move ahead, but only onto another line. Please don't go anywhere until we know more."

"You want us to just stand here like idiots?" one man shouted out from the group by the stairs. Others who'd wandered down from the men-only car began to grouse, their voices raised in cacophony.

The conductor held up his hand to ease the discord. "Of course not, sir. We'll have a better idea of how long our delay will be as soon as we see what equipment this town has."

Immediately, the conductor was assaulted with questions. Mitch led Victoria and the children out of earshot, to the short side of the depot's main building. "It looks like we'll get more fresh air than we planned, but I'll still go ahead and purchase some food."

"When were we supposed to arrive in Proud Bend?"

"Tuesday morning. I had scheduled it all out, even chose this route because of its speed. But now, I can't say." He didn't want this delay. He had a ranch to run, and needed to brand the heifers he planned to keep. Several other ranchers had been interested in purchasing the rest of them. He needed that quick infusion of cash to pay his quarterly mortgage installment or that bank manager would be using the default as an excuse to force Mitch to sell him his mineral rights.

Victoria glanced over at the crowd. "I need to send a telegram to my uncle to tell him of this delay."

She wasn't traveling to a beau? His heart took a treacherous leap. Determined to ignore it, he answered, "Fine. I'll do it. What is his name?"

In answer, Victoria opened her small drawstring purse and pulled out a folded paper. "Here's the telegram he sent my mother. All the information is on it."

Mitch took it and unfolded it. The name at the top was as clear as if she'd spoken it aloud. Walter Smith.

His stomach turned. That cad of a bank manager and Victoria's uncle were one and the same man.

Chapter Five

Mitchell's expression went from concerned to filthy angry as quickly as Victoria could blink. "Walter Smith is your uncle?"

With raised brows, Victoria nodded. "Is there a problem?" She could have counted the seconds that passed as Mitchell swept his narrowed gaze down her frame and back up again, as if seeing her for the first time. When that same look crossed the breadth of her shoulders and up to her face again, she knew one thing. Mitchell MacLeod didn't like what he saw. A chill ran through her, despite the bright sun on her.

Mitchell opened his mouth to say something, but Ralph tugged hard on his father's jacket. "Papa, why was that man mad?"

And, as if picking up on her older brother's cue, the baby in Victoria's arms began to cry. For once she was grateful for the sound. She welcomed the break from the inexplicably dark moment that had passed between Mitchell and her. "I need to change Emily and see that she's fed." She looked around, and then finally dared to settle her gaze on Mitchell. Whatever was going through the man's mind was a mystery to her, but the fact remained that her duty at this moment was to the child and not the father.

Still, she needed that telegram sent away. "Will you please see to the telegram?"

"Yes."

A colder word there wasn't. Refusing to be bothered by the change of mood, Victoria set off for the sleeper car. As she reached it, she glanced back, hoping to find Mitchell's mood improving while he explained the situation to Ralph, but instead, her own cautious gaze collided with his.

Mitchell was watching her. Closely. Running her tongue over her dry lips, Victoria tore her gaze away and allowed a young black porter to help her climb aboard. She offered him grateful thanks and, spying the woman who'd agreed to feed Emily sitting in her seat, she pushed the disturbing thoughts of Mitchell from her mind and hurried toward her.

Mitch swung his stare from the car, all the while trying to ignore feeling as though he'd been punched in the gut.

Lord, what are you doing to me? First Agnes, then this?

No, first Walter Smith, subtly cunning, pressuring him to sell his mineral rights. Then Agnes's betrayal. Now Victoria's.

Is hers a betrayal? You sought her out, not the other way around.

Only on Lacewood's recommendation, he argued stubbornly to himself. What if the three of them together had schemed up a plan to force him to sell his rights?

He had entrusted Lacewood with his dead wife's affairs, confiding in him details of the ranch's ownership and the difficulties with Walter Smith's bank. Had Lacewood seen an opportunity and set up this plot with Victoria, getting her to convince him that keeping his mineral rights was a selfish gesture?

"Papa?"

Snapping out of his paranoia, Mitch peered down at his youngest son. Those wide, innocent eyes, along with the stares of the rest of his children, met him in earnest. "Why was that man angry? Is the train broke? Why are you mad at Miss Templeton?"

Mitch pulled in a stilling breath. *Lord, help me.* His children were far too observant for their own good.

Still, his gut tightened and bitterness blossomed on his tongue. A gust of wind delivered the foul smell of oily smoke to him, at the same time fluttering Victoria's telegram. He quickly shoved it into his jacket pocket. "I'll explain what's happening in a few minutes. But it's nothing serious, Ralph. We just need to send a telegram."

"So you're not mad at Miss Templeton?"

Mitch couldn't miss the concern in his children's eyes. They didn't want him mad at Victoria, probably because they were afraid she'd leave them like their mother had done. Mitchell blew out a sigh. They were getting far too attached to her. "Miss Templeton surprised me, that's all."

Matthew, being old enough to pick up on what his father was now attempting, grabbed his brother. "It's nothing, Ralph. The train tracks are blocked with trees and Papa knows Miss Templeton's uncle. Don't you listen?"

"I do listen! I'm a good boy!"

Matthew pushed his brother. "You weren't when Momma died. You threw a tantrum!"

"Enough, both of you!" Mitch raised his hand, palm out. "Mary, go help Miss Templeton. Matthew, keep an eye on John for a minute. I won't be long." Taking his youngest by the hand in an effort to thwart a fight, Mitch made a straight line for the telegraph office.

But at the entrance to the office, Mitch stopped, holding open the door as a middle-aged couple and a young, attractive woman exited. The depot bustled, a beehive of activity. Inside the ticket office an argumentative man voiced his opinion loudly, and the line in the telegraph office coiled around like the back end of a snake. This delay would be costly.

Mitch turned, wanting to make sure his children were mindful of his instructions. Mary was climbing aboard the sleeper car, hauling herself up the steep steps as the young porter who'd helped Victoria offered his hand. Below, Matthew and John were kicking a small rock back and forth underneath the first set of windows.

Beside them, the middle-aged couple who'd exited the telegraph office paused a moment, the man holding the older woman's hand as she fussed with her shoe. Having fixed whatever it was, she smiled her gratitude up to her man, and in that moment, he leaned forward to steal a kiss. Playfully, she batted him lightly, while the young woman laughed.

The intimate moment clenched his stomach, stalling him briefly. The love that couple shared glowed like a fine mountain sunset. How had their love survived the turbulent times, he wondered. What did they know that he didn't?

He caught a glimpse of Mary skipping through the

train car, stopping halfway when she reached Victoria. Victoria was bending over the seat. She turned her head when Mary approached, then, a moment later, as she lifted the tiny Emily up into her arms, she looked out the window.

Again, their gazes crashed together like rams in season. Her gaze was wide, curious, and cautious. He knew then why he couldn't share a love like the one he'd seen in that middle-aged couple. Because he had chosen poorly, both in wife and in occupation.

All he'd wanted was to build a life for his family. He'd left them in Boston, his wife's hometown, so they wouldn't have to deal with the hardships of ranch life without even a roof over their heads for the first little while.

It had taken time to build a house. Even now, Proud Ranch wasn't finished. He was gone long hours, sometimes days, fixing the fence that his neighbor had objected to. And if there was one thing he'd learned, it was that separation wasn't good for a marriage.

He couldn't do a thing about his family, except what was right, and he couldn't do a thing about his occupation, either.

But he could prevent more personal humiliation.

Mitch ground his heel into the gravel beneath his feet as he spun away from the train and deeper into the telegraph office, putting his back to Victoria and her soft, beguiling eyes.

No more humiliation.

Victoria watched Mitchell stride into the telegraph office. It wasn't hard to see the man was upset. He'd taken one look at her uncle's name on the telegram and had gone from frustrated by the sudden delay in the train's schedule to just plain angry. But why?

Her shoulders drooped. She knew so little about her uncle that she couldn't even begin to speculate. He owned the bank in Proud Bend, a large one, according to her mother. Victoria had secretly assumed Abigail was exaggerating the size. How big could anything be out West?

Not for the first time, Victoria grated against her mother's belief that women should avoid all financial matters. Thanks to that silly notion, Victoria's business sense was limited to her basic math. Yes, she'd listened in on several marital arrangements and the exchange of money that invariably accompanied them, but that was the extent of her experience. Mercy. No wonder Mitchell seemed surprised that she believed she could find employment.

In her arms, the baby fussed. "Can I hold her, Miss Templeton?"

Victoria smiled down at Mary. "Of course, but just for a moment. She will need to be fed as soon as the other baby is finished."

She glanced over at the young mother across the aisle. Victoria had honestly believed she'd done what was right by securing this arrangement, but Mitchell believed otherwise.

Mary sat down on the seat and Victoria set the baby in her arms. "Support her head, dear. She isn't as strong as you."

"Her grip sure is strong. She got ahold of Ralph's curls once and wouldn't let go."

Victoria chuckled. "Was she born at home?"

"No. Mama went to the hospital."

Victoria sat down opposite Mary, feeling her heart

squeeze shut as she remembered how Mitchell's wife had died. "Did you see much of Emily after she was born? Before your father arrived?"

"Some ladies from the church came and got us."

Victoria gasped. "You children weren't living alone, were you?"

Immediately, Mary clamped shut her mouth and dropped her gaze. Her eyes narrowed as she refused to answer.

Leaning forward, Victoria touched Mary's small hand as she splayed it over the side of Emily's head. The baby was rooting around, looking for food, and would not last long before she fully protested. "Mary? Did your mother tell you not to say anything about living at home alone? It's okay. No one will get into trouble. And I'm glad you had some ladies help you."

Mary continued to say nothing, although glanced up one time. Her eyes were filled with tears.

Oh, dear. Victoria felt her own eyes water. Oh, she was not good with children. Look at her, all ready to burst into sympathetic tears with this little child. She should be strong. Who would have thought Victoria Templeton, once a prominent socialite in Boston, and half the time a mother to her own mother, could be reduced to tears just because a small girl's eyes watered?

"I lost my father when I was a little older than you," she said, digging out her hankie from a small pocket. "I still think about him all the time." She dabbed her eyes, noticing only then that the mother across the aisle was finished and was watching her with keen interest.

This would never do. She shouldn't be embarrassing herself like this. "It's okay to be sad. It shows you loved your mama." Standing, Victoria took Emily from Mary and gave her to the young mother. Once the baby was settled, Victoria returned to her seat. "But you have your father back now. And you're going to a new home built just for your family."

Two fat tears rolled down Mary's cheeks, and, surprising Victoria, she slipped off the seat and up onto her lap. Victoria's arms automatically wrapped around the little girl and held her close. Mary's little body shook and vibrated as her crying increased.

With a hard swallow, Victoria blinked back her tears and glanced away from the young mother's prying stare. She looked out the window. She could see only Matthew's head, but occasionally, she could see John's pop into view as they played some game.

"Matthew told us."

Victoria looked down at Mary. "What did Matthew tell you?"

"Not to tell anyone that we were alone. He said we should tell everyone who asked that Momma was resting. He said it wasn't a lie. That she was resting with Jesus now."

Victoria stifled a small gasp. "And the baby? Where was Emily at that time?"

"The hospital kept her."

Victoria frowned as she glanced over at Emily. The baby was only about a month old, Mitchell had mentioned. When had he arrived in Boston? She looked down at Mary. "Were you and your brothers alone at home? The nurse shouldn't have allowed that."

Mary shrugged. "Matthew said it would only be until Papa arrived. But the ladies of the church came. One lady made us molasses cookies, and they all made us drink hot milk." Mary looked up at Victoria. "Your face is wet."

Finding her handkerchief again, she quickly dried her tears. With a weak smile, she shrugged aimlessly. "So you weren't alone for long?"

"The reverend came by. We told him what Matthew had said, but he told Matthew it was wrong to lie. But it wasn't a lie! Mama *is* resting now!" Mary paused and seemed to calm down a bit. "I miss her."

Victoria sighed and hugged the girl tightly. "It's okay." While her grief was honest, the assumption that they were alone for weeks on end would probably prove to be false. It had to be, Victoria reasoned. Outside the window, Matthew jumped, and she could see his entire head briefly. He was a proud boy, determined to protect his family.

She had a feeling he'd acquired those traits from his father.

As if on cue, Mitchell appeared at the telegraph office door with Ralph in tow. His broad shoulders, stiff and proud, turned as he squeezed out past a young man hurrying inside. He wore a simple sack suit, dark gray in color. Her sharp eye told her it could use a brushing and a pressing with a good flatiron, but it was suitable for travel. He must be warm, for the day was heating up, but he had not loosened his bow tie or undone any of the closely tailored jacket buttons. As if by habit, he tipped his head as he donned his Stetson. When he raised his head again, Victoria found her breath catch ever so slightly. He cut a fine figure.

The couple Victoria had noticed earlier called out to Mitchell. Following them was the young woman, her small carpetbag pulled up to her waist as if for protection as the four stood and spoke at some length.

What were they talking about? Was Mitchell already looking to replace her, having spoken to them inside?

Most likely. Victoria really hadn't done an adequate job caring for his children. She'd pawned the baby off on another woman. And at one point while Mitchell had been sleeping, she'd scrubbed those boys with her soap. Had they complained and in so doing, shamed their father into looking for a way to rescind his offer of employment? Could he even do that? Was she going to be abandoned here in this little Midwestern town whose name she didn't even know?

Mitchell was frowning. Then he swung his gaze over and looked directly at her. Victoria swallowed hard at the indiscernible expression as a fearful chill rolled through her.

Chapter Six

"Mr. MacLeod, you and your nanny are perfect for this. I can pay you, if you like. Please consider it."

As the stranger spoke, Mitch tugged his gaze away from Victoria, who wore an expression similar to a newborn calf torn from its mother. He wasn't sure what he should do. It wasn't about the money, although as a man with a hefty mortgage held by a greedy banker, he would be wise to take what was offered.

And have this man know how desperately it was needed?

No. Besides, since this man was asking only that his well-dressed niece travel with them to Proud Bend, her expenses paid for, and with cash of her own for incidentals. Mitch hardly saw a reason to take this man's hard-earned money for such little work.

He had yet to figure out what to do about Victoria. Was that guilt he saw behind the fear in her eyes? Why else would she be fearful of him now that he'd discovered who her uncle was? Unless she feared that her part in some plot to relieve him of his mineral rights was now exposed?

You're being paranoid, MacLeod, he told himself. She'd given her uncle's name freely. Surely that proved she had no role in any scheme Walter might have devised.

Unless it was a misstep on her part. She *was* naive, after all. But Mitch wasn't sure, nor would he speculate. He'd been wrong about his wife, so he didn't dare accept his own assumptions anymore.

He straightened his shoulders. He would take his situation one moment at a time. Turning back to the man before him, he spoke firmly. "Sir, Mr.—"

"Walsh. Robert Walsh. This is my niece, Clare Walsh. She only needs a companion for the rest of the trip. A family emergency requires that my wife and I return to Boston. I trust her. She's a wonderful young woman. Smart, too, but I would feel better if she traveled with someone. First class is full, as is the women and children's car. She's going to Proud Bend to her parents. She's been away at college."

Mitch held his tongue until the man finished his lengthy and unnecessary explanation. "You don't need to pay me, Mr. Walsh. I would be happy to keep an eye on her. But our seats are assigned, and I have seven in my group."

"I can see that she gets a new seat near you, sir. She won't be any trouble."

"Uncle Robert, I will be fine—"

The man shook his head at her. "Clare, your father does not think so. This isn't college, you know. There may be a moment when you will need Mr. MacLeod's help."

"There are porters and conductors on this train, Uncle." Clare swung her gaze to Mitch. "I don't need much care, sir. I might provide some assistance with your children, even. Being the oldest child in my family, I have a great deal of experience."

Her innocent remark cut through him. He did not need another woman with obvious breeding helping with his children. Look what Victoria had done, foisting her duties onto another woman. He disregarded the fact that Emily looked a whole lot happier having been taken off that baby's milk. It was the principle of it all, Mitch told himself.

He stole a fast glance at his boys. Ralph had joined his brothers playing beside the train. Looking into the train car, he noticed Victoria holding tight to Mary, whose head was pressed against her bodice. What was going on? And where was the baby? He needed to get back on the train and sort it out. Urgency swelled in him.

But Walsh was not to be deterred. "Mr. MacLeod, please. I have run out of options and I can pay handsomely."

Out of options? Mitch knew the feeling well. He looked again at Walsh. "I would be only too happy to keep an eye on your niece and I'm sure the task would hardly be so strenuous as to require payment." He peered at Miss Walsh. "Do you have your ticket already?"

The young girl beamed as she held it up. "Thank you, sir. I appreciate this very much."

Mitch nodded, and after shaking Walsh's hand, he called to Matthew to say he would be right back and then set about assisting Miss Walsh in climbing aboard.

The young porter finished that task, allowing Mitch to make a beeline for his seats. He found Emily asleep in her basket, and a sleeping Mary clinging to Victoria.

"What's wrong?" he barked out, somewhat more roughly than he'd planned.

* * *

Victoria was going to ask that same question, but held her tongue. Behind him, coming down the aisle, was the porter, followed closely by the young woman Mitch had met on the platform. Her heart sank, but she held herself stiff. "Shush," she admonished. "You'll wake the children. Nothing is wrong."

"Then why are you holding Mary? And you look like you've been crying."

She wanted to ask her own questions, but Mary didn't need to hear that Victoria was leaving her to the care of another woman, if that was indeed the case. She certainly hoped not.

"Mary misses her mother," she whispered. "We're just having a spell, that's all. She told me about how Matthew didn't want anyone to know they were alone."

The blood drained from Mitchell's face. Then, after a moment of staring into her eyes as if he was as much a child as the little girl in her arms, the same blood rushed back into his cheeks. "I don't know what Mary told you, but they weren't alone. At least not for more than a day. Agnes's church family cared for the children."

"I figured it out." Victoria smoothed Mary's hair. She wanted to remind Mitchell that his children were mourning their mother, and this behavior might go on for months.

Behind him, the young woman bustled past, smiling at Victoria as she did so. The porter found her seat near the young mother, who had decided to leave the car for some fresh air. Victoria rolled her cautious gaze up to meet Mitchell's. "Is there something wrong?" she asked. "You spoke at some length with that young lady and the older couple."

"No." Mitchell took the opportunity to glance out at the boys. "She needs someone to keep an eye on her for her trip to Proud Bend. I declined her uncle's offer to pay me. We will hardly be doing anything to warrant money."

Relief washed through her. "Oh."

Mitchell frowned. "What did you think it was about?"

"I thought you were securing another nanny to replace me." She gripped Mary tighter. The little girl shifted in her arms but didn't awaken. Thank goodness. Who knew how she would interpret this conversation? Victoria didn't want her to think she was losing her as she'd lost her mother.

Mitchell's frown deepened. "Replace you? Why?"

"Because of what I did with Emily."

At the mention of the baby, Mitchell glanced down at her. Victoria saw again that inscrutable expression and wondered what it meant. Would Emily always remind Mitchell of the loss of his wife? What a terrible legacy for a child to carry.

His eyes met hers again. "I have hired you to assist me with these children. I don't renege on such matters, unlike what you have done." He shut his mouth to a firm, thin line.

Victoria bit her lip. Her misstep had been completely accidental. "Mitchell, you must try to understand something."

He cut her off. "I don't wish to discuss it, Victoria." He held out his arms. "Give me Mary. You need to stretch your legs and collect the boys."

Then he pulled one arm back to dig in his jacket pocket, offering her a small coin purse. "Why don't you take them to find a general store and buy some food? We can't be expected to live on what's left in your treat box."

The cool dismissal was obvious. If it wasn't for the guarded look in his eyes, she would have simply told him off for such rudeness. Instead, carefully, she handed him Mary and then rose, finding her hand stretching out to take the coin purse.

When she stepped into the aisle, she caught sight of the young woman who'd just arrived. She'd settled in her seat as though the train was going to pull out of the station at any moment. Hadn't the conductor told her of the delay?

Their gazes met. There was nothing in the young woman's stare to raise Victoria's ire, but when the stranger's eyes strayed curiously to Mitchell, Victoria couldn't help but feel irritation blossom within her. Then shame.

For what? She had done what she felt was best for Emily.

Victoria sat down again and glared at Mitchell. "Are you saying I have reneged on a promise made to you?"

His eyes narrowed. "Didn't you?"

"No, but you won't allow me to explain."

"What is there to explain?"

Victoria tamped down her growing discontent, refusing to raise her voice within earshot of so many strangers. "I believed the milk you'd purchased for Emily was making her sick. I made arrangements to have her fed properly."

"The doctor said an upset stomach would happen for a while but would go away. He said it's better for her."

Victoria thinned her mouth as she folded her arms. "I disagree."

"And on what do you base your belief?" He lifted an eyebrow. "A few fussy moments on a moving train? Are you an expert on babies?"

"Well, no, but—"

"Then how can you say what's good for her?"

"Take a look at her, Mitchell. She's sleeping like a baby should sleep. She's not in pain anymore. How can this other stuff be good for her if it causes her pain?"

It was Mitchell's turn to shut his mouth.

Victoria leaned in and lowered her voice. "This isn't about what I arranged for Emily, is it? I am not going to be so rude as to pry into your personal life, Mitchell, but you should not be blaming me for something I didn't do! It's unchristian, and frankly, it's rude." With that, she sat back and pressed her lips into a thin line.

He then leaned forward, close enough to her that she fought the urge to back away. Mary shifted in her father's arms, her pinafore scrunching up around her chin as she, still sleeping, turned her head so as not to be smothered against Mitchell's jacket. "Then, why don't you tell me why you're really going out to Proud Bend?" he asked her. "Because I have a pretty good idea."

Shame flooded through her, this time for a very good reason. She was penniless and homeless, and to hear him accuse her of it was like a heavy stone falling deep in her stomach.

She swallowed hard. "What do you know? What did Mr. Lacewood tell you?"

Mitchell's mouth hardened. "So Lacewood is part of this, is he? Was he the one who thought it up?"

She sat back, unsure how to answer. Yes, Mr. Lacewood had found her temporary employment. Was that what Mitchell was asking?

"The plan won't work, you know," Mitchell warned. "I will see to it."

What plan? To find work? Or did Mitchell know about

Walter's plan to marry her off to his aging partner, for surely the widower would be at least as old as Walter Smith? Her cheeks burned even hotter than before. Mr. Lacewood was supposed to be discreet, even though her mother had probably told him far too much. Abigail Templeton-Smith talked a good line about maintaining decorum and appearances, but once alone with Lacewood, she must have, in order to convince the solicitor of the need for secrecy, spilled out every shameful detail of her daughter's life. Victoria had no money, no decent marriage prospects, and she was headed into what was surely going to be an awful life of marriage to an old man and being a puppet to her uncle.

Tears sprang unbidden into her eyes. She would not answer Mitchell. She would not tell him to mind his own business and thus confirm what he'd just said.

Mitchell leaned in closer, his eyes glittering as if he was taking personal offence to the decisions foisted upon her. "Why don't you tell me everything?"

Tell him, like her mother had blathered to their solicitor? Victoria was already enough like her mother, thank you very much. She would not be foolish to boot. Mitchell MacLeod may have guessed much of her life, but she refused to relent to this demand for confirmation. "Mr. Lacewood was supposed to say nothing." She glared at him. "If you think this plan isn't going to work and you have the ability to stop it, then why should I bother to give you the details?"

"So I can nip it in the bud and save you the humiliation when it all becomes public knowledge."

Public knowledge? That must never happen. Pride stiffened her shoulders, an action tempered only by another nervous swallow. And in that moment, she felt the horror of another realization, something as bad as the people of Proud Bend knowing her embarrassing circumstances, her stepfather's suicide, the theft before that and her absolute lack of hope for happiness in life.

Victoria gasped. She was as proud as her mother. She jumped up and fled from the sleeper car.

Chapter Seven

Mitch gently set the sleeping Mary on the bench seat opposite him, smoothing her rumpled pinafore and pulling her dress over her stockings. He then sat back, exhaustion draining him. He dragged his hand down his face and throat, hating the itchy burr caused by his need for a decent shave and hating that he was so dog tired.

And also hating how the truth was coming out. So Lacewood was part of Walter Smith's plan to buy his mineral rights. The solicitor had seemed honest and reliable, but who knew nowadays? Mitch shut his eyes. He hadn't been able to trust Agnes, either. Those letters she'd written him over the past year had been one farce after another. All those words about how it would be good to see him again. They were all lies.

He shook his head. Had she lived, she no doubt would have lied about Emily's birth date, too, saying something about poor health making the baby smaller than she should have been. All to hide what she'd done.

Lacewood had lied, too, but his plan was now exposed.

Yes, Mitch's business with Lacewood was pure happenstance, but Lacewood had mentioned that he knew Victoria was planning to travel.

Mitch nodded to himself. *Of course.* Lacewood knew Smith. The diplomas hanging in both men's offices were from the same university. He remembered seeing Smith's the day he applied for the mortgage. And that morning a few weeks ago when he'd first sought out Lacewood, Mitch had sat in his office with the solicitor's diploma in full view, all the while casually mentioning that his banker in Proud Bend wanted his mineral rights.

Lacewood knew even more. He'd helped Agnes write her will, which left everything to Emily, for he had a copy of her will on file. Then after learning of Mitch's troubles, he'd helped Victoria's mother. Lacewood could have easily seen the opportunity presenting itself and telegraphed or sent a letter by courier to Walter Smith with an idea. He knew of Victoria's financial troubles, too. Her need for money that would make her a willing accomplice.

Lacewood's treachery was one thing, but hearing Victoria practically admit it aloud was something else entirely. It left a hollowness in his stomach. The thought that Victoria was embroiled in this cut him to the quick, a betrayal that he hadn't seen coming.

And she'd just rushed out, after blushing as bright as a cherry. The retreat had sealed her guilt.

Mitchell opened his eyes and turned his head to spy Victoria herding his boys down the street that led away from the depot. She held one of Ralph's little hands, while Matthew held the other, and his youngest boy had already begun to swing and jump between the pair. For just a second, he caught her smiling down at Ralph. Then the three boys all laughed.

He was as stuck as she was. He couldn't dismiss her and have his children suffer. Yes, they'd only just met Victoria, but despite her inexperience, she was good with them. More importantly, they were already responding to her natural affection. He couldn't rip that away from them, not so soon after they'd lost their mother.

But he would not trust her one iota, using the Greek term his mother had often used. Victoria would not use her wiles to convince him to sell his land's mineral rights to her uncle.

Had that been what she'd started to do when they'd discussed his parents' farm? Obviously, her skills at small talk were keenly honed. He would have to be more careful in the future.

Lord, give me the strength to protect what You've given me.

Victoria peered over the counter at the various foodstuffs. Still gripping Ralph's hand, lest he wander away and force her to pay for whatever mischief he wreaked, she asked the prices of some of the items. She wasn't sure what she should purchase. A loaf of bread and a pot of preserves were obvious choices, but the prices seemed high and Victoria didn't want to get into another spat with Mitchell.

She couldn't believe he just expected her to admit her family's shame in public. She'd thought he was a decent man. So much for her skills at judging men.

Still weighing her best options for food, and asking Matthew what he would normally eat in the run of a day, Victoria added some cheese, tinned meat and some biscuits, carrots and tea.

She watched as the clerk wrapped up her purchases.

Pride still stung her, even as she carefully counted out the money. Anytime she'd purchased something, it had been billed to her stepfather. *Ladies don't deal with the crassness of money,* he used to say. Even now, feeling as though she couldn't afford the food, which she couldn't personally, she felt her cheeks burn as the clerk peered down his nose at the less-than-abundant contents of Mitchell's small change purse.

Pride made her snap it shut after she'd handed over the few coins. Then, catching Matthew's curiosity, she thinned her lips. Foolish pride, already tender from Mitchell's harsh words. What of it if she was penniless? No doubt some in Proud Bend would guess her situation soon enough.

No, she would not let it mold her into being so ridiculously haughty that at the slightest hint of scandal, she would flee, as her mother had done.

Victoria shut her eyes. Hadn't she done exactly that a few minutes ago on the train?

Mitchell's demands—no, his threats—should not force her hand, she told herself. Accepting her purchases and dividing them up between the boys to carry back to the train, Victoria decided she would speak to Mitchell. She refused to be bullied, plain and simple.

But there was no point in asking for Mitchell's discretion. Her mother had asked for that from Lacewood and she'd seen how that had ended.

Bustling the children out of the general store, while ignoring Ralph's plea for brittle, Victoria met with a sudden strong gust of wind. The weather had changed. Gone was the scent of morning, newly cleansed by a good thunderstorm. A cluster of colorful leaves fluttered past as if hurrying away from an impending storm.

What she really needed were a few dollars, so she wouldn't have to stay with Uncle Walter. So people wouldn't assume she was a penniless relative. Then any of Mitchell's shaming threats could be ignored.

But she had less than one dollar, let alone a few.

"Ouch!" Ralph cried out. "You're holding my hand too tight, Miss Templeton!"

She eased up on it immediately. "I'm sorry. I didn't want you to wander off."

"Is that why you're frowning?" John asked, falling in step beside her as he hefted up his share of the foodstuffs. "Because Ralph would run away, you know."

"I would not!"

"Hush, both of you. I was frowning because my mind was elsewhere." It was right back at square one, like a silly game of chutes and ladders when your man lands on a chute and you end right back at the beginning. She had no choice but to carry on with this trip, regardless of the tears welling up in her eyes and her future looking as bleak as the graying skies.

As they stepped onto the wooden platform of the depot, the young porter hurried over. "The tracks are cleared, ma'am."

"So soon? I thought it would take all day."

"We did, too. But the engineer has announced that we can move along soon. I think they hurried it up on account of another storm coming our way."

Victoria looked up. Indeed, the wind had risen and the sky had filled with dark-bottomed clouds. She'd read about those big storms coming from the Midwest and wondered if this was one of them, but, Victoria realized, she wasn't even sure how far into the Midwest they were. She'd ask the porter. But when she dropped her gaze from the sky, she found he had left to round up the rest of the passengers.

"Let's get on the train," she told the boys, hurrying toward it. "Your father is probably hungry."

"So am I!" announced John.

The older children climbed easily aboard. She helped Ralph up, and as the wind threw up some debris, and her skirt, she stalled in her own climb. Within the car was Mitchell.

Lord, take away my apprehension.

It had been more a sense of duty that had compelled her mother and stepfather to attend church, but Victoria had found comfort and solace in her prayers, especially after her father's sudden death a decade ago. His heart had not been good, the doctor had said, and even today, she missed his easy laugh and friendly wisdom. He'd often chided, with good Christian patience, her mother's desire to stay within their class.

Oh, to receive his advice again, but she'd been so young that even his face was lost to time.

Spying a family bustling toward the car, Victoria allowed Matthew to quickly help her up. The outside air smelled of fumes and rain and she was glad to be aboard.

Once up those few steps, for the porter had not set out the short stool for her to use, she decided that whatever had caused Mitchell's sudden surliness, he and his late wife had taught their boys well. She plastered on a smile as she thanked Matthew.

At the thought of Mitchell's wife, Victoria felt her heart squeeze. She had to keep reminding herself of his grief.

But should that grief be an excuse to threaten to tell any and all of her dire circumstances?

She threw back her shoulders. Just as her pride should not trump his grieving, his subtle threats to expose her plan—to find employment and not be seen as a penniless relative relying on charity—could not be allowed to stand.

Indignation spurring her on, Victoria brushed down her dress and with a hand on his back she urged Ralph down toward the center of the car. Ahead, Mary was peering over the back of the seats and smiling at her. The nap must have been exactly what the little girl needed. And Matthew, bless him, was helping his father stow away the food she'd purchased.

Victoria stiffened her spine and sat down. Mitchell needed to know that she would not be cowed by any threats.

He had changed seats with John and Mary to allow them to sit facing the direction of travel, and the two children were already looking out the window with keen interest. She sat beside them.

Keeping herself as straight as she could manage, she leaned toward Mitchell. He leaned toward her, no doubt expecting her to speak.

Just as she opened her mouth, the steam whistle sounded and the train lurched forward.

Mitchell was pitched into her arms.

Chapter Eight

Victoria had no time to react, only to feel her body being tossed back as the train car bumped forward. Already off balance, Mitchell splayed out his hands, his palms landing on either side of her shoulders. Since she shared a seat with Mary and John, her attention snapped to them, to ensure their safety.

And Emily! As Mitchell fell on her, Victoria leaned forward to check on her in her basket. But all she saw was Mitchell's strong chest.

She shot up her head. His face brushed hers, the start of his beard scraping her cheek until finally the train found its speed and Mitchell pulled back slightly. Still, he remained shockingly close to her. She could see deep into his dark brown eyes, the color polished and shiny, a richness one found only in fine quality furniture.

His lashes were long and curled, lush and enviable. His whole attention focused on her, making her heart race as it stole her breath for that terrible, yet exciting moment.

When his gaze dropped to her lips, she felt them part

of their own accord, her bottom lip falling ever so slowly forward into a tiny pout.

Even over the din of the engine and the clacking of the train's wheels, she could hear his sharp intake of breath. What was that for? And why was she leaning closer to him, her own lids slipping shut? Did she—?

"Are you all right?" he whispered, finally easing back ever so slightly. "I didn't hurt you, did I?"

She couldn't find her voice. She could only widen her eyes and swallow hard. No man, not even Francis, had been this close to her. Her cheek still burned where his short growth of beard had brushed. Finally, Victoria managed to shake her head and speak. "No, but is Emily okay?"

He blinked at that moment, and whatever it was vanished like a soap bubble popping. Immediately, he straightened and looked down. Victoria followed his gaze. Emily, thankfully, was not touched.

Victoria turned to look at John and Mary. "Are you two all right?"

They both nodded, their attention ever watchful.

Though Mitchell had settled back into his seat, Victoria still felt his presence close to her. Her heart continued to race and her stomach flipped foolishly. "Well," she said, straightening more and trying to make light of the incident. "I didn't think the train was going to move so soon. It's a good thing that we boarded when we did."

"Why is your face red?" Mary asked loudly.

More blood rushed to her cheeks and Victoria stole another glance at Mitchell. He was looking away, uncomfortably, if she read his expression correctly. She cleared her throat and forced out another smile. "Well, I wasn't expecting your father to jump into my lap, that's all. For a moment, I thought he was Ralph."

Thankfully, her attempt at humor was successful and the children laughed. Instead of seeing if Mitchell also laughed, she busied herself checking on Emily and then her dress. Both were secure and unruffled. She then touched where her cheek still burned.

"You wanted to say something to me?"

Victoria turned to Mitchell, his expression calm, his eyes hooded, unlike a few seconds ago when he was so close to her. Her silly joke had lightened her thoughts, as embarrassing as it was. Around them, the other passengers were returning to their own business, the distraction no longer of interest. The train rumbled on, and Victoria could see they'd already left the small town behind.

The mood had changed, and she had no desire to rehash his threats until there wasn't any other choice. It would be an even more difficult trip otherwise.

She shook her head. "It's nothing." The center of a public train car was no place to tell Mitchell off. But if she didn't speak to him, would he follow through with his threat, leaving her in worse shape than when she was in Boston?

Mitch was sure whatever Victoria had wanted to say was more than just "nothing," but he didn't pursue the matter. He knew better than to force a woman to speak when she'd changed her mind. Besides, his main concern from now on was to be careful when moving around her. The engineers must have switched off, for this one had a rough touch, unlike the one this morning who'd eased the train to a smooth stop.

He clung to the armrest, willing his heart to slow. He

didn't need to be pitched into her arms again like a sack of dirty laundry.

"I'm hungry."

At Ralph's announcement, Mitch looked down to his youngest son. This was the first time he'd been grateful for his children's unquenchable appetites. "Then we should taste what you and Miss Templeton bought for us."

Victoria was already up, stretched on her tiptoes to access the food he'd stowed above them. Mitch jumped up to help her, steeling himself against her closeness, not to mention against her faint scent so like the roses that had sprouted at the side of his barn.

"Let me get it."

"No. It's my job to care for the children." Immediately, she clamped shut her mouth.

Mitch frowned. Did she regret her words? Because he'd voiced his irritation at her impromptu trade?

In that moment, he did regret his surliness, but shoved the reaction away. Whereas he could have had more tact back then, the reasons were still valid and it was better for him to keep that attitude between them. A nice emotional distance would make it less likely that she'd succeed in her part of that scheme with Smith.

He yanked down the food he'd stowed away.

"Thank you. I didn't get much because I wasn't sure if it was too expensive." She said the words quietly, as if the children should not hear.

"It's always too expensive," he replied. "The merchants know the travelers don't want to eat train food or those inedible messes offered at the depots. They have us over a barrel."

She sighed with relief. "I just hope it's enough. I didn't want to waste your money."

He stilled. These weren't the words of a scheming woman. His hand brushed hers as he retrieved the pot of preserves that had rolled to the back of the shelf. Victoria was warm, her hands soft, and he was noticing things about her that he shouldn't.

Seated again, he discovered she'd purchased well. A thick, dense bread that was sure to fill the children, along with the pot of preserves, some cheese and vegetables. She'd also chosen a tin of meat, and he pried off the key attached to the top and opened the lid with a few good twists of his wrist.

Mitchell listened as Victoria explained to the children that they should not take too much, for it was to last a while. For a woman who'd been part of Boston's elite, she was surprisingly thrifty. Although, it was a trait of Bostonians. They could stretch a penny until it broke.

Or was she purposely ingratiating herself with him? Again, doubt rushed in.

"But what if we're hungry after?" John asked with a worried frown.

"This has to do, I'm afraid. If we eat slowly, and enjoy the food, it will make us full." Victoria sat down and took the bread.

"What if there is no food at the ranch?" John pressed.

"Then I will get you some," she answered calmly. "I won't let you starve." Victoria shot Mitch a fast, cautious look.

"But you have no money," Matthew pointed out.

Mitch saw Victoria freeze. She swallowed before speaking. "What makes you say that?"

The boy shrugged. "From that day we went to your house. You said that you needed money. And when you dropped your coin purse at the train depot in Boston, I noticed that it was nearly empty."

Mitch looked back at Victoria in time to see color rising brilliantly into her cheeks. She cleared her throat and glanced around, as if afraid that someone was listening in. "Don't you worry about that. Just eat." She set about slicing the bread. He noticed she saved the small heel for herself, with only a sliver of cheese.

With a grimace, Mitch recalled the conversation Victoria had had with her mother the day he'd first met her, the one Matthew had so innocently and astutely mentioned. Victoria and her mother had been arguing over money. There hadn't seemed to be any and her mother had seemed deathly afraid that people would discover that fact. Lacewood had suggested that Victoria would be very interested in being hired for the trip. It had sounded odd, but Mitch now understood what was happening.

Shocked, he sat back. Victoria was penniless, and like her mother, she was appalled that someone in Proud Bend would guess as much. Surely, her relatives would know, but it was possible that they would keep it a secret.

He sagged. So that was what she thought he'd been talking about when he'd warned her that he knew what was going on. It wasn't about a plan to force him to give up his mineral rights at a fraction of their worth. He was sure of it.

It all made sense now. He'd jumped to conclusions about her. And what about his threat to tell everyone her part in Walter Smith's scheme to own his minerals rights? She must believe that he'd threatened to tell everyone about her embarrassing situation.

He should apologize immediately.

The children were greedily accepting Victoria's careful portions of food, potted meat pressed into thick hunks of bread with layers of cheese on top. They were happy and occupied.

Now was his chance. Yet, all he could do was stare at Victoria. The pink in her cheeks didn't subside. The color actually complemented her appearance. It went well with the dark gold of her hair. When a wisp fell from behind her ear to brush those warm cheeks, he reached out.

What was he doing? Mitch pulled his hand back. He had been preparing to slip the tendril back over her ear, as if she belonged to him. Was he insane?

Just as that thought hit him, Emily let out a scream.

Victoria leaned forward and scooped her up. She was getting better at supporting the baby's head and not so afraid she'd drop her. She needed this kind of confidence.

"Who would like to come with me while I change this little one?" She was expecting at least Mary to join her, but occupied by food and the fact that Matthew now pointed out some deer in the open field they passed, none of the children were interested in their sister. There was wildlife to be spotted and sandwiches to eat.

With a small smile to the young mother, who nodded and said she would be ready in a few minutes, Victoria took the things she'd need and walked toward the rear washroom. Since Emily had had a day of normal feedings in her, her disposition had greatly improved.

"May I join you? You're just changing the baby, aren't you?"

Victoria turned. The young woman who had boarded the train with Mitchell at the last stop stood behind her. "I have a small spot on my dress that needs attending to immediately," the woman continued. "I won't take up much room."

Indeed, she wouldn't, Victoria thought. She was as thin as a hand rail and probably only a year or two younger than she. Victoria nodded and stepped inside the washroom.

While she busied herself with the baby, the woman dabbed a spot on her skirt with her dampened handkerchief.

"I'm Clare Walsh, by the way," she called out over her shoulder.

"Victoria Templeton. You're going to Proud Bend, also?"

"Yes. My parents moved there while I was in college." She smiled. "I hope to get a job there."

"Doing what?"

Clare shrugged, her expression unconcerned. "I could work at the bank, but I hear the land registry office could use another clerk."

"How long were you at college?"

"Three years. I earned my degree."

Victoria stared up at her as the rather proud Clare finished her small task. Briefly, she wondered if the spot had been imaginary, an excuse to strike up a conversation.

"Do you have a college degree?" the woman asked.

Blankly, Victoria shook her head.

"So you're not expecting to work. You could if you weren't too discriminating."

"Discriminating?" she echoed.

"You could work as a barmaid." Clare batted the air with her handkerchief. "But you are too refined for it. Which makes me wonder why you're working as a nanny. Not that I wouldn't have done the same for the chance to sit by that fine figure of a man."

Fighting offense, Victoria could only gape. Did Clare really think that Victoria had taken the position solely because Mitchell was handsome?

Or was she offended because she didn't have the skills Clare had? But hadn't Mitchell already pointed that out? She cleared her throat. "How old are you? You seem too young to have a college degree."

"I'm twenty. When I told my father I refused to marry, he sent me to Smith College. I think he was afraid I'd end up doing terrible things, like becoming a barmaid."

Victoria lifted her brows. "As you suggested I become?"

The woman's hand flew to her mouth. "Oh, I can't believe I said that! I always spew out like a hot volcano! Please forgive me!"

She should, however insensitive Clare's words were. But as she stood watching this peculiar woman, she struggled to talk herself into accepting the woman's apology. At the same time, she was appalled at her own stubbornness. "So what was college like?" she asked with forced interest.

"Wonderful. My professors say that women have the right to our own opinions, and not to be pressured into things like marriage."

Now finished her task, Victoria hastily pulled down Emily's little dress. "I don't really have an opinion on that subject. Nor am I as educated as you." She blinked several times. "I'm going out to live with my uncle for a while."

"How nice. It will be like a mountain holiday for you."

Victoria looked away.

"Oh."

She looked back, to find Clare frowning at her. "It's not going to be, is it?"

Victoria tightened her jaw, refusing to answer. After a distinct and rather long pause, Clare dug into a small pocket and produced a roll of bills. She thrust them toward Victoria. "Here."

Victoria stared at the money. The thick roll could have been only ones, but regardless, it still represented more money than she'd seen in a long time. "What's that for?"

"My uncle gave me money to pay whoever might accompany me to Proud Bend. Since Mr. MacLeod refused it, I expect my uncle wants me to keep it. But I can tell by the look on your face that you need it. And you're obviously well-bred enough to spend it wisely."

This was the strangest woman Victoria had ever met. Still, all the hopes she'd recently had rushed back at her. All the things she could do, the things she could escape from if only she had money. She shifted Emily to free up her right hand.

Chapter Nine

Mitchell's words rang in her ears. She remembered him saying he didn't think it was right to take money for so little work.

The hand she held out began to tremble slightly.

The money could help her in so many ways. She could rent a room at a women's boardinghouse. She wouldn't owe Uncle Walter, or be forced into a marriage to his partner. Even if it was only ones, the amount of money Clare Walsh thrust out toward her was still substantial. It was freedom.

Her face heating again, Victoria shut her eyes. *Lord Jesus, do not test me so.*

She lowered her hand. Whether it was divine intervention in the way of new strength or simply the fear of humiliation, she didn't care to decide. She found herself saying, "Mitchell said we'd hardly be doing anything to warrant payment. So, no thank you."

Clare reached out and grabbed Victoria's elbow with her left hand. In her right was still that wad of bills. She hastily shoved it into her pocket before taking both of Victoria's elbows. "I'm so sorry! It was crass of me to offer you money. I can only blame my professors. They encouraged us to be forceful."

Victoria struggled to stop the embarrassment still flowing through her, for both her and Clare. "Should you blame your professors?"

Clare dropped her arm. "No, I shouldn't. I apologize for being completely out of line. This is not the way I was raised."

After hefting the sack containing the diapers, Victoria opened up the door. She wanted to add an admonishment, but held back. If she did, she'd be no better than Clare with her outspokenness.

Instead, she left the woman alone as she shut the narrow door and stepped into the aisle. Emotions roiled inside of her as she moved within the rocking car toward Mitchell. She'd done the right thing by declining the money. So why did a small, shamefully insistent part of her regret it?

Mitch took the baby from Victoria when she returned to the seat. Beside him, Ralph was chattering on about the animals he saw, insisting loudly that Mitch watch out the window at the beating rain that had begun.

He smothered a yawn. Tomorrow morning, they would wake up in Denver, and then take another train down to Proud Bend. It would feel good to finish this trip. He'd love nothing better than to take his horse, Bruiser, out for a long gallop, to breathe in the fresh mountain air and be done with this stuffy train car.

Ralph poked John, who hit him back. Up until that point, they'd been well behaved, but Mitch knew it wouldn't last. "Whoa, both of you!" He immediately divided the boys.

Victoria hurriedly took back Emily and handed her to the young mother across the aisle for a feeding. "Here, allow me," she told Mitch as she moved between the boys. Immediately they folded their arms across their chests and glared at each other.

Mitch frowned. He had no idea which son to reprimand, having not seen how the incident started. And he had no idea how he was going to handle his family once they were at the ranch. There would be no taking Bruiser out for a good run anytime he felt the urge. His life was changed forever.

Resentment bubbled in him, and he worked hard to push it down. He'd had the luxury of time when he'd started this trip, but that was slowly being eroded, like the embankment at the end of his high pasture where the surveyor had inspected the minerals. With each passing hour on this train, the indulgence of not thinking of his new life at the ranch was disappearing. He knew what he had to do. As he stared silently out the window, he ran through a plan to find a housekeeper. There had to be plenty of capable women in the area. His pastor would know whom to ask. He would discuss the matter with him as soon as they reached Proud Bend.

The day was waning and thankfully the storms both inside and out were also. They were scheduled for one more stop before evening fell, but he heard the conductor tell the passengers it would be short in order to make up the time lost to the trees on the tracks.

Once night fell, the porters made up the beds. Victoria busied herself with the smaller children, saying nothing but a brisk good-night to him before slipping into the lower berth.

Mitch turned to see how that young Miss Walsh was

faring. She'd taken a seat with an older woman and then taken the upper berth. Its curtains were closed, her belongings tucked away with her. With all the seats now opened for sleeping, the aisle had narrowed considerably. A single, dull kerosene lamp lit each end of the train car, to allow the porters to watch for thievery and mischief. Their oily scent hung in the still, hot air.

With a heavy sigh, he climbed up for another uncomfortable night with the boys. The novelty of bunk beds had long since worn off for all of them.

Victoria silently thanked the good Lord for firm ground, even if it was just dust and gravel, rutted deep from the last heavy rain. The town of Proud Bend was spread out at the base of the mountain, all wooden buildings with false facades and rough streets. Beyond the town limits, great, stunning mountains rose, their peaks already dusted with the autumn snows. Below, mixed with the evergreens, the yellow leaves had turned to brown. There didn't seem to be as many reds or oranges in the fall foliage as in Boston, though she was sure that the peak had passed. In the southerly wind lingered a foul smell of coal and sulfur burning. Not overly strong, but since it was late in the afternoon, it could have been waning for the day. Somewhere to the south was a good deal of industry, Victoria guessed.

She stepped down on wobbly legs and across to the wooden platform, taking Ralph's and Mary's hands as she went. Mitchell followed somewhere behind them, carrying the basket that held Emily.

One quick sweep of those meeting the train told her who Walter Smith was. She hadn't seen him in nearly a decade, but the family resemblance was uncanny. He had her mother's pale hair, although his was graying more than his sister's. The older woman with him could only be Aunt Louise. Still gripping Mary and Ralph, she hurried over to them.

The greeting was awkward. Aunt Louise seemed kind enough, albeit wary, but Walter's keen eye rolled up and down Victoria's dusty frame, appraising her worth, no doubt. She'd slept poorly last night, her mind churning through the previous day's events. Clare's odd offering still lingered in her thoughts, taunting her, although the woman had been piercingly correct in her assessment of Victoria's situation.

And then there was Mitchell, who had remained inscrutable for the rest of the trip. He'd said precious little to her since he'd been pitched into her arms. She'd felt an uncharacteristic leap to her heart—in fact, to all her senses—and the experience had left her flustered and bewildered, so she was thankful for the brevity of their ensuing interaction.

Somewhere behind her was Mitchell, for the crowd of passengers and townsfolk had thickened and no doubt split them. He had accused her of being penniless and going West to secure an affluent lifestyle and had threatened to expose her plan. It was hardly a crime, but he'd certainly made her feel like a criminal.

"Your trip was good?" Aunt Louise asked, reining in Victoria's errant thoughts.

"As well as can be expected," Victoria answered, still hanging on to the small children and grateful for them, for they prevented her from wondering if she should at least shake hands.

"Who are these brats?" Walter demanded, peering down his long nose at the children. "They can't be yours.

Abigail didn't mention any grandchildren when she wired me about taking you in and paying your expenses. I won't take any children."

Victoria bit her tongue to avoid snapping out something equally rude. The children were tired and cranky, but they were not brats. And did she look old enough to have birthed a seven-year-old and a five-year-old? Apparently the train trip had been harder on her than she realized.

"I assisted a gentleman who was bringing out his family," she finally gritted out, also realizing that Walter didn't seem to care who overheard her need for a home. "Their mother died in childbirth and Mr. Mac-Leod needed help with the children. In return, he paid my train fare. I told my mother not to ask you to send money because there was no need. I had decided to telegraph you with my arrival time from one of the stops along the way."

Walter's eyes narrowed. "MacLeod? These brats are his?"

"Yes, these *children* are mine."

Victoria glanced to her right, where Mitchell had come to a stop, setting down the wicker basket. Walter's expression narrowed further as he glared at Mitchell. Aunt Louise, on the other hand, merely peered into the basket that held Emily. Her eyebrows shot up, but she said nothing. The appearance of the baby seemed to surprise her.

Walter spoke to Victoria. "So you've been working on the train? Abigail had promised you would be rested. I should have known something like this would happen when she didn't ask for the fare." He flicked his glare up to the car from which she'd alit. "Second class?" He sighed, as if long-suffering. "You may as well have been traveling with the cattle."

"I doubt first class could have been any more accommodating. The service was excellent and the beds comfortable." Victoria could hardly believe that she actually rose to her uncle's provocation.

The older man flicked his attention back to Mitchell. "MacLeod. What a coincidence it was you who employed Victoria. It's not cheap to bring the whole family out."

Completely irritated, Victoria spoke before Mitchell could answer. "What would you expect he do? Abandon his family? Give up a baby because her poor mother didn't survive childbirth?"

Aunt Louise's gaze flew directly to Walter, but the man didn't acknowledge it. Victoria frowned. Was she expecting her husband to retort? Uncle Walter continued to ignore his wife and turned instead to Mitchell. "You're going to need a woman to care for them," he warned.

Mitchell stiffened. "I believe that's my own business, Mr. Smith, and not yours."

"Walter!"

Everyone turned at the sound of the loud, gravelly male voice. A rotund man of about fifty toddled over. He wore an expensive coat over what looked like a fine suit, and on his head was a beaver pelt top hat of excellent quality.

"Clyde! Here, meet my niece, Victoria." Although the words sounded pleasant, Walter's expression seemed guarded. "Victoria, this is Clyde Abernathy, my business partner. Sorry, Clyde, for her disgraceful appearance. She traveled second class, of all things."

The man peeled off his hat to reveal wisps of flyaway

gray hair over a peeling and oily scalp. Victoria gripped the children's hands even more tightly.

"I'm so glad you have made it here safe and sound. The delay had us all concerned." Clyde grinned widely at her.

Oh, dear, he's missing teeth.

"She's lovelier than you described, Walter. Not at all disgraceful. I can't wait to escort her on a tour of our fine town. It'll be an excellent opportunity to get to know each other."

So the pair had obviously been discussing her as a potential bride, even though Uncle Walter hadn't sent any money that he might use as leverage. She averted her gaze from the unseemly man and her eyes lit on Clare Walsh. The young woman was greeting her parents with great affection.

The wad of bills flashed through her mind and she had to tell herself again that she'd made a sound decision not to accept the money Clare had offered. She pushed away those thoughts and looked back at Clyde. "I'm afraid that won't happen for some time, Mr. Abernathy. I am very fatigued from my trip." She stepped back again, and took the children with her.

"And if you'll excuse me, I see my ranch hand has arrived." Mitchell lifted the basket, and turned to Mary and Ralph. "Let's go. Say your goodbyes to Miss Templeton."

Mary and Ralph gaped at him. Neither moved a muscle. In fact, Victoria felt Mary's grip tighten in hers. To her own surprise, she found her hand squeezing it back. She pressed out a tight smile. "Walter, I have several bags. The young porter knows which ones they are. Could you please direct him to your carriage while I say my goodbyes to the children?"

Walter scowled, then catching sight of the young porter tossing someone's bag down onto the dirt below, he strode off to ensure that Victoria received all her luggage in good order. Most likely he had no wish to replace any items should they be damaged. Aunt Louise remained, but a small smile hovered on her lips. Clyde made no effort to help Walter, either.

Suddenly, the children threw their arms around her waist, with Mary letting out a loud wail of full-out terror.

Chapter Ten

Mitch gently peeled the crying Mary away from Victoria, but the child wrenched free of him and clung to her again. Bending her knees, Victoria looked up at him. "Give me a minute with the children, please?"

Their gazes locked. Her pale eyes were filled with tears, and it gripped him unexpectedly. She gave the two young children a soft smile as she gently extricated herself from Mary's tight grip. "Now, we're not going to say goodbye, are we?"

Mitch heard a small catch in her throat as his two young children shook their heads.

"Why aren't you coming with us?" Ralph asked.

"I came out here to visit my uncle and aunt," she said. "I'll be in town and when you come in, you can come to see me. Be good for your father, and always help him out."

"Who's going to take care of Emily?" Mary whined.

Victoria's shoulders stiffened. "Your father will find someone. She'll be just as nice as me. You'll see." Even as she said it, Mitch heard the plaintive note in her words.

He stole a swift glance to the fat man standing beside

Mrs. Smith. Abernathy was watching Victoria, all the while licking his thick lips.

Mitch's fingers dug into his palms, even the hand holding the wicker basket's handle.

"We need *you*, Miss Templeton," Matthew said coming up beside Mitch. The boy was usually cautious with his words, but those few he spoke summed up perfectly how they were all feeling.

Except Mitch. He didn't need a socialite in his house. It was obvious to him now that her trip here was to find a wealthy husband. But the thought cut through him.

Victoria would be the mistress of one of the fancy houses with their rose-colored rhyolite facades. She'd have an assemblage of servants to do her every bidding. There were plenty of men and women here in Colorado who had discovered that mining was harder work with poorer pay than they'd expected. Many of the women ended up working as servants in fine homes or in the local saloon. Since working as a maid was the preferable choice, they'd probably line up to be hired by Victoria. She'd have her pick.

He needed a solid, hardworking housekeeper, preferably older, willing to come out to his house every day, a woman who knew how to care for children. Victoria cared *about* his children, but she couldn't care *for* them. She didn't know the first thing about that. She needed money, but that was no reason to hire her.

She looked up at Mitch as he frowned at her. He would *not* hire her to look after his children, no matter how soft and watery her gaze became. Their mother had abandoned them, albeit unwillingly. The minute Victoria realized she couldn't care for them, she'd abandon them, too. Only willingly.

Mary threw her arms around Victoria's neck, and Mitch watched her cling to the child fiercely. He stiffened, refusing to be moved by the poignancy of the moment. For the few days on the train, he'd allowed himself a bit of foolish, ignorant luxury. He'd lived for the moment, not worrying about how he was going to both ranch and look after his children. Now he was paying the price for it. With thinned lips, he knew he had to break up this cozy moment before it swelled out of control.

Victoria finally released Ralph and Mary. "Be good, and when you come to town, ask your father if you can see me, all right? I'll always be here."

With a long series of sniffles, Mary nodded. Victoria straightened. With sudden coolness, she said to him, "Thank you for employing me. I hope you will all settle into a routine without too much trouble." Her attention strayed to Abernathy and her voice dropped. "As soon as you get your finances sorted out, I would appreciate my wages."

Tight-lipped, Mitch reddened. Did she think he'd forgotten it? With a nod, he looked away to discover his ranch hand, Jake, pulling in closer with the cart, and just in time, too. He gruffly corralled the children. The sooner they were out of town, the better.

"MacLeod!" The rough voice stilled him. He turned. Walter Smith was striding toward him, having abandoned his supervision of Victoria's luggage. From the right, Jake was approaching just as quickly. The ranch hand was young and, while generally good-natured, he could turn into a guard dog in the blink of an eye. He knew the history Mitch shared with Smith and wouldn't mind stepping in between the pair if he had to.

Mitch held out his hand to Jake. This wasn't the first time he'd had to pull in the reins. Jake stopped.

"Get our stuff," he ordered his ranch hand. "Matthew, show Jake where it is."

Jake grabbed the basket at Mitch's feet, and immediately Mitch reached out his hand. Only when Jake peered into the basket did he let it go. The obvious question rolled over his features, but Mitch crushed it with a shake of his head.

Matthew peeked up at the scene with cautious curiosity, but mindful of his father, he led Jake away.

Mitch turned to Smith. The older man's gray eyes glittered like rock washed with melting snow.

"Did you want something, Mr. Smith?" It bit at him to be so polite, but he refused to be anything else.

"Got your family all back, I see. Did I hear correctly about your wife?"

Mitch's jaw tightened. "Yes, she passed away during childbirth." He waited for the inevitable questions, but they didn't come. Then he realized why. Smith didn't attend church. He wouldn't know that Mitch had been there every Sunday for the past year.

"I'm sorry to hear that, MacLeod," Smith said. "But life goes on. I expect you will be bringing in the necessary paperwork for the changes to the mortgage."

"As soon as it's all finalized, you'll be the first person I see." Stalling the man wasn't his intention, but Mitch needed to get his family settled, find someone to keep house and mother Emily and, after that, see about ensuring he had enough money to make his quarterly mortgage payment. In that order of importance. Walter Smith and his "necessary paperwork" were not even on the list yet.

Smith took a step closer. "I hope you'll be smart

enough to reconsider my offer on your mineral rights, MacLeod. I'm offering a fair price and you'll need the money for your children."

Fair price? Smith's offer was laughably low. The banker must have thought that Mitch was like most men out here—ready to make a fast buck and spend it just as quickly on liquor and women. But Mitch's parents didn't raise a fool. This past winter, Mitch had done some research. Only a few deeds created when the government began selling land actually included the mineral rights. That offer had been rescinded quickly, letters to ranchers like himself had been sent, demanding they sign on to new deeds. But those few ranchers had rallied together and won their case. They could keep their mineral rights, Mitch included.

"I'll be keeping my mineral rights, Mr. Smith, until I decide to sell them on my own terms."

"Shame." Walter's face hardened, his mouth twisting into an ugly sneer. "You'll be needing cash when the mortgage payment comes due. And it's coming due soon. Oh, and make sure you have all the necessary papers concerning your wife's untimely passing. I wouldn't want there to be any mistakes that might mess up the timing of your payments."

Mitch threw back his shoulders. "I have heifers for sale and buyers lined up. I'll be making my payments right on time—don't worry."

Smith's eyes brightened, and for a brief instant, Mitch wondered if he'd erred by mentioning his plan. He stepped closer, enough for the brim of his Stetson to touch the brim of Smith's fine hat. "If you'll excuse me, I have more important things to do." With that, he ground his heel into the dirt and strode away.

Fifteen minutes later, Mitch flicked the reins of the team to move them faster now that they'd put the town behind them. Mary and Ralph huddled on the seat between him and Jake, while Matthew and John bookended the wicker basket in the bed of the cart. Mitch could hear the baby fussing. He had a tin of that new baby milk, and made a mental plan to rise early in the morning to get the additional tins that he would need. He'd store it in the well between feedings.

As the team trotted along, he could feel Jake's stare on him. "Go ahead and ask. I know you want to," he muttered.

"I think I should wait until these young-uns are sleeping."

Mitch grimaced. Of course. "Fine, whatever you want."

The trip out to his ranch took over an hour, all uphill. With Castle Rock, and its namesake mountain behind them to the southeast, they faced the wide expanse of the Rockies.

He blew out a long sigh. It was good to be home again. He would get out of this suit, then bathe and shave and pull on his favorite pair of work pants and a sturdy cotton shirt. Then slip into those boots he'd left by the door, the ones perfectly molded to his feet, and narrow enough to slip into a stirrup in that single swing into the saddle. They weren't fancifully embroidered like Jake's were. The man liked to spend money. Mitch preferred the suppleness of one sheet of fine leather, without the encumbrance of extra stitching.

The wind picked up, delivering to them the scent of pines and streams. He inhaled deeply. Yes, it was good to be home, even if he still had to feed the children and tuck them into bed before he faced Jake's inevitable questions.

* * *

Only when she was refreshed by a bath, a nap and clean clothes did Victoria realize how draining the long trip had been. Her aunt had asked her to come down to the parlor for tea before supper, and when she'd arrived, Victoria discovered the woman had set everything out between two fussy Queen Anne chairs.

From the tall nearby window, she could see the wide front lawn, the picket fence and the vista of mountains behind the few homes across the street. This late in the day saw few people, and yet the Rockies behind the town still caught the waning, late autumn sun.

Victoria sank into her seat and accepted a steaming cup of tea from Aunt Louise. It tasted wonderful. The older woman sipped her own before glancing toward the closed door of the well-appointed parlor. Victoria watched her over the rim of her cup, trying her best to gauge the woman who would be her hostess for an indefinite period. Aunt Louise didn't seem to resent her arrival. Actually, she almost seemed pleased to have a member of her sister-in-law's family here. Victoria was sure her own mother would not have been so accommodating.

Taking another sip, Aunt Louise looked again at the door. Victoria set down her teacup. "Are you expecting someone, Aunt Louise?" After dropping the women off at the house, her uncle and Mr. Abernathy had returned to the bank.

"No, of course not." She smiled and refocused her attention on Victoria. "Your telegram surprised us. We were waiting on a request for money. There was none, but it was rather a short note, even for a telegram. It just said when you would arrive."

"I'm not surprised. It was Mitchell MacLeod who sent it, not I."

Aunt Louise leaned forward and sipped her tea again. "Another surprise, your showing up with a strange man."

"Mitchell needed a woman to help him with his children. The solicitor we shared suggested me, because Mother had told him I was coming here. Mr. Lacewood suggested to Mitchell that he might avail himself of my assistance, and in return, Mitchell paid for my fare and a small recompense."

"Walter *was* prepared to send you money," Aunt Louise chided softly, hiding the lower part of her face behind her teacup.

Victoria frowned. Her words sounded almost like a warning. Or was Aunt Louise baiting her?

She took her time answering. How much did her aunt know of Uncle Walter's plans to marry her off? Did she know that Victoria had been penniless and alone and had to vacate her home immediately? Mr. Lacewood felt that the house would sell quicker if it was empty. Victoria could feel the heat of shame rise in her cheeks just remembering when she and her mother listened to his advice, the day after Mitchell had visited.

"I didn't want to impose on either of you any more than I am," she answered with caution. "Not when I could earn the fare."

"But second class? With all those children? And a baby, too? It must have been terrible for you."

"I had the baby and the little girl in the bunk with me. It was cramped, but not intolerable." Mary had kicked several times during the nights, and the basket took up far too much room. Yes, the nights had been difficult, but Victoria had survived them.

She smiled to herself. Yes, she had.

With a frown, the older woman set down her cup. "You said that Mr. MacLeod's wife died in childbirth. Was that the baby she delivered?"

"Yes." Even now, Victoria felt her heart wrench at the thought of those poor children. Their wide, haunted looks as they'd said goodbye.

"How old is the baby?"

"A little more than a month. She was born in early September." Victoria blinked as she looked out through the lace sheers. Evening had descended and the delightful mountains were easing into darkness. When would Walter come home, Victoria wondered. A shiver ran through her. Would he bring Mr. Abernathy with him?

"Are you cold?"

Victoria lifted her teacup. "No. I was just looking at the mountains."

"They are lovely. We take breakfast in the morning room. On nice mornings, I sit outside. From there, you can see Castle Rock and the town, plus the Proud River. It makes for pretty scenery."

"Does the river bend here?"

"Yes, that's why the town is called Proud Bend. It's a good town. But like any out here in the wilds, it has its seedier side. Fortunately, your uncle will have no part of that." Her tone tightened. "We from Boston are here to, how shall I say it, lift the standards? Do our part, that is."

A few days ago, Victoria might have agreed, but the words now sounded snobby. Aunt Louise arched her brows. "It's common knowledge that our class has had to move West to preserve our finances." Abruptly she laughed. "In order to preserve our way of life, we've had to move away from it. Can you imagine?"

Victoria didn't appreciate the irony the way her aunt did. "Was that why you married Uncle Walter?"

"Well, of course. Walter's from a banking family and Proud Bend needed a bank. Mr. MacLeod is probably here to make his fortune, too." Aunt Louise paused, then leaned forward. "Do you know where he ranches?"

"No." Victoria didn't understand why her aunt kept bringing him back into the conversation.

"It's an hour southwest of here, if you push the horses. He has a prime piece of real estate, Walter says." Her tone turned sly, as if testing the waters. "Perhaps you'll see it."

She doubted Mitchell would welcome her. But surely he had arranged to hire someone for the children and was off doing things ranchers needed to do.

And if he wasn't?

Thinking of Mitchell struggling to keep Ralph and John apart, or consoling Mary, all the while feeding the baby, made Victoria's throat close. She was here, cozy and comfortable, waiting while the servants prepared a delightful meal in the distant hollows of this sprawling house.

How could she even eat?

No. Mitchell wouldn't let his children go hungry. In fact, she could see him forfeiting a meal in the course of his day to ensure they'd have theirs. Recalling how it felt to have him close that moment when the train lurched forward, she felt her cheeks redden. "I don't expect I will ever see his ranch."

"I hear the house is mean. It will be a very rustic start for those children. Did Mr. Macleod discuss his family at all with you?"

Victoria eyed her aunt. The woman appeared to be skirting an issue she wanted to discuss, but her manners could not allow her. And it involved Mitchell. "No. He had all but his wife with him, remember?"

Her aunt didn't answer. When silence descended on the parlor, Victoria set down her cup again. "You seem like you want to tell me something. What is it?"

"Do you know how long a woman is pregnant?"

"Of course. Nine months." Victoria shifted in her chair, uncomfortable at the turn of the conversation.

"If the child was born early September, then when was she conceived?"

Victoria's face flushed brilliant red. She stood. "I don't think we should be discussing this. What Mitchell and his wife did within the bonds of marriage was their own business, not ours."

She'd made it to the door before the older woman simply called out, "Mr. Macleod isn't that baby's father."

Chapter Eleven

Victoria spun. "What do you mean?"

Aunt Louise finally gave her a look that Victoria found easy to define. Smugness. "Mr. MacLeod was here in Proud Bend early in December. You see, the church's stove needed to be replaced. We'd known for some time the new one was coming, and when it finally arrived, Mr. MacLeod and several other men installed it."

"That's a lovely story, but what does that have to do with Emily?"

"Bear with me a moment. It was a blessing that they replaced the stove when they did, for an early winter storm arrived that next day. We were cut off from everything for some weeks. No one left town. Mr. MacLeod had to keep his horse in town and snowshoe back to his ranch to tend his animals. It was a week before Christmas by the time the train with the plow came through. We were expecting presents for Rachel and they arrived just in time."

Victoria had forgotten about Rachel, her uncle and aunt's only child, and even now wondered where she was. But that wasn't the issue at hand. She sank into her chair again. "Perhaps the child was born prematurely?"

The smugness dissolved, and patience washed over Aunt Louise's features instead. "Mr. MacLeod has been at church every Sunday for the last year. He sits behind me, and when the service is over, he always lets me leave ahead of him. Even if the child was born late or prematurely, there's no escaping the fact that he couldn't have fathered her."

"Perhaps the mother came out here?"

"And leave her other children? If any of them came, why didn't we see them in church? Unless his wife refused to raise them as Christians."

Victoria blinked and frowned. That was highly unlikely. The children knew Bible stories and had mentioned going to church at Easter. If their mother took them to church in Boston, surely she would have shown up at the one in Proud Bend where her husband worshipped.

There was no getting around it. Mitchell was caring for a child who he knew wasn't his.

Tears formed unbidden in Victoria's eyes for some inexplicable reason. What was he doing right now? Settling the children in their beds, no doubt. Did they even have beds? Aunt Louise called the ranch house mean. But he'd bought bedding. Still, he wouldn't have been prepared for Emily.

Victoria glanced uneasily around. Upstairs in her bedroom, she had everything she could possibly want. Downstairs somewhere, supper was simmering away and here she could sit in a warm and cozy room, sipping piping-hot tea until her meal was ready. Everything around her was restful and quiet. All a person could ask for.

Suddenly, the delicious scents emanating from that distant kitchen soured and the overstuffed chair beneath her turned to cold steel. She rose. "I don't know what to say."

"You don't have to say anything, my dear. But just keep in mind that if Mr. MacLeod is caring for a child that is not his, there has to be a reason."

Well, of course, there was a reason. Because it was honorable.

Her aunt leaned forward, her stare reading Victoria's thoughts. "It may *seem* honorable, but let me tell you something. I am married to a man whose intentions *seem* very honorable, but they really aren't."

Victoria barely contained a gasp. "What do you mean?"

"Walter has given me a fine home and a daughter, and I love them both. But they've come with a price. He's not as upstanding a man as he wants people to believe." The smugness returned and she took another sip of tea as if to shield her attitude. "So just be careful of men. They claim women are fickle, but they are as sly as foxes. They twist women around their fingers or, worse, bully them." After another sip, she set down her teacup.

Victoria played with the lace at her collar. She wasn't sure how she felt about the older woman's words. She just knew she didn't care to be enjoying anything tonight. "If you'll excuse me, I think I'm not as rested as I first thought."

"Supper will be served as soon as Walter arrives home."

Victoria's head suddenly started to pound. She knew right then that she didn't want to sit about like a silly socialite waiting to be served, not while Mitchell was out at his ranch trying to be both mother and father to his children.

And to the one who was not even his.

"Excuse me, but I think I will retire early. You shouldn't set a place for me, either. I won't be much company, I'm afraid."

Before Aunt Louise could try to convince her otherwise, Victoria fled the parlor.

Mitch spread out the children's things on his kitchen floor. This way, he could keep an eye on the kicking and squirming Emily as he sorted out what each child had. Ralph considered it a game and he and Mary sorted the items first according to color, but then, thankfully, according to whom they belonged. Jake also helped.

There were so few things, it cut him to the quick. He'd sent money home to Agnes, as much as he could, but he knew there usually wasn't enough. Matthew's clothes were the newest looking, the rest had hand-me-downs, and Mary owned only one other pinafore.

There were no toys, save a small wooden game and a book of children's stories. His mother would be appalled if she saw this.

"What is this thing?"

Mitch turned. He'd asked Jake to unload what food was left, hoping they could scavenge something to feed the children quickly.

"It's a bottle to feed Emily. You can't figure that out?"

"There's a lot I can't figure out, Mitch, but I'm doin' my best."

Mitch grimaced. "There should be a tin of milk in that

sack. Heat it up for me, will you? Not too hot, though. I'll show you what to do next."

"Where'd you learn that stuff?"

"The nurse at the hospital showed me." Mitch returned to his sorting. "And dig out some food for the children. There's got to be something there they can eat."

"Do we have to go to bed right after supper, Papa?" Mary asked looking up from her task. "Can we see the horses first?"

"It'll be dark soon."

"You can use a lantern," John reasoned, slipping close with a hopeful expression. "We have good eyes."

"We'll see." Mitch dug back into the large box he'd acquired for the bedding. No doubt the porter had helped Matthew pack everything. Those young men on the trains did commendable jobs and Mitch was grateful that in the turmoil of disembarking, he'd remembered to tip the man.

His hands scraped against something wicker. Lifting it out, he found it was Victoria's treat box. The porter knew it was Victoria's, for he'd helped her find it, but must have presumed she was also coming out here to the ranch.

"Treats!" Mary cried out, jumping up and forgetting about the horses. "I want some!"

"No!" he snapped, a bit more harshly than he planned. All the children shrank back. Mitch gritted his teeth as he set the box on the table. His back turned, he shut his eyes.

Lord, give me strength.

"This doesn't belong to us," he said to no one in particular. When he turned, all the children were standing close looking as though they'd been told a favorite pet had died. Even Emily had stopped her squirming.

First thing tomorrow morning, he would see Pastor Wyseman. He would know a reliable woman who could help, Mitch told himself. But before that, he'd return this wicker basket, as much as he didn't want to darken any doorstep at that address. He'd just drop it off at the door. No, he'd drop it off at the tradesman's entrance. Less chance to run into Victoria if he showed up at the back entry.

She was a guest at the finest house in Proud Bend. He was a rancher in what could be the smallest ranch house in Colorado. He glanced around. That first summer, after he'd acquired a few cattle, he'd built this place. A three-room log house, which included the kitchen with a stove, a counter and some cupboards. In the front room, a table and some ladder-back chairs, four beds, each with a tick Matthew had been charged with making up. His own tiny bedroom was tucked in back. The place had two windows and one door. What would Victoria think of it if she saw it?

Oh, yes, it was good that he and Victoria had parted ways.

His gut clenched at the thought, but he smiled at the children, albeit forcedly. "Why don't we see those horses now? I have a couple of yearlings that don't have names yet. Maybe all of you can help me with that?"

Smiles wreathed the children's faces, and though they did much to dispel the pall he was suddenly feeling, nothing rid his gut of the chill.

A light rap stirred Victoria from her doze. She rolled in her bed and called out, "Come in."

She was expecting Aunt Louise, and as much as she

was grateful to her, Victoria didn't feel like dealing with her anymore tonight. Her aunt was polite, but underneath, she seemed to be a woman who felt trapped in her own web.

"Miss Victoria? Am I disturbing you?"

It was the maid, Sandra, carrying a tray. The smells of fresh bread and lamb stew wafted over to her. Her traitorous stomach growled. She didn't want to think of food. There were too many churning emotions within her. And they all starred Mitchell, as if his name was centered in a marquee above a famous theater. Victoria quickly straightened. No reason for the maid to see her as a slouch.

"Mrs. Louise told me to bring supper to you," Sandra explained with a short, bobbing curtsy. "My ma did a wonderful stew."

A small smile hovered over Victoria's features. "Thank you, but I'd rather prepare for bed."

Sandra set the tray down on the small table between two chairs in Victoria's spacious room. "Yes, miss."

"Sandra? Does your mother run this house?"

"Yes, miss. She's the housekeeper."

"Where is your father?"

"He looks after the grounds and the horses."

"And your quarters?"

"Me and my sister—she's the kitchen maid, miss—we sleep up in the attic, but my parents have a cottage at the back of the property."

"Thank you." Victoria wasn't sure why she asked all this, except to perhaps learn about the household. It seemed pretentious to be here and not know. She bit her lip. Wouldn't it have been better if she focused on a plan for employment?

Where would she start? Even that young woman from the train, Clare Walsh, wasn't sure. The land registry office was big, she'd said. That was the only lead Clare had.

Not very hopeful for the woman. And even less so for Victoria.

Chapter Twelve

Victoria found the morning surprisingly warm, and she opted for breakfast out on the back patio, probably the only time she'd do so before next spring. As promised, she could see Castle Rock, a squat pillar of stone jutting up from a hill. Mine trappings spoiled its natural beauty, but the view of the nearer Proud River made up for it. If it wasn't for the dry air and curious butte in the distance, she could have been in a country home in western Massachusetts, with that charming little log cottage peeking out from a copse of trees at the bottom of the yard.

One thing, though. She missed the brilliant reds and oranges that colored the autumn leaves out east. The trees here offered mostly yellow and gold.

Having risen at a time she considered early, Victoria had expected to see Aunt Louise around, but Sandra reported that her mistress often slept late. Uncle Walter, on the other hand, had already departed for the bank.

Victoria was thankful for that small mercy. She knew that sooner or later, Walter would pick up where he'd left off with this business about Clyde Abernathy. But for the time being, she was glad that his work distracted him.

"Where is Rachel?" Victoria had also asked Sandra earlier, not wanting to monopolize the girl if her cousin needed her.

"Miss Rachel stays out very late." Sandra's voice had dropped to a whisper. "She sleeps in until noon. But when I helped her prepare for bed, I told her you'd arrived."

It was curious that her parents didn't admonish her for this shocking lifestyle even if she was an adult. Did they not know?

"Perhaps she has a beau?"

"No. Miss Rachel said there ain't no decent men here."

Victoria's brows had shot up. A scathing remark. No wonder she was still single.

She was still pondering that more than an hour later as she sat outside. The door opened and another maid brought out Victoria's breakfast, effectively ending her speculation. The young woman offered her a hasty good-morning in a rather shrill voice, set the tray on the linen covered tablecloth and soon disappeared. After grace, Victoria lifted the lid covering her plate and found several slices of toast with marmalade, and a boiled egg. Coffee sat in a small pot, as it was expected of her to pour her own. Victoria filled her dainty cup, idly pondering the different climate here. The air smelled cleaner, fresher and, today, warmer. Such a rare treat, this weather. All she needed was her light tailored jacket. Dry air felt warmer, she decided. And she would enjoy it as much as possible.

Her stomach growled, reminding her that last night she'd left her lamb stew and fresh bread untouched.

After stirring her coffee, Victoria set down her spoon, feeling guilty at the waste. She should eat. It was funny how her sudden poverty had made her appreciate what she'd always taken for granted.

Victoria took a small bite of her toast, her actions stalling when a series of sudden noises reached her. She turned, but couldn't see anyone through the shrubs that fenced in the patio. Someone with a deep voice shushed another, and a sharp rap on a door rang through the morning air. A delivery man must have arrived.

She heard a murmur, but couldn't make out the words. The tradesman's entrance would no doubt lead to a cellar, its downward steps cut out of the rocky ground. Sounds would bounce off the hard natural walls before filtering through the shrubbery and waning flowers of autumn. Victoria heard the young maid's rather shrill voice cut the dry air. "Oh, Miss Victoria is up on the terrace now, sir. I'll ask her if she wants to see you."

Victoria stilled, feeling her face drain of color. Her heart stopped. Was this Clyde? *Lord, please let it not be Clyde.*

No. He would never come to the back door.

"That's not necessary." The voice was clear, and Victoria's heart went from cold stillness to a fast gallop. Mitchell?

"But, Papa, I want to see Miss Templeton!"

That was Mary! She felt her lips curl into a smile. What had brought them here?

Victoria stood and hurried over to the shrubs to peer down at the small entrance. Packed inside the stony alcove in front of the door were Mitchell and his children, including baby Emily in her wicker basket. "Hello!"

The older children looked up. The maid spoke. "Miss Victoria, this man wants to see you."

"Come up, please!" She'd no sooner spoken the words

when Ralph and John scrambled up the short wall. Ralph squeezed through the shrubbery, while John vaulted over it. They both rushed at her. Mary looked plaintive, for her dress and pinafore would not have allowed such a climb. Behind her, Matthew stood with his usual reserved look. He held Victoria's wicker box in his hands.

Not so long ago, Mitch had vowed he'd never come here as long as Walter Smith kept badgering him to sell his mineral rights. But here he was. He should have come alone. That way, he'd have hastily asked the maid to return the box and been gone in a flash. But his traitorous children had other plans.

He'd come to town to purchase some foodstuffs and arrange for the sale of several heifers who'd been bred late in the spring. Several ranchers had agreed to buy them, and Mitch had told Jake just this morning to finish up the sale of them, while he completed this short detour.

The maid led him and the other children through the house and quietly shut the terrace door behind them. John and Ralph were still hugging Victoria as he stepped out into the morning sunshine. Mary tore off the second she spied Victoria, while Matthew, ever cautious, set the box on the chair and allowed himself to be hugged.

"What brings you all here?" Victoria asked.

"We came to return the box," John announced. "Papa wouldn't let us eat any of it."

"I'm hungry," Ralph announced.

"Ralph!" Mitch had had enough. That boy couldn't be hungry. Before they'd left, he'd ensured everyone ate a decent bowl of oatmeal, washed down with a cup of fresh milk. Tightly, he added, "We're here to return the box, that's all."

Beaming, Victoria hurried over to it. She sat down and removed the lid. "I can't even remember what was left in here." She whispered to the children, "Let's finish it off right now."

Mitch felt his jaw tighten. She was brushing off all of his attempts at discipline. The children needed to learn control. "That's not necessary, Victoria. And I would rather you not indulge the children."

Too late. She'd already doled out the remaining food, breaking the biscuits into halves and crumbling the cheese into large chunks onto a plate. The children ate like starving cats. Mitch rolled his eyes. "I said, enough!"

They stilled immediately. "We have to leave," he told them. "Say your goodbyes and your thank-yous."

"No, wait!" Victoria closed up the box and told the children, "Go down to the yard and play for a moment. But don't go near the river, especially you two, John and Ralph. I want to speak with your father."

Immediately, Mitch stiffened his spine. Did she want to remind him to feed his children? Or make sure they washed their hands and faces? He knew how to be a good father. It wasn't the ideal solution, being a father and a rancher, the latter being better off alone, but he would do just fine.

He waited until the children were out of earshot before he turned to peer down at Victoria. She was particularly beautiful today. Her dress and short jacket were a deep purple, both cinched at a small waist he was sure he could span with his two hands. Her hair had been fancifully arranged and she smelled of lavender, too, just enough to entice him to inhale deeply.

"Yes?" he asked, refusing to allow his lungs the pleasure of a deep breath.

She looked up at him, her expression mixed with nervousness and anxiety. "I know I shouldn't ask, but I will, anyway. This is terribly ill mannered of me—"

"Then don't do it," he grated out.

She pursed her lips, but a moment later, she burst out, "Is Emily your child?"

He folded his arms. "Does that make a difference?"

It doesn't, Victoria told herself firmly. *So why are you asking?*

Because it changed how she saw Mitchell. Yet she wasn't sure if she should accept that reason. He wasn't a part of her life now, but he lingered in her thoughts. So proud. She suddenly ached to smooth away the slight wrinkle in his forehead.

He'd shaved and abandoned his suit for a sturdy pair of saddle pants, a plain cotton shirt, with the sleeves rolled up enough to reveal a long sleeved undershirt. His vest was leather, and his scarf checkered. Victoria could only stare. Even in this ordinary outfit, Mitchell was a handsome, rugged figure of a man.

It was best if she think of him only as a simple cowboy raising his family. She needed to focus on employment, doing something that required her skill set, such as it was. And that skill set didn't include children and babies and keeping a mean cabin up in the mountains.

Victoria glanced into the basket that Mitchell had set down. The baby was watching her. Could Emily see her properly? Was the smile the infant wore for her?

Emily would never know either of her parents, if what Aunt Louise said was true. Victoria frowned and worked her jaw. She'd lost her father a decade ago. No child should suffer through a loss like that.

"It doesn't make a difference at all who Emily's father was," she replied. "It was just that I heard that you couldn't possibly have—" She cleared her throat and started again. "That you couldn't possibly have fathered her, and, well…" She thought quickly, hoping her words would catch up with her speeding thoughts. "I was thinking of the children. What if someone torments them about it? People talk, you know."

"So I see. But they won't be in town enough for that to happen," he ground out. "And they will be well cared for, too, if that's your next question."

"So, it's true?"

Mitchell picked up the basket and turned. He called for his children before facing Victoria again. "Since it doesn't make any difference, I'm not going to tell you."

Victoria bit her lip as the children advanced toward the house, Matthew hauling a reluctant Ralph, and Mary and John skipping ahead.

It must be true.

She should not assume anything, she told herself sternly. She should be thankful she'd been a part of these fine children's lives even for a short time.

And a part of Mitchell's. He stood in front of her, his lips a thin line and his spine as stiff as the side of a highboy. He hated answering her, and she hated that she even asked. What was wrong with her that she acknowledged her aunt's gossip with a question that embarrassed both of them?

An apology sprang to her tongue, and she opened her mouth to utter it, but was stopped by a voice from the doors leading to the house.

"What do we have here?"

Victoria turned. A smiling woman about a decade

older than her breezed through the terrace doors that she'd held open with both hands. She wore a conservative but expensive outfit and her hair was immaculately coiffed. A small brooch pinned to her high collar was her only jewelry. Her long features resembled a younger Louise, and Victoria knew immediately that this was Rachel her cousin. The woman released the doors and strode out.

"Victoria, I presume. I'm Rachel." She held out her hand.

Still feeling a bit surprised she would meet the woman so early in the day, Victoria shook it. Rachel's was a firm, warm handshake, and she added to it by covering Victoria's hand with her free one.

Victoria looked down. To her amazement, Rachel's hands were rough, her fingernails and cuticles chewed nearly to the bone. Calluses filled her palms. They were the hands of a stable boy. How was that possible?

Yet, Rachel held her head high and regally, as if she hadn't done a single thing to give herself working hands.

"So nice to meet you, Rachel," Victoria murmured. She looked to Mitchell, who was watching the older woman with his own expression of surprise. "This is Mitchell MacLeod."

"I know Mitch well." Rachel rolled an assessing look down his frame. "He has been very helpful in our church."

Rachel's tone didn't match the simple explanation, but Victoria couldn't say why. "I assisted Mitchell in bringing his children out here," she answered. "His family had stayed in Boston until his ranch house was ready."

"I know."

Again, the light, self-assured tone rang clearly through the still morning air.

"Sadly, his wife was not able to see the ranch," Victoria added. "She recently passed away."

Rachel's expression fell. "I didn't know that." She turned to Mitchell. "My condolences, Mitch. What a shock for you and your children."

Victoria waited for an explanation of how they knew each other. From either of them. It didn't come. But surely it was more than just worshipping together.

Miss Rachel stays out very late. No! She would not speculate. If she would not do so about Mitchell's private life, she would not speculate about his relationship to Rachel. Nor would she judge her cousin.

Victoria plastered on a smile. "Mitchell was returning my box of treats that somehow made it into his luggage."

Rachel laughed. "Were the treats still in it, with all these children about? I can't imagine that."

The children stood between Mitchell and Victoria. She could feel Mary's small hand slip into hers. Ralph was grinning at Rachel, but the other two had stepped cautiously back.

They didn't trust her. Self-satisfaction rose completely unbidden in Victoria, and she crushed it immediately. Those same children had acted in a similar way when they'd visited her brownstone only a week ago. Victoria reminded herself not to judge Rachel, whose bold, self-assured manner had not been unlike Victoria's own behavior that day in her parlor.

"We should leave, children. Good day, ladies." Mitchell touched the brim of his Stetson first to Rachel, then to Victoria. Then he took Mary's and Ralph's hands.

The doors to the house were once more pushed open and the same maid—Victoria really needed to learn the girl's name—stepped out. "Miss Rachel, Miss Victoria? This man is here for Mr. MacLeod."

A young man stepped onto the terrace, his Stetson in his hand and an anxious look on his face. He focused on Mitchell.

Mitchell released his children's hands. "Jake, what is it?"

"The men you sent me to, Mitch. All of them. Roberts and the Miller brothers, they say they can't buy your heifers. There ain't a buyer in the county, Mitch. No one wants your stock."

Chapter Thirteen

It felt like a punch in his gut. Mitch took a step toward Jake, whose own deep concern mirrored his. "They *can't* buy them, or they *won't* buy them?"

"Both, Mitch. Roberts said he couldn't, but one of the Miller brothers said he won't. He said he'll get new heifers someplace else. I asked him why, but he wouldn't say."

Mitch tightened his mouth. He had a pretty good idea. This was his fault. He should have kept his mouth shut at the train depot yesterday when he mentioned to Walter Smith that he planned to sell some heifers. He knew it wouldn't have taken too long to figure out which of local ranchers wanted to buy them.

Frustration swelled in his gut. What was he supposed to do now? Fighting irritability, he took up Ralph's hand and the basket, and gathered the other children.

He glanced at Victoria. It was best he leave now, mostly to figure out his next step, but also to put some space and time between him and this house.

He needed to get away from Victoria, too. She'd already judged his children. He'd seen her disgusted look when she'd stared down at the baby. He had better leave. She was distracting him from figuring out how to counter her uncle's wily tricks.

Walter Smith would do anything to gain Mitch's mineral rights and the way to that end was forcing him to default on his mortgage payment.

Refusing to walk through the grand rooms with the expensive wallpaper and fussy furniture, Mitch stalked around the house, leading the children. Reaching the long, wide drive, he eased up on his rushing steps.

"Mitchell!"

He heard her call out but he would not turn. Her question and her disgust pricked his pride.

Victoria hurried up to stop him, racing around in front of him with concern etched into her face. "Are you all right?"

The baby cried a bit, and he automatically took the basket and rocked it gently. Then, after thinking a moment, he turned to Matthew. "Take your brothers and Mary to the wagon. I'll be right along."

With those wide eyes and cautious expression, Matthew obeyed. He was such a great boy. Mitch knew he needed to spend more time with him, but with the list of chores growing each day, and now this setback, he wasn't sure when that would happen.

"Mitchell," Victoria began again after the children were out of earshot. "This sounds serious. Is there anything I can do?"

He cocked his head. "Yeah, you can buy all my heifers."

She recoiled, ever so slightly, for her fine manners and polite concern had been able to temper her shock at his biting remark.

"I—I'm sorry." She looked away, blood rising into her cheeks. "Y-you know I can't do that."

He pulled a face and relaxed slightly. "I was being sarcastic, Victoria. I know you can't buy my heifers."

The flush deepened, spreading to her neck and contrasting brilliantly with the white lace of her high collar. Mitch's gut hurt. Why did he have to say that? Victoria was proud, an heiress fallen on hard times for a reason that was none of his business. Her mother had foisted her upon wealthier relatives. He didn't need, nor did he really want, to make her feel any more miserable. He knew the feeling well. It didn't need to be spread around.

All the more reason to get out of there. Mitch walked around her. As he took that first step, she caught his arm.

He looked down at her hand, then into her face. That moment in the train car when it had lurched forward suddenly returned to him, when he'd found himself falling on her. Her scent had been…what? Lavender like today? Automatically, he inhaled, only to be rewarded with another head full of fine, soft perfume.

"There must be something I can do, Mitchell. What about the children? Whatever this is, it will affect them, and you need help—"

He pulled back his arm. "I don't need any help, thank you." He leaned toward her. "And what can you do, anyway? You have only ever fed Emily once. After that, you pawned her off on another woman."

"I could help—"

"Victoria, listen to yourself." He flicked his gaze up to the big, stately home behind her. The fine rhyolite facade was only just catching the late-morning sun, its curious tans and pinks glittering as the rough surface played with the oblique rays. It was a ridiculously opulent mansion.

Too fine a home for him. "You can't help. We both know that. Honestly, do you even know where the kitchen is in this place? Could you lead me directly to it?"

She opened her mouth. Then shut it.

"Do you know how to start a fire in a cold stove, or how long bread takes to bake? Or how much water oatmeal needs?" he added. "All these things are part of the help I need. The other is to sell my heifers. You can't do either of them."

Her stricken expression intensified. Though Mitch's tone was gentle, he knew his words stung. He hated them, but they needed to be said.

"We were talking about selling my heifers," he continued. He noticed her slight frown. "Do you even know what a heifer is?"

She swallowed. And for a moment, he'd hoped that she would know that much, but no. He could read her expression. She didn't.

He shook his head, berating himself for his behavior. For a man who didn't want to hurt a lady, he was doing a pretty poor job of sticking to that promise. She may not be the silly socialite with irritating ideals that he'd thought her to be—no, she was gentle and kind—but that didn't mean she could help him. She cared, yes, but she knew nothing of the regular things that regular people did in the course of a day. If she did, he would have honestly considered her offer of help.

No. He wouldn't allow her to make a fool of herself, and he didn't want her to sweep into his and his children's lives only to realize later that she couldn't handle it and then leave. It would hurt his children too much.

And you, too?

No.

Abruptly, he turned and stalked away, and this time, thankfully, Victoria let him go.

Victoria blinked back the wellspring of tears that threatened to burst forth from her eyes. All she could do was watch, uselessly, as Mitchell climbed aboard his wagon and flicked the reins with a bit too much harshness. As the horses responded, the children turned their heads. Mary lifted her small hand to wave a sad goodbye.

Mitchell was right. She *was* useless. She'd wanted to tell him she knew exactly where the kitchen was in this mansion, but it wasn't her Boston brownstone, with its layout as simple as it was elegant, with the garden level having the kitchen, the parlor level, the receiving room and library, and two more levels above. Victoria turned and viewed the expansive home in front of her. It was so wide and sprawling, the kitchen in this home could be anywhere in the back.

This wasn't fair. She'd only arrived last night, and refused her evening meal because of the silly, confusing emotions she'd felt when she'd learned that Mitchell could not have fathered Emily. She'd had no chance to learn the layout of this grand house.

But how hard could it be to figure it out? Mitchell had walked around to the tradesman's entrance, and it would be by the scullery, which obviously would lead to the kitchen. That way, the only thing workmen saw were a few drying dishes.

So somewhere down there lay the kitchen, but Victoria knew she would not be able to walk straight to it with confidence. The house had too many closed doors.

A man strode around from the back of the house, equally anxious to be gone. It was Jake. He tipped his hat to her as he passed, heading toward the horse tied up at the end corner of the fence. When it was clear he wasn't going to stop, she called to him. He turned.

"Do you work for Mitchell?" she asked.

"Yes, ma'am. I'm his ranch hand."

"Did he give you heifers to sell?"

"No, ma'am, he just wanted me to make the final arrangements for pickup and collection of the money. Mitch had already arranged the sale and would have done this all himself, but he needed to get some food, plus his young-uns wanted to return that box and see you." He smiled suddenly. "I can see why."

She flushed. He reddened, also. "Sorry, ma'am. What I meant to say was that you gave those kids the rest of your treats. Of course, they'd want to come by. They knew you would."

"Jake, why did the sale of those heifers really fall through?"

"Well," he began slowly, as if reluctant to speak. "I don't quite know the full reason. Two of the men said they couldn't buy them, but I figure that they're too scared."

"Of what?"

Jake's gaze darted to the house, but when Victoria glanced over her shoulder, she saw nothing amiss. Not even a servant peeking out a window. "Ranchers around here owe the bank in Proud Bend. It ain't right, but they need to stay on the bank's good side."

Oh, so that was why he glanced back at the house. Uncle Walter. She should have known, especially after Aunt Louise's blunt admission last night. She knew she'd married a cad. Was that why she tolerated Rachel's late nights? Because she felt guilty for giving the woman an unsavory father? Victoria blew out a heavy sigh. "There must be something that can be done for Mitchell."

"I wish there was, ma'am. Mitch needs the money. And these heifers were older and have been bred. They're good stock, too. It's a shame, really. I'd best go catch up with him." He tipped his hat and moved away toward his horse.

Victoria stood there, biting her lip and fighting frustration. Again, she was proving that she wasn't meant for this frontier, as they used to call Colorado. Before she left Boston, she'd read one of Ovando Hollister's books. He felt this state was still a frontier. Regardless, she couldn't possibly find her place here. Out here, no one wanted a socialite whose greatest skill was small talk.

"That's quite a pickle he's in."

Victoria turned as Rachel walked up to her. "How much did you hear?" Victoria asked her cousin.

"Enough. And I know how it works in town. Father is a tough banker, as is his partner. I expect some of those mortgages are up for renewal. Those ranchers have the right to be nervous."

"Uncle Walter should be ashamed of himself."

"Yes, he should, but owning the only bank in Proud Bend does that to a person." She shrugged. "He'll try getting his own way with you, too."

"How so?"

"He's expecting you to marry Clyde."

Victoria swallowed hard and Rachel smiled. "That was my reaction, too, when he said that to me."

"He wanted you to marry Clyde?"

Rachel nodded. "For several years, when I was younger, until I told him a flat-out no. He was furious for a long time, rarely speaking to me, but he got over it. Then he learned you were coming."

Victoria turned away, spying Mitchell's wagon far down the street by the general store.

There was a pause before Rachel added, "Do you want to help Mitch?"

"I do." Victoria looked back at Rachel. "If I had the money, I would buy those heifers, and then sell them quietly to those men at the same price."

"An interesting idea." Rachel was smiling as she spoke.

"It's the logical thing to do. They can't buy the heifers from Mitchell, but they could buy them from someone else. If I had money, I'd buy them because I don't have a mortgage at your father's bank."

"But you *do* owe him."

The blood drained from Victoria's face.

The older woman laughed and reached out to squeeze her hands with her own calloused ones. Victoria looked down at them. Why did Rachel not care for them? Where had those hands been? Why, Victoria hadn't even touched reins or a bridle without gloves, let alone anything else that could harden her skin.

"Now, how about you and I go into the heifer business together?" Rachel asked. "I have the money, and I can give it to you. You buy the heifers from Jake, then sell them right away to those other ranchers. When the men give you the money, you return it to me."

"Why don't you just do it?"

Rachel smiled. "And not allow you the opportunity to help?"

Victoria's mind churned. Was Rachel looking for a way to punish her father or did she want Victoria to share in the chance to help Mitchell?

"You have that kind of money?" Victoria asked. "And you'd go against your father?"

"Yes, I have the money, and let's just say I have gone against my father before. Allow me to worry about him."

Victoria paled. Then hesitated. She'd already leaped into a situation she hadn't fully appreciated when she'd accepted Mitchell's offer of a job. She shouldn't be doing the same now, especially where money was concerned, and these heifers, whatever they were, sounded expensive.

But what would happen to Mitchell if she didn't do something?

Rachel leaned forward. "If you like, I'll make all the arrangements."

"Why are you offering this?"

"Because there's a need." Her smile faltering a bit, she led Victoria back around the house. "I'll send the errand boy to bring Jake back. We'll sort out the details over breakfast. Do you have any more questions?"

Victoria stalled her steps. "Yes, just one. What on earth is a heifer?"

Chapter Fourteen

As the children tucked into their evening meals on Thursday, Mitch heard Jake blow out a sigh as though they'd dodged a stampede of wild horses. Was it because he was afraid the meal wasn't good enough for them? Hardly. Jake was a pretty good cook for a cowboy. He'd even insisted that Mitch plant some herbs around the door so that "food didn't taste like old socks," as he'd once said.

No, Jake's relief couldn't be about the cooking. Was it about the sale of the heifers? Yesterday, Jake had disappeared, right after Mitch had left Victoria and her shocked expression. But during that time, he'd somehow managed to convince the other ranchers to buy Mitch's stock, a task for which Mitch was very grateful. Then, he'd shown up with the money, adding that they needed to deliver the heifers by week's end. Saturday.

Mitch hadn't gone to the bank yet because the mortgage wasn't due till next week. First he wanted to pay his bill at the general store. He also wanted to send Jake to pay Victoria for her help on the train. It was better if Jake went. Victoria had commanded Mitch's thoughts every second since he'd last seen her, especially at night. He needed sleep, not to be reminded of the hurt in that woman's eyes when he asked her if she knew where the kitchen was.

All right, that hadn't been a fair question. But the point had hit home. She wasn't meant for frontier life. Oh, it was fine for her to play the fancy visiting heiress, but as much as she might want to help, he knew it would be a miserable failure.

"What's wrong, Mitch? You're pushing good food around the plate like it's a game."

Mitch looked down at his plate. Jake had cooked up some meat, made a decent gravy and managed to boil potatoes just right.

"You haven't touched your food," Jake pointed out. "It's good. Look at the kids."

Mitch glanced around the table. All the children had polished off the plates set before them.

"It was good," Matthew assured.

Mitch's gut tightened. "What did you normally eat for supper?"

"Beans and bread. And porridge."

"Did you have any meat?"

Matthew shrugged. "On Sundays when the ladies from the church came around with it."

Mitch pushed his food away. John and Ralph looked at his plate with interest. What had happened to the money he'd sent to Boston every other month? How had Agnes spent it? There had been nothing in her apartment. He'd searched it thoroughly. Had the cost of living in Boston increased so much that Agnes hadn't been able to keep up? Shame welled up in him.

He scraped back his chair and stood. "All you kids help Jake clean up. We have a big day tomorrow."

"Are we going back to see Miss Templeton?"

Mitch looked down at Ralph's hopeful expression. "No. We have work to do here. I have an errand for Jake, so I'll need you all here to help me."

Jake shifted in his seat. "Okay, but I'm still workin' on that list of chores you gave me before you went out east." He paused and when Mitch said nothing, he continued, "Don't forget that you need to go to the land registry office. You need to take your wife's name off the deed."

And put Emily's on it, Mitch added to himself.

Jake was still talking. "Not to mention getting that money put in the bank." He looked over at Emily. "And ask Pastor Wyseman if he knows of a woman who can come out here. You might have an errand for me, but those things you need to do."

Mitch grimaced. He'd been looking forward to catching up on the rest of the work around here, but Jake was right. Only he could do those tasks.

When he'd gone to town last, yesterday, his time had been taken up with getting supplies and seeing Victoria. By the time everything was loaded into the wagon, both the bank and the land registry office were closed. Yesterday, he'd worked on getting a routine started, but Emily had fussed with the milk he'd purchased. Even now, in her basket, she squirmed. He grimaced. Could Victoria have been right about the milk?

No. She knew nothing about milk and babies. And while on the train, she had sloughed off her duty onto another woman. Well, he wouldn't slough off his. He would raise the children. And he'd give Victoria her salary instead of sending it in with Jake. He would do what was right.

He grabbed his plate. "I'll go first thing in the morning, but you'll have to keep the children here. I'll make sure Emily is fed first."

"That milk makes her sick," Jake announced. "I should bring the ewe close to the house. Maybe her milk is better. Her latest lamb is ready to graze on his own."

Mitch rubbed his forehead. He'd only been following the doctor's orders. Babies sure were complicated little things. And they generated a whopping pile of laundry, too.

He needed help and he needed it fast.

The morning sun had just reached the top of Castle Rock when Mitch met Pastor Paul Wyseman. The man was just finishing his prayers at the front of Proud Bend's only church. The day, like most in midautumn, had promised and was delivering warm sunshine. If only Pastor Wyseman's answer had been equally welcoming. The pastor had listened without comment as Mitch asked if he knew of a potential housekeeper.

He held his breath now. "Let me make some inquiries," Paul finally said. "But we're a small town and I can't think of any woman off the top of my head. I can ask in Castle Rock, if you like, but why not hire the woman who traveled with you?"

Working his jaw, Mitch folded his arms. "Do you know who that was?"

Paul shook his head. "No. I just know you hired a woman in Boston to act as a nanny."

"That was only a temporary position. She's come to live with the Smiths. She's their niece."

Paul's expression brightened. "I think I know of her. Do you think she's unsuitable?"

Mitch didn't want to say anything, but how could he make his pastor understand why it would be a mistake to hire her without revealing too much? Yet, couldn't he trust the man to be discreet? "Victoria pawned off the main task of caring for Emily onto another woman. She said the milk I bought was making Emily sick."

Paul cocked his head as he studied Mitch. An uncomfortable flush rose in him.

"Did she know how to care for Emily? In my ministry, I see young girls finding themselves with child and unable to care for them simply because they've not learned to do so. We can't expect a man to be able to build a barn without being trained, and I can see that motherhood is the same way."

"Perhaps so, but that doesn't change the fact she traded a dress for my daughter's care."

"So she pawned off her duty on another woman? Did she not want to care for Emily?"

"It wasn't that," Mitch explained. "She said she had Emily's best interests at heart."

"Isn't that what you have?"

"Of course!"

"Why?"

"She's my daughter."

Paul frowned reproachfully. "We both know that Emily isn't your daughter, Mitch."

Head flooded into Mitch. "That's got nothing to do with it."

Paul leaned forward and gripped his arm. "I'm not being argumentative, Mitch. I just want you to see another point of view."

"She didn't even try with Emily."

"It seems to me that Victoria tried her best under unfamiliar circumstances. It sounds like her life has been turned upside down, as well."

Mitch didn't want to hear any sympathy for Victoria. She'd only end up hurting the whole family. Okay, maybe he could forgive her for trading Emily's care, but that didn't mean the woman who popped into his thoughts at the most inopportune times should be in his family's lives.

Lord, why is this happening?

Paul released his arm. He was a calm, plainspoken man who had heartfelt compassion for all his flock. "My condolences on the loss of Agnes. I wish I had known her."

Bitter pride rose in Mitch. "Why? We both know what she did."

"It was hard for you here, Mitch, but it was hard for her back east, I'm sure. I don't condone her actions, but we are all sinners. You're doing right by your wife, as you should, but we have to remember that all sin is equal."

Mitch tightened his jaw. What sin in his life was equal to that? He scowled at his pastor. "But the consequences aren't equal."

"Nor is doing right going to erase the sin in your own life," Paul added. "We all have it. Slothfulness, idolatry. Pride."

Mitch stiffened.

There was a distinct pause. "Is there anything more I can do for you?" Paul finally asked, his tone gentle.

Though the words were polite, Mitch knew that his pastor meant them with the fierceness of Mitch's own words. But he shook his head.

He needed time alone. To consider the words meant to teach him.

"Here's my advice, Mitch," the pastor said into the ensuing silence. "While I ask around about a woman who can help you, take time to consider what it all means. Prayerfully consider it. And ask yourself why you have Emily here."

"What do you mean?"

"Why did you bring her here?"

"Are you suggesting I brought her here to prove my sin is less than my wife's? That I am a better person?" Mitch didn't want his pastor to believe that. "Because that's not why."

"Then did you take her because she needs a family or because of another reason?" Paul held Mitch's gaze. "I remember when you first got your ranch, and how you had Agnes own half of it. Did she have a will? Did she leave her share to you, or the children, including Emily?"

Stunned, Mitch eased back. Paul was a smart man to guess who co-owned the ranch, but did he really believe that was the only reason Mitch had brought the baby here? It was unfair.

The pastor correctly assessed his reaction. Still staring at Mitch, he lifted his brows. "So, if I can be mistaken about that, think of how you could be mistaken about Victoria. Perhaps there is a plan in all of this with her."

"I'm not mistaken, and there is no plan that includes her." He straightened. "Thank you. As you might assume from correctly guessing Agnes's will, I need to see to the deed changes. I can only hope the staff is discreet."

Paul pondered the idea, then nodded. "At the recorder's office? I believe they are. Most are in my congregation and understand there is a certain expectation of privacy. Your pride won't be tested there, I'm sure."

There he went again. Gentle words that were heavy with admonishment. All Mitch wanted was to remind them of that expectation of privacy, and not set tongues a-wagging after he left. Because he didn't want anything hurting his children. He knew how that felt. He'd been devastated when he'd learned that his favorite uncle had been killed in the war. He'd been left in the street crying when a little girl, a tattletale, had repeated the words she'd heard over the back fence. The sad news should have come from his parents.

That was the only reason why he wanted discretion. To spare the children.

Still, a voice inside of him whispered, *Are you sure it's not your pride?*

He focused on Paul again. "I thought at first that Agnes had changed her will because she believed her end was near, but she didn't specify a guardian. Now I believe she did it to force me to raise Emily."

"There is much more to being a father than just being there at conception."

Just like there was more to caring for a child than putting food on the table. Mitch felt his jaw clench at his own admonishment. Still, bitterness and pride pricked him. "I have work to do," he groused to his friend. "Good day."

With that, he stalked out of the church.

So there Victoria was, pushing open the recorder's office door, all the while searching the dim, quiet interior for Clare. The woman had sent a note early this morning, inviting her to lunch. Since it had been the only exciting thing to happen since she'd arranged to buy Mitchell's heifers, Victoria had jumped at the diversion.

She hadn't realized how full her days on the train had been until the days here loomed ahead of her like the mountains loomed above Proud Bend. Rachel slept in most days, and Aunt Louise was always running the household. Victoria was left to stare at the walls.

Her heart squeezed at the memory of the train ride. How was it possible to miss the children so much?

And Mitchell? Did she miss him? A part of her wanted to see him, but at the same time, a part of her found him infuriating. Honestly, what on earth was it about him that both interested and frustrated her?

The pain behind his expression? Mix that with stubborn pride and one had a man like Mitchell.

Or was she frustrated at her inability to help?

Inside the recorder's office, Victoria glanced around, refusing to answer her private questions. From the back of the office, Clare, quite cheerfully, lifted her hand in greeting.

Victoria swallowed the jealousy suddenly rising in her. Why was she this way? Frustrated at Mitchell, jealous of Clare? She was a poor Christian, indeed. She should be happy that Clare found a position so quickly. Victoria forced out a smile and waved back.

Perhaps if she learned what Clare did in the office, Victoria could apply for a job there, too. She had to find some employment, for last night Uncle Walter had suggested a dinner party so she could meet Clyde Abernathy properly.

Victoria's stomach soured at the thought. She needed to do something. She wasn't Rachel with her courage to refuse. She was the poor relation.

Clare hurried up to her, her closely tailored skirt swishing as she squeezed between a pair of desks. In fact her whole outfit, a lovely blue shirt and skirt, with an ecru tie and dark vest was perfect for her new job.

"I'm glad you were free," she said brightly. "I know so few people here I was beginning to think I was some kind of outcast."

Victoria sympathized with her new friend. "How did you get a job so soon? It's only been three days. I've barely left the house."

Smiling and shrugging, Clare rolled her eyes. "My father knew I wanted to work, so he made some enquiries."

"So liberal of him."

Clare laughed. "My mother convinced him to put my college skills to good use. So here I am."

"What do you do?"

"Come to the back behind the screen and I'll show you. I have to lock up for lunch soon. It's part of my duties. I've brought us some things to eat. My lunch is only half an hour, but I thought that we could walk down to the bandstand and eat there."

"I didn't even know that Proud Bend had a bandstand."

Again Clare laughed. "We tease my father about that. He lobbied for one to be built, even though Proud Bend doesn't have a band."

Victoria smiled, trying her best to push aside her jealousy.

Clare continued her chatter. "I've discovered that the only eatery in town is more suitable to miners after a hard night. It's open far too late, too. Our home is down the street from it, and they woke me up last night. Honestly, you would not believe the people who go in there at all hours! I saw a rather tall, regal woman with black hair just strolling past with a young man as if she was out shopping. It was very odd, indeed."

Victoria's heart lurched. Her cousin Rachel was tall with long, black hair. Could that woman have been her? She bit down on her lip to stop herself from saying something she shouldn't.

"Come, Victoria, sit here while I finish up. They've put me way in the back to recopy some of their ledgers that were damaged when the roof leaked. It's a boring job, and frankly I'm capable of so much more, but I keep telling myself that it's a start and I am still young."

On the desk were several ledgers, all stained brown. A fresh one and a good quill and ink set had been arranged in front of the only open ledger.

"Let me lock the door first, so we don't get any more customers." Clare hurried around the screen.

Victoria sat down, her attention falling on the open ledger. She caught sight of the name at the top.

Mitchell Tyrell MacLeod.

His name leaped from the page at her, and like a moth to a lamp, her gaze drew in closer. He'd registered his deed to the ranch, citing his wife as co-owner.

Louise's words that first day here returned to her. There was a reason for everything. And Mitchell returning to his ranch home with a baby that wasn't his needed a reason, also.

Could it have something to do with the ranch?

The bell on the top of the door jingled, causing her to jump. She hastily slipped back farther behind the screen as she heard Clare's light voice call out, "Mr. MacLeod! We were just about to close."

"Miss Walsh? I hadn't expected to see you here."

Entering the office, Mitch held open the door, wondering if the young woman was leaving, but she carefully turned the Open sign over.

"I work here now. It's just a temporary position transcribing some ledgers that have been damaged, but I hope to be hired full-time after this." She beamed at him.

About to ask if she could deal with his request before lunch, for he didn't want to stay in Proud Bend any longer than necessary, Mitch cleared his throat. Then the door behind him opened and in walked a young man whom Mitch recognized immediately as the assistant to the county recorder. Noah Livingstone, if Mitch remembered correctly. The man had dealt with Mitch when he'd recorded his deed several years ago. Noah was tall, but where Mitch was slim and wiry, this man was thick shouldered and looked as strong as an ox, odd within the office environment.

With a nod to him, Mitch began, "I'm running late with my errands. I would appreciate it if you could take care of me before you close for lunch. I have to change a name on my deed." Mitch gave the date he'd registered it.

Mr. Livingstone consulted his watch. "I think we can see to it. We're usually closed at this time, but I forgot something and had to return. Let's see if we can get you sorted out right now." He turned to Miss Walsh. "Please pull the ledger for that year."

"I have it out already, Mr. Livingstone," she answered with a flush and a smile that sparkled a little too brightly for such a simple task. Mitch frowned. Was there a romance budding here?

Noah lifted his brows with a nod. "Of course. That ledger was damaged. Please bring it here."

Mitch watched as Miss Walsh slipped around the few desks to stand beside a back screen. Ledgers were stacked up on the desk that was partially hidden. The pleats in the plain, off-white cotton that made up the majority of the screen suddenly ruffled and shifted. Mitch saw Miss Walsh peer across the desk into the depths that were hidden from him. Did she just give a short, almost imperceptible shake of her head to someone?

Mitch pondered what he should do. He wanted only to finish his errands and return to the ranch as quickly as possible. He'd stopped at the Smith house, but only the maid was there and Mitch had been reluctant to leave Victoria's salary with her. He would try again after this errand. Jake had the children and would be itching to return to his chores.

Should he ask Miss Walsh if she had been alone? What would happen if she had someone back there? Mitch had no desire to get her into trouble, but he didn't want to be overheard, either.

"What do you need recorded?" Noah asked as Miss Walsh returned with the ledger.

Mitch straightened his shoulders. He didn't have time to ask Noah to search behind the screen. He would just have to risk it. He lowered his voice. "My wife has died, and she passed on her share of my ranch to her youngest daughter."

While Noah gave no reaction to Mitch's pronouns, Miss Walsh flicked up her head and frowned slightly. Mitch could have waited for more, but pulled in a deep breath and hastily added, "My wife's new baby has inherited her share of my ranch. So I hope you will understand my desire for discretion here. This is a delicate matter and I now have five children to consider. The children—the four I share with my late wife and this baby—shouldn't suffer for their parents'—" he paused, swallowed, "—mistakes. Can I count on you to be discreet?"

"Absolutely, Mr. MacLeod." Noah's chin hardened as he stood even straighter. "While the records are always public and cannot be denied someone who requests to see them, we are certainly not going to gossip about what we see. Are we, Miss Walsh?"

The young woman's eyes widened. She looked as if she'd been dunked in hot water as she answered, "Absolutely not, Mr. Livingstone."

Mitch gave Noah all the information that he needed to update the deed. All the while, Miss Walsh's eyes grew wider with the answer to each question. Mitch almost expected her to fly apart at any moment. He quickly thanked Noah, nodded to Miss Walsh and left.

As he dipped his head to don his Stetson, Mitch noticed Noah following him out. "I see you go to church," the man said conversationally.

Mitch nodded as they walked slowly toward the corner of the building. There they stopped. "Yes, though I don't see you there."

"I sit in the back. I pick up several of the widows on my way. They're always tardy. I told them once they're going to be late for their own funerals."

Mitch laughed, but as he glanced toward the door, the laugh died.

Victoria was slipping out of the office.

Chapter Fifteen

As she stepped over the threshold, Victoria's gaze slammed into Mitchell's. Her heart stalled at the look of shock on his features.

For a moment she couldn't speak, though her mind whirred. She'd had no intention to eavesdrop on Mitchell's plea for privacy. But she had, and in her guilt, she'd hurried out of hiding to escape outside.

Now, captured by Mitchell's cold stare, she fought the urge to turn tail and run. Though it had been a few minutes since both he and Mr. Livingstone had departed the recorder's office, she'd assumed Mitchell would be gone from sight.

But there he was, and written boldly across his face was all the proof she needed. He realized she'd heard all of what he'd said to the assistant county recorder. She'd heard the words his pride had not wanted her to hear the other day when she'd asked him about Emily.

The urge to race over to him rushed through her so quickly, she felt her legs tense in preparation. But what could she say? That Emily's paternity didn't matter? It had for some reason, or else she wouldn't have asked. She was no better than Aunt Louise.

Her aunt's words echoed in her memory. Had Mitchell brought the baby out here only because she owned half of the ranch? Victoria bit her lip, unable to answer and hating that such an answer meant something to her.

Before Victoria could move, Mitchell turned and walked around the corner. The young man with him— Mr. Livingstone, she assumed—nodded and, oh, so thankfully, did not glance toward the door, but rather walked in the opposite direction.

Spurred into action by her need to say something, anything at all, Victoria lifted her skirt and hurried to the building's corner. Surely if she talked to Mitchell, told him that she hadn't meant to eavesdrop and that he had nothing to be concerned about, he'd understand.

Victoria hurried around the corner, her expression hopeful, and yet she was half-scared that Mitchell would be waiting for her, arms folded, scowl lining his suntanned features.

But he was gone. She heard hooves pounding the ground, and quickly peered down the intersecting road.

On his horse Mitchell had already retreated down it. She had no idea where the road led, though she assumed to a trail that took him back home. Her heart squeezed.

"What's wrong?"

She turned to find Clare had approached. "Mitchell saw me leave the office."

Clare blanched. "Oh, no!"

"Don't worry. Mr. Livingstone didn't see anything."

"That's not the point." Her shoulders dropped. "I will have to admit to Mr. Livingstone that I hid you behind the screen."

"You didn't. I just sat there for a moment while you locked up. There was no intention to deceive. It was just an accident."

"No. Although I wasn't told I couldn't bring anyone in here, I should have said something. I need to admit my error to Mr. Livingstone." She took Victoria's arm and led her away. In her other hand swung a small pail that contained their lunch.

Victoria stole a fast glance at her new friend. The woman had strong, determined morals. Such a good quality.

She looked away. She also needed to admit her part in this accident. To Mitchell. But how?

Throughout their lunch, Victoria felt the growing need to see Mitchell. Finally swallowing the last of her cress and cheese sandwich, she took the damp napkin in which her meal had been wrapped and wiped her hands.

"Do you know where Mitchell's ranch is?"

Clare blinked. "No. But we can go back to the office and look at the map. It's available to the public." Clare consulted her pendant watch. "We have time, if we hurry. And, yes, I can read a map. That's one of the reasons I feel I can do so much more than transcribe ledgers." Hastily, she gathered up the remains of their meal, then as she began to stand, she stopped and peered hard at Victoria. "It wasn't your fault, you know. Are you planning to apologize to Mr. MacLeod for eavesdropping?"

Needing to do something with her hands, Victoria took the small tin from Clare as they strode to the office. "I should." She offered a watery smile. "It's the same reason you feel the need to apologize to Mr. Livingstone."

"Is it?" Clare's soft, breathy question surprised Victoria. She looked at her new friend, finding the woman searching her face. What on earth for?

Suddenly, Clare's smile returned. "Come on. The map is on the wall beside the door." Her expression turned conspiratorial. "I understand completely why you need to go."

Victoria was still mulling over Clare's odd tone when, two hours later, she turned her mount in past the wide sign that read "Proud Ranch."

The mare, a piebald pony, was excellent, as good as any she'd ridden at the stables north of Portland, Maine, where their summer home was. Her mother had insisted she learn to ride at an early age, and right now, Victoria was as thankful for the lessons as she was for Aunt Louise being willing to loan out her favorite mare for the afternoon.

She was also thankful for Clare's ability to read a map and set out detailed directions. Victoria had written them down carefully.

Now, paused at the entrance and facing the small log home down a long lane, Victoria struggled to draw a breath. She shouldn't be nervous. Asking forgiveness was a good Christian trait. But perhaps she should have waited until Sunday at church to explain and ask Mitchell's forgiveness.

The words she'd rehearsed faded in her mind.

Just as Victoria spurred her pony forward, she caught sight of Mary. Immediately, she pulled back on the reins and the calm mare stilled.

Oh, dear, why hadn't she thought to bring something for the children? She hated that she'd forgotten them. She would lavish them with hugs and love instead.

If Mitchell didn't send her packing immediately.

Urging the mare forward, Victoria kept her spine straight and her face plastered with a worriless smile. Mary, bundled up in a coat against the cool air of the mountains, ran up to her as the mare came to a stop. With care, Victoria slipped from her sidesaddle and to the ground. She'd been trained to have a stool and a groom, but many years ago, her instructor had insisted she learn to mount and dismount from a sidesaddle without assistance. She was glad for it now.

Mary stood there, looking slightly paler than she had a few days ago. "Hello," Victoria said with a bright smile, expecting a greeting far more enthusiastic than the somber look she was getting. "Where is everyone else?"

"In the house."

"On a nice day like this? Or are you doing chores?"

"Only Papa is. He's cleaning the throw up."

Victoria gasped. "Who is sick?"

Mary remained unsmiling. "All the boys."

"I need to see your father." Head down, Victoria bustled past.

"I'm here."

Victoria flicked up her head at the sound of his voice. Mitchell, with his arms folded, stood in the doorway.

All of her courage drained away and she could no longer recall her apology.

Get ahold of yourself.

Victoria smoothed her outfit and adjusted her gloves. With a quick straightening of her shoulders, she lifted her chin. What had happened at the recording office had been an accident and she was ready to do the Christian thing.

She stalled that thought. It didn't matter as much anymore. Not while the family was sick. Behind him, deep in the house, Emily wailed. Hoping the baby wasn't sick, as well, for far too often they could not fight even the slightest flu, Victoria hurried up to Mitchell.

"What's happened? Are the children sick?"

He walked back inside. "It's not that bad. Just a stomach ache or two. You needn't have come out."

Determined not to be brushed off, Victoria followed him inside. "I didn't come here about that. I came to apologize."

"For eavesdropping on me?"

She looked around the small kitchen. Dishes were piled high in the dry sink, while food had been prepared and then forgotten on the table. The stove was stoked so hot, Victoria found it almost too hard to breathe. And the place smelled like a sickroom.

Turning back to Mitchell as he stopped in the doorway to the other room, Victoria sighed. "It was an accident. Clare had invited me to lunch and asked me to wait at her desk behind the screen until she locked the door. We were planning to eat at the bandstand, but she—"

"Why there? It's a stupid place. Proud Bend doesn't even have a band."

"Clare's father lobbied to have it built. I don't know why, nor do I care. We simply chose to eat there. While Clare gathered her lunch, I stepped outside and that was when I saw you talking to Mr. Livingstone."

"Oh, so you have come here to ask me not to make a formal complaint against Miss Walsh?"

Frustrated, Victoria sighed. "No. Clare said she would apologize to her supervisor. I came here to ask your forgiveness for my mistake and tell you that I won't repeat a word of what I heard." She wanted so much to tell him that it didn't matter if he hadn't fathered Emily. But the question still lingered. Had he brought the child here because she owned half of the ranch? Relinquishing guardianship would have meant that Emily's new guardian, whoever that would have been, would control her share.

Oh, Victoria ached to ask Mitchell.

But his eyes narrowed. He filled the doorway into the other room, blocking her passage should she have wanted to investigate the soft sounds beyond. Through the bottom third of the doorway she could see a small, rustic bed, with bedding she recognized from the train, mussed as though the sleeper had thrashed all night.

Eyes watering and heart pounding, Victoria moved her gaze back up to Mitchell's stern expression. "Your children are sick. Let me help."

There must have been something soft and coaxing in her strained whisper because his shoulders drooped slightly. He took a step toward her, just as his gaze dropped to her mouth.

In the heat from the kitchen, with her full riding outfit still on, Victoria felt suddenly warm. Mitchell tilted his head and lowered it. She felt her eyes widen. He was so close.

Then he spoke. "Have you learned anything more since our last discussion? Can you run a household, Victoria? Can you nurse children back to health?"

Her face heated further. She blinked rapidly. It was as if Mitchell had stripped away all her pride, all that she'd held dear. "Please don't ask that," she whispered. "I want to do something." She leaned toward him, and heard his indrawn breath.

Then he shut his eyes. "Victoria, I know you mean well. When I first met you, I doubted you could even polish a fork. I can see you care for the children, but caring isn't enough." He paused and opened his eyes again. "Even love isn't enough. Ranching is a tough life. It's not meant for families."

His voice hitched as he continued. "Please leave, Victoria. I don't want the children hurt. I don't want to be—" He cut off his hoarse words.

She reached out and touched his arm. The cotton was rough, durable, the muscles beneath firm. It was as if she could trust this man with her life. He seemed so salt-of-the-earth dependable. Hardworking stock. She had to shut her eyes for a moment, for surely he was stealing her focus. "I can help. I can learn to—"

He took her wrist and pushed her hand away. "No, you can't help. Now, leave before I do something stupid."

She leaned closer. "Like letting me try?"

He shook his head. "No, like kissing you."

Chapter Sixteen

Mitch watched Victoria blush the deepest red he'd ever seen. And worse, she did not back up.

Whoa. He stepped back. She had no idea what she was doing and he would not allow her into his family's lives, into his *life*, only to have her realize how hard it could be here. She hadn't even experienced a winter in Colorado.

Speaking of which, it was getting late in the afternoon, and the sun would soon dip down behind the mountains, plunging everything from his ranch to the far side of Proud Bend into a chilly twilight. It wouldn't be safe for her to be out riding at that time, and with Jake still up in the north pasture—he'd taken the dog Growler with him to help keep the herd back while he fixed a portion of fencing—Mitch could not leave here to escort her home.

He tightened his jaw. Victoria wanted to stay, and if Mitch was truly honest with himself, he wanted her there, as well. But his wants had to be ignored. The family would suffer and he didn't feel like being betrayed again. Yeah, he was unwilling to admit that his pride had been hurt when she asked about Emily. A moot point now, he told himself. Victoria knew Emily wasn't his child.

With straight shoulders and a gruff tone, he added, "Go home, Victoria. It's going to be dark soon and when the sun goes down, it gets a whole lot colder than you have ever experienced in Boston. It's not safe after dark, either."

Victoria's eyes strayed to a spot behind him, and Mitch turned. His heart plummeted. John and Ralph had roused from their sickbeds to peer around the corner at them. "Back to bed, both of you."

"I'm thirsty," Ralph whined. "I want Miss Templeton to give me a drink of water."

"*I* can do that in a minute. Now, go lie down."

Thankfully, both boys returned to their beds. Mitch watched them with a heavy heart. When he heard a slight sobbing noise, he turned back to Victoria.

Her hand to her mouth, she was fleeing out of the door. By the time he got himself in gear and rushed toward her, she was already at her mount, a beautiful piebald mare slightly smaller than average and with a dainty, English sidesaddle.

He stopped and gripped the jamb as he watched in fascination. With one single, flowing movement, she unclipped her apron skirt, revealing fine linen breeches the same color as her skirt and tall black boots. Within seconds, she'd mounted astride. Then, the obedient mare lowered her head, allowing Victoria to swing her right leg over to the left to fit into the sidesaddle pommel. She was remarkably agile, a testament to her good training, for he'd never before seen a woman mount sidesaddle without assistance.

Victoria then whipped the apron skirt back over her lap and fastened it quickly in place at her right hip. She gently tapped the pony's off side to lead the well-trained piebald to a gentle trot.

And she was gone, tearstained face and all.

Mitch sagged. It was for the best, he told himself. All of them, Victoria, too, would have been hurt if she'd stayed. She was magnificent, not only in her beauty, but in her ability to adapt, but this would be too much to adapt to.

Mary was suddenly at his side. She was the one who'd fought this flu the fastest, and he'd sent her outside for fresh air. She didn't need to breathe in the sick air all day. Although she still looked pale and hadn't moved more than a few bored steps around the house, she tugged his hand. "Papa, why did you send her away? To get a doctor?"

"No. She can't help, that's all."

"What if John and Ralph and Matthew get sicker? What if they die?"

Mitch's heart hitched and he pulled his daughter into his arms and held her tight. "No one is going to die, Sweetpea," he crooned, using the little pet name he'd called her when she was just a toddler. "We'll all be fine in a day or two. Come on in and help me with the broth for your brothers."

"Can I feed Emily? Jake milked that momma sheep and Emily likes it. Can I feed her, please?"

Mitch hadn't wanted to leave the baby in Mary's youthful care, but he didn't want Mary working around the stove ladling hot broth, either. He would just have to keep an eye on her as he made the meal. Decision made, he nodded.

He'd no sooner found the milk Jake had set in the well when pounding hooves drew his attention away. Victoria? His disloyal heart leaped, but he crushed the expectation and looked up.

Jake rode straight into the barn. Across his lap lay Growler, the dog limp and bouncing with the horse's gait. Mitch rushed over. "What's wrong?"

"Trouble." Jake dismounted quickly and laid the dog on the nearby hay. "Those half-breed mongrels of Donner's got into the north pasture. Five of them took down the donkey before Growler got at 'em."

Mitch bent down. Growler lifted his head and licked his hand. Blood matted his fur in several spots that were obvious puncture wounds.

Jake busied himself with his horse, calming the animal who was clearly spooked. "Growler will be fine. I'll clean his wounds in a minute. But the herd isn't so good. They stampeded out to the west into that pasture that leads to Blue Gulch. That's all I can say right now. But I got the fencing pulled closed, so they can't move." He looked over his shoulder with a grim expression. "We've lost a few of the heifers you sold. They fell into the gulch. I hadn't even delivered 'em, yet. Those men are gonna want their money back, Mitch." He sighed. "You aren't going to make that bank payment."

Mitch's gut twisted. Jake had been fixing the fence with the barbed wire Mitch had ordered in from out east. He was thankful Jake wasn't hurt in the stampede, and that he'd had the presence of mind to close up the pasture. Noting Jake's shredded shirt, he knew his ranch hand had torn strips off his clothing to tie onto the wire to warn the cattle away.

Mitch had only just started to fence in his herd. Most ranchers allowed their cattle to wander the foothills and the fields around their ranches, only corralling and sorting the herds in the fall. Mitch owned his land and wanted his herd to stay put. The grass was plentiful, the water source fresh, and he could keep an eye on them that way. Donner, his neighbor, never liked that. But to punish Mitch by allowing his dogs to harass Mitch's herd and therefore ruin his ability to meet his mortgage payment? Could Donner do that? Mitch didn't want to speculate.

"At first light, we'll have to move the rest of them out of there. I used the fencing that was supposed to go along the side that touches Donner's land." Jake peered at Mitch. "You need to get over to Donner and tell him to tie up those mutts. This isn't the first time they've roamed in a pack and killed. I heard they ran up to the Westwind Ranch this spring and took down some calves."

Mitch had heard that the Westwind Ranch had financial hardships. The deaths of their calves had no doubt added to those hardships. They were still operating, but how, Mitch didn't know.

He would confront Edgar Donner, all right, but it wasn't a task he relished. Donner was well-known to be one of Walter Smith's cronies. He was argumentative and cared little for his herd. Mitch had secretly wondered where the man got all his money. He never sold any of his stock but rather allowed them to wander the various upper pastures, expecting the other ranchers to deliver them at the end of the summer.

Jake's question intruded on his thoughts. "I saw someone galloping down the lane as I was coming in. Looked like a woman, what with the long skirt."

"It was Victoria."

"Why was she here?"

Mitch tightened his jaw. "She came to apologize."

Finished with the quick grooming of his horse, Jake led the animal into its stall. "For what?"

"Never mind," Mitch growled. "She's gone. And for good."

"Too bad she didn't offer to help around here. We both should get up to the pasture in the morning."

"She did offer. I sent her packing."

Jake snapped his head around. "She offered to help and you refused her? What's wrong with you?"

Mitch didn't want to hear he'd made a mistake, especially from his ranch hand. "Don't you start. It would never have worked out."

"How do you know?"

"I know, all right? Now, give it a rest."

With a shake of his head, Jake went to tend to the dog.

"Is Growler going to be all right, Papa?"

Mitch jerked around. Mary stood there, holding a whining Emily in her arms.

His foolish pride had sent Victoria packing.

When pride cometh, then cometh shame.

His pastor's words echoing in his head, Mitch strode over and scooped up both Mary and the baby. There was nothing he could do until he hired a decent housekeeper. The day after tomorrow was Sunday and by then, the children should be healthy enough to attend church. He'd ask his pastor again. It would all work out, he told himself fiercely. He'd done the right thing, sending Victoria away.

So why did it not feel that way?

Victoria rapped lightly on Rachel's door. It was still early, not yet suppertime, so she might be able to catch her cousin before the woman left for the evening. Victoria refused to ponder where the woman went. Her activities, however disconcerting they were, were none of her business.

Allowing her hand to drop, Victoria cringed. She'd ridden home at a brisk pace. Her riding outfit and corset were both rigid, forcing her to lean back uncomfortably. Her legs ached, too, for she hadn't ridden in such a long time.

Mitchell had been correct when he said it turned cool at night. She managed to reach the stables just as the sun dipped down behind the mountains. By then her feet had been frozen, and even now, standing before Rachel's door, she found herself still shivering.

She'd shed more than a few tears, too. Mitchell would sooner let his family suffer than take her help, but now, in retrospect, she understood. She would have only made things worse. He'd been right and it hurt so much, she'd cried most of the way home.

But it was Mitchell's soft plea for her to leave that had really flustered her. It was as though a part of him wanted her to stay. Did he not trust himself? Her heart hitched. Had he really wanted to kiss her?

How did she feel about it? A few weeks ago, she'd never have entertained the thought that a rancher, a man who worked with his hands, would try to woo her. Nor had any man ever stated so bluntly that he wanted to kiss her.

It was a dangerous desire.

She fought back the heat that flooded into her face just as the door opened. Rachel stood there, her outfit simple and modest, but warm. A lovely, fashionable hat perched on her head and Victoria's trained eye spied a discreet pearl pin holding it secure. Obviously, Rachel was preparing to leave.

"I know you plan to go out, and I won't take a moment, but I need to ask a favor."

"Come in," Rachel said briskly as she backed away from the door.

Once inside with the door closed firmly behind them, Victoria began. "I need your help, but I'm not sure you can even help me. I don't want to ask Aunt Louise or Uncle Walter. They may not approve."

Brows raised, Rachel walked over to her dressing table and began to put small notebooks into her purse. "I'm intrigued. But saying my parents may not approve doesn't mean much. Father misbehaves more than anyone I know. I can't imagine what he wouldn't approve of."

Victoria blushed. Rachel was nothing if she wasn't candid. And what were those small sheets of paper she was tucking away? They looked like tiny newspapers. Or Bible tracts.

"So," Rachel said as she pulled on the drawstrings of her purse. "What is it?"

"I want to learn how to run a household. More specifically, how to run an ordinary household."

"Mother could teach you that."

"I'm not sure. Can Aunt Louise build a fire and make porridge and do laundry?"

Rachel laughed. "That kind of household! I can see why you are reluctant to ask her. I don't think she's ever done laundry in her life. And since Father wants to marry you off to Clyde, I would say he wouldn't approve of your request, either. By the way, I should warn you. Today is Friday and Friday evenings are when Clyde makes his appearances. And why I choose to avoid supper and leave early."

Victoria swallowed. She didn't have the luxury of

being born the daughter in this household. Or have the boldness that Rachel wore with the ease of last season's fashions. Could Victoria merely refuse to see Clyde? She'd met him at the train station and that had been enough for her. Even now, the memory of his assessing look made her shiver.

But if she stood up to Uncle Walter, what would happen to her? Would she be tossed out onto the street?

Before dealing with Clyde Abernathy, she had another problem to address.

"Rachel, I don't have any idea how to do even the simplest household tasks. My mother was adamant that we maintain the appearance of wealth, but you and I both know what happened to my money. That's why I'm here."

"And my mother was probably quick to remind you of that?"

"Not really." Victoria didn't want to add that she thought her aunt was a gossip.

"How odd. Mother married Father for his money, and he married her for the prestige of a good Boston family. It was an arrangement that suited both parties. Did you know the real money is here out West? Father promised her the lifestyle she was used to, but don't be fooled by her decorum. Father isn't maintaining the high standards Mother was born into, so she prefers to walk around with blinders on. In other words, Mother believes that if she can't see Father's less than stellar behavior, it therefore doesn't exist."

What a scathing assessment of her parents, Victoria thought. And while Victoria hadn't sensed that behavior in her aunt, it did give her pause. Had her own perception of her life in Boston been like her aunt's here? Had she been deluding herself into thinking she had been living in an idyllic world?

"So," Rachel said, changing the subject. "Do you want to live on your own?"

Victoria blinked. "Yes, but it's not quite that simple. Should I find employment, I could board at a nice establishment, perhaps a widow's home. If that happens—"

"You'd have the luxury of being treated like a daughter without the familial obligations. Not to mention avoiding everything here. Interesting hope, although you may not find it quite that way in Proud Bend." Rachel studied Victoria carefully. "Do you really want to learn the basics of running a home just in case you can find a job or a widow who needs company?"

Victoria paused, just long enough for Rachel to smile. But it bore a gentle, but fatalistic edge. "Times are changing, Victoria, and you, being completely penniless, need to change, too. There is a middle class emerging, and these people will want the finery you and I have grown up with." Rachel lifted her brows. "Or is there another reason?"

Victoria thought of Mitchell. Was that what he'd planned for his family? To have the good things in life?

Then, after studying her a moment, Rachel set down her purse, and rang her bell for the maid.

Victoria was not sure what her cousin planned. She had come looking only for advice, but now felt as though she was being swept out to sea on the riptide that was her cousin's no-nonsense attitude.

Well, whatever was happening, she could do it. Mitchell had intimated that she was someone who would find menial work distasteful. That couldn't be further from the truth.

"This will take a while," Rachel was saying, tugging off her gloves. "You will be at it for most of the evening, not to mention all day tomorrow. These things take time to learn. I shall convey to Father that you're not feeling well. It will keep both Father and Clyde out of the upstairs."

"But I feel fine."

Rachel peered hard at her. "Where have you been? I mean, you're still in your riding outfit and you were shivering up until a moment ago."

"I went to Mitchell's ranch. His children are sick."

Rachel's brows shot up. "All the more reason you should not be around too many people. Who knows what you could spread?"

It was a logical decision, but Victoria still didn't feel right about it. "What are you planning? Am I taking you from your night's activities?"

"No. I'll still go, but later. You have to understand, Victoria, that my evening's activities are very important to me. I consider them more important than anything that can happen in this household." She patted her cousin's hand. "I know it sounds awful, and makes me look terrible, but just trust me on this. I don't mean any of this to be offensive."

Victoria was about to say she wasn't offended at all, but Rachel's tone turned fierce with commitment. "Nor can I elaborate right now. Just suffice it to say that nothing, *absolutely nothing*, in this household could drag me from going out each evening. I may be a bit late tonight, but I will send the errand boy to warn of my tardiness."

Victoria flushed. Did Rachel have a paramour? Should she tell her older cousin just how awful her lifestyle appeared?

No. Suddenly, something didn't feel right about her assessment. She held her tongue.

The maid arrived, and Rachel ordered wood, laundry soap and a bowl of hot water, after instructing the girl to tell her father that Victoria believed she may be coming down with an illness and would not be present at suppertime. Sandra nodded, confusion in her eyes as she curtsied to her mistress.

"I also need to know how to make oatmeal," Victoria added.

"One thing at a time. Tonight, we learn how to start a fire, and scrub laundry. This way, you'll be out of the way. If you pick it up quickly, we'll go downstairs tomorrow and make a loaf of bread and fry meat and onions. Oh, and we'll teach you how to make a decent cup of coffee and a pot of oatmeal porridge." Rachel shook her finger at her cousin. "You'd better take notes, Victoria. You'll need to refer to them later."

Victoria gaped at her. "I was just expecting you to speak discreetly with the housekeeper to allow the cook to show me what to do. I didn't expect you to have to learn it at the same time."

With a laugh, Rachel brushed off Victoria's words. "I learned these skills ten years ago, when I decided that God wanted me out there helping those women who need a bit of compassion, not judgment."

Victoria bit her lip. What women? "I don't understand."

"Never mind. Go find a small selection of clothes that need to be washed. We have a decent wringer downstairs, but this will do as a start." A bold smile grew on her face. "You'll be able to work in *any* household by the time I'm done with you."

Chapter Seventeen

Victoria squirmed like a small child in her pew the following Sunday. She ached all over, even where she didn't think she had muscles. All day yesterday, Saturday, Rachel had kept her busy. They had slipped down the servant stairs, with Rachel somehow managing to convince the staff to keep their presence below a secret. And from there, Victoria had crammed a lifetime of rudimentary tasks into eight grueling hours.

The cook, a robust woman with a booming voice, showed Victoria everything. Armed with a pen and notebook, and wrapped in a coarse, cotton apron, Victoria carefully followed all the directions fired her way by the cook.

She cringed and gingerly rolled her shoulders, but she now knew how to do everything from wash laundry to pluck a chicken. Victoria shuddered at the memory of that task. She was sure she would never eat fowl again.

"Stop moving or mother will demand you remove yourself," Rachel whispered from beside her on the pew.

"I don't understand. Didn't you tell her I was sick?"

Victoria hissed back. She still hated that they'd stretched the truth about Friday evening.

"No. When Mother came to my room asking about you, I told her the truth."

Victoria shut her eyes. Would her aunt tell her uncle? "Why did you say that?"

"That way, you could come to church today." She glanced over her shoulder and turned smug. "Good thing. Here comes Mitch."

Immediately, Victoria spun in the hard, wooden seat. The Smiths always sat up front, she'd been told and she now realized in horror that she faced the entire congregation. Aunt Louise clicked her tongue at her, and Victoria turned back around. Without seeing Mitchell.

Wait, how did Rachel know?

Rachel chuckled, giving away her ruse. Blushing madly, Victoria sat rigidly beside her older cousin, all the while willing her face to return to a normal color.

Behind her she heard someone slide into the pew. Victoria noticed Rachel toss another fast look over her shoulder, then snap it back a moment later, almost in horror.

Mitchell? Victoria jerked around.

No. There sat a broad-shouldered man in a plain black suit with a lawman's badge. Victoria's gaze dropped to his waist, but thankfully the man didn't appear to be armed.

But he was staring a hole in the back of Rachel's head. And her cousin was refusing to do anything but stare up at the altar. What was that all about?

"Sheriff, how are you this morning?" Aunt Louise asked coolly.

"I'm quite well, Mrs. Smith," the sheriff answered. "And where is Mr. Smith this morning?"

The congeniality on Aunt Louise's face slid away. "Alas, Mr. Smith doesn't share my devotion. Rather, he was up and gone very early this morning."

Victoria frowned. Not early at all. She'd been downstairs before her aunt and cousin and had seen Uncle Walter speaking with a man at the front door. Neither man saw her, but it was obvious that the conversation had been argumentative. In fact, she'd caught a few of the words, her uncle saying he would do it himself, after the stranger claimed he would not jeopardize his land or his herd.

Uncle Walter had then warned the visitor that he would regret not doing as he was told.

Horrified that she had been eavesdropping *again*, however accidental both times had been, Victoria had hurried into the dining room, and thus pushed the incident from her mind until now.

From the corner of her eye, she saw another tall man slipping into the sanctuary, a child in his arms.

Mitchell, with Mary. Where were the other children?

She had no time to wonder, as the service began.

Afterward she was filing toward the door with the rest of the family when a gravelly voice called her name.

"Miss Templeton?"

She turned, and found herself staring at Clyde. He lifted her hand to kiss it, but she yanked it back. "Mr. Abernathy, please. This is a church."

"I'm so sorry I missed you this past Friday. Perhaps I can beg Louise to have me over today for lunch?"

Victoria opened her mouth to remind him that such would be far too short a notice when she was suddenly besieged about her skirt by small, but strong arms.

She looked down into Mary's bright eyes. The girl

had greatly improved since Friday, for she was smiling broadly and her cheeks bore a healthy glow.

"Miss Templeton! I go to the same church as you!"

Victoria laughed. "There's only one church in Proud Bend, but nevertheless, I am glad to see you." Her heart leaped as she looked up behind the girl, her curious gaze bumping into Mitchell's. Feeling suddenly awkward, she scooped the little girl up and was rewarded by a tight hug about the neck.

Clyde shrank back. "Has this child ever been taught manners?"

Victoria bristled, turning Mary away from him. "She's merely happy to see me. Don't you have any children, Mr. Abernathy?"

"My late wife and I were fortunate enough not to have any. They are messy, bothersome creatures."

Victoria glanced over at Mitchell, whose expression had turned dark. He peeled Mary free of her embrace. "Allow me to remove my bothersome daughter from your presence, Mr. Abernathy. And I can assure you that my late wife taught our children excellent manners. Good day, sir." With that, he squeezed himself through the crowd of worshippers and was gone.

"Now, my dear, where were we?"

She spun back to the old man, ignoring the crowd moving past to shake the pastor's hand. Another time would have found her calm and collected, never once showing anything but the best manners ever. Public displays of anything but cool politeness were for the less cultured, her mother always said.

But something burst inside of her, and words and emotions that would have curled her mother's hair now poured from her. "We were nowhere, Mr. Abernathy.

And we never will be anywhere." She barely drew a breath as she continued. "Children are a gift from God. Manners are important, yes, but it's more important to simply love children for who they are. And never abandon them or not want them at all! That little child has been sick and since I didn't see her brothers, I can assume they are still sick. It's a blessing to see her out and about and happy and healthy!"

With a shocked look, Clyde pulled his handkerchief from his jacket pocket and covered his nose and mouth with it. And not from shock of her outburst, either, although she now realized that it was probably a mistake for her to berate her uncle's business partner.

No, Clyde covered his face because he was afraid of catching whatever Mary had come down with. Poor little thing. She didn't deserve to be treated like a leper.

With a huff, partially to stop from saying even more, Victoria gathered up her skirt and pressed into the crowd. She had to find Mitchell to ask how the boys were. And Emily. A sickness in a house often saw the baby perish first.

Please, Lord, let them be all right.

Breaking free of the crowd at the entrance, she spotted Mitchell and called out his name. He turned, a frown still chiseled into his face. Victoria hurried toward him. "How are the boys? And the baby? Are they still sick?"

Though he replied, his words were cool. "Yes, but Jake thought Mary and I should get out of the house. He volunteered to look after the rest."

"Even the baby?"

"He likes children." Mitchell's attention was diverted by a scurrying figure. Clyde was hurrying away, his handkerchief still covering his mouth.

Suppressing a remark at the sight of the cowardly man, she focused on the concerned father before her. "And what about this week coming? What do you plan to do?"

Mitch had learned that with children, planning his days in advance was an exercise in flexibility. Yesterday he'd needed to get out and check on the herd. Instead, Saturday had found him caring for the children, while Jake fixed the fence and moved some of the herd back to the main pasture. When he'd returned in the evening, Jake reported that five of the heifers he'd been set to deliver to other ranchers were dead.

Mitch would have to return the money. Now he would not be able to make his bank payment.

Rubbing his forehead with his free hand, for the other held Mary's tightly, Mitch had to push that worry away. The children needed him more.

He looked at Victoria, splendid in a navy outfit with a matching hat and purse. The hem of her closely cut skirt was deeply ruffled and her long, snugly tailored jacket had contrasting piping. How she'd managed to hurry over to him in that skirt was beyond him. But then again, on Friday, he'd witnessed Victoria mounting a sidesaddle unaided, deftly flipping free a detachable skirt in the process, and then reattaching it just as quickly once she'd settled against the pommel.

What had she just asked? He'd been awake much of the night and fatigue was stealing his attention.

"I asked what your plans are," Victoria said as if guessing that his thoughts were miles away.

"I plan to go home and relieve Jake. Victoria, you don't need to worry—"

"I'm coming with you."

"What?" He gave her a stern look. "You don't need to. Whatever happened to the day of rest?"

"Let no man judge you in meat or in drink, or in respect of an holyday."

Mitch stepped back, his eyebrows shooting up. She'd quoted a Scripture verse he'd heard many times from his father when there were cows to milk. It rolled off her tongue with the ease of a woman who'd studied the Bible diligently.

"Now give me fifteen minutes." Before he could say another word, she yanked up her skirt and spun away. He watched her hurry over to Rachel Smith, speak quickly with the woman, and then rush away in the direction of her uncle's house.

Like when she mounted that horse, Victoria could be quick and efficient when she needed to be. If she kept that pace up, she'd be back at the church in less than five minutes.

His tired gaze roamed back toward the church and bumped into Rachel's. She smiled at him, far too smugly, he thought. He moved on.

Behind the church stood a long, open stable, manned by several volunteers whose jobs before the service were to unhook the horses and lead them out of the sun. Some farmer had donated the hay and feed while several young boys, some he was sure as young as Matthew, watered the mounts. As he approached now, one man led his horse out of the stable to the line of empty carriages and wagons.

He should just bundle Mary onto the wagon and be on his way before Victoria could make it back. But she would probably follow him and it wasn't in his nature to be rude.

"Come on, Sweetpea," he told Mary gruffly. "Let's hitch up the horse."

Mary held back. "But what about Miss Templeton?"

He sighed and looked down at Mary. "We'll wait for her." Perhaps one quick afternoon to convince Victoria that she couldn't handle a household. The kids were sick, anyway. They wouldn't miss her when she scooted out in horror a quarter of the way to suppertime. By then she'd have learned how tough life out here could be.

Mitch stopped when he noticed that the Smith carriage, a gold-trimmed black coupe that looked more suitable for royalty than the town's banker, was parked in front of the wagons and carriages.

Walter Smith stood beside it, smoking a cigarette, obviously waiting for his family and not caring that he blocked the rest of the congregation from leaving. Mitch hadn't seen him in church, but he'd noticed the rest of the family immediately upon entering.

All right, he'd noticed *Victoria* immediately. She'd looked briefly around, but had then quickly turned to face the front. He was sure she hadn't seen him slip into a back pew with Mary, instead of the usual one behind the Smith ladies.

But the point was that Walter Smith hadn't been in church, but was here now waiting for his wife and daughter. Bold of him.

Mitch turned, noticing that Mrs. Smith and Rachel were still talking to the pastor's wife, seemingly in no hurry to leave. So why was Smith waiting dutifully here for them?

"So, MacLeod," Smith began as he approached. Mitch was determined to squeeze his wagon past the sleek and small carriage. "I hope you're still able to make that mortgage payment no later than Monday. I heard you had some trouble."

So that was why he was here. As in any small town, news traveled fast, but since he hadn't yet confronted Donner about his pack of wild dogs, and Jake was likely too busy to have mentioned it, Mitch took a stab at what really happened. Had Smith convinced Donner to set his dogs on Mitch's herd? He had seen Donner and Smith drinking together on those few evenings he'd spent escorting Rachel on her mission work, as per the pastor's request. Smith was probably here to gloat. Or maybe put even more pressure on Mitch.

Mitch gritted his teeth. "Don't you worry about my payment. It will be on time."

"And the herd? How's it doing? What about that spot of trouble?"

"I still have plenty of heifers to sell, Mr. Smith. They've all been bred, too, and are safe up in a fenced pasture."

"Fencing doesn't make good neighbors, MacLeod. You're more than likely going to get some opposition for that. The herds have to roam and get water."

"It's my land and I am not blocking access to water." With that, Mitch scooped Mary into his arms as he passed Smith.

The banker blew smoke into Mitch's face as he passed alongside him. Mary coughed. Mitch fought the urge to set his daughter down, rip the cigarette from the man's lips and grind it into the dirt beneath their feet. But what would that teach his daughter? That violence was the answer? No, he wouldn't do it.

"Don't think I don't know what you did with that sale, MacLeod. I'm not stupid."

"What are you talking about?"

"You finagled the sale of the heifers. I don't know how, but it won't happen again."

Mitch went cold. The ranchers had backed out of the purchase of his heifers, only to change their minds. They all had mortgages or loans with Smith's bank. Had Smith threatened them? Yet Jake had convinced them to risk it. How? Jake wasn't that silver-tongued.

As soon as he returned to the ranch, he'd ask him. Until then, Mitch hefted Mary higher and walked past Smith to his wagon, grateful for the young man who'd just finishing hitching the horse. With a thank-you, Mitch set Mary on the bench and climbed aboard beside her. Squeezing past the Smiths' fancy coup without scratching it was tough, but he did it.

Smith stood on the opposite side, his expression like the twisted growl of an ugly dog.

Mitch swung to the left to come out onto the road in front of the church, an easier feat since most worshippers had departed for their noon meals.

"There's Miss Templeton!" Mary cried out, pointing down the road in the direction of the Smith mansion.

Mitch groaned. Victoria was hurrying along the road, still dressed in her fine Sunday outfit, the feather in her small, velvet hat fluttering backward in the breeze she created with her haste. The ties of the big bow under her chin danced as if in full merriment. Over one forearm was her small drawstring purse, and being gripped tightly in her other hand was a small portmanteau that Mitch immediately recognized as one of Victoria's many pieces of luggage.

As he pulled alongside her, he noticed her attention yank away. He looked over his shoulder. Donner, his cantankerous neighbor, was down at the stables speaking with Walter Smith. Both men's demeanor was stiff as if they had yet to sort out an argument.

Mitch looked back at Victoria. "What's wrong?"

"Nothing, really. I just noticed that my uncle is here. He didn't attend the service but must have come to collect Aunt Louise and Rachel. Who is that man he's talking to?"

"Edgar Donner, my neighbor. Why do you ask?"

"Does he attend church?"

"No. In fact, he's rarely in a decent enough state to get up early on a Sunday morning. Something must have happened."

"He came to visit my uncle early this morning. I saw them arguing, right at the front door."

Mitch had wanted to ask what they'd said, but refused to participate in gossip. He liked to think he was above that. But both men were the argumentative type and Donner was well-known to be inside Victoria's uncle's pocket. Who knew what mischief they could be into?

Hopping off the bench, Mitch took the bag and hefted it as if weighing it. "Are you planning to spend the night?"

Victoria looked confused. "No. Why do you say that?"

"Because of all of the luggage you're toting."

"This one little bag?" she asked as he helped her up onto the bench seat. "I'd need more than this if I planned an overnight trip."

He tossed the bag into the wooden bed behind him and climbed up beside her. Without urging the horse on, he asked, "Then what is in it?"

"My working clothes." Victoria sat primly on the seat, moving only slightly to allow Mary to climb onto her lap and press her cheek against Victoria's fine, velvet-trimmed waistcoat.

"*You* have working clothes?"

Victoria tossed him a sharp look. "You need help and I am now fully capable of helping you. So tuck away your pride, Mitchell, and do the right thing." She sat ramrod straight on the bench, her chin high. "Let's go."

Despite his dignity prickling him like a field of thistles, Mitch laughed and flicked the reins. The horse moved forward.

"What's so funny?" she snapped.

"Absolutely nothing." He sobered, knowing that he shouldn't have laughed. After all, he was bringing her home to teach her a lesson. Now, with Mary contentedly curled up in Victoria's arms, her own little hand reaching up to finger the still-dancing ostrich feather on Victoria's cap, he realized he should not have agreed to bring her at all.

But then Victoria smiled at him, a soft smile as contented as Mary's snuggle, with shining eyes and the satisfaction of a cat with cream.

Something caught in his throat and he fought the urge to smile back. This wasn't going to work out, and he was a fool to allow it to start in the first place.

Chapter Eighteen

Victoria pulled a very unladylike face. So Mitchell didn't think she had working clothes? He'd soon see. She had a perfectly good dress in last year's style.

When they arrived at his ranch, she asked for a private room in which to change. Emerging a few minutes later—well, perhaps a bit longer than that, Victoria amended silently—she pulled from her pocket a small leather-bound notebook, something she'd studied with due diligence most of Saturday evening after that long, tiring day in the kitchen.

She looked around. The small room from which she'd emerged, ready to work, had been relatively orderly; judging by the bigger bed, it was Mitchell's. But this room and the kitchen were both disasters. Clothes were strewn around and whichever child had slept in the bed closest to her had thrashed all night. Although the day was sunny, the room was dark. In one corner, a small lamp burned, adding its pungency to the already distasteful smell.

The boys stared at her, each face pale and wan. In her basket, Emily slept. Thankfully.

Apprehension swelled in her throat and Victoria pushed it down with a hard, determined swallow. She hurried over to the window and threw up the sash. It creaked in protest. When she turned, she saw Mitchell in the doorway, still in his Sunday best, much like he'd done Friday, his arms folded and his expression as closed off as the bedroom behind her.

"Okay. You wanted to help," he muttered.

So that was it. He was setting her up to fail. Indignant, she marched passed him into the kitchen. She needed hot water. Testing the contents of a large cauldron sitting on the stove, she found it tepid. With growing determination, she stooped, opened the stove door and peered in. Only a cooling bed of embers. Jake had allowed the fire to die out.

With a sniff, she pressed open her notebook and laid it flat on the floor beside her. Thankfully, she'd not only taken notes, but sketched out a few diagrams. She read through the page again.

"What are you doing?"

She looked back at Mitchell. "I'm putting on a fire. I need hot water if I am to clean this place and make a meal."

"Do you plan to burn your notebook?"

"Of course not. It's showing me how to start a fire. Now, go out to your barn." She flicked her hand. "Check on your cattle or do whatever Jake is doing. I'm fine here."

Mercy, she wasn't fine. She didn't even know where the firewood was kept. In her uncle's house, there was a separate room off the kitchen for it, one that led to the outside so that a servant could restock the firewood but not allow a constant winter draft to flow in.

But here, well, the wood had to be outside. But she should first stir the embers to see if they would light.

They didn't. She needed a match and kindling. Still stooped, she waited for Mitchell to leave the house. Then she'd find what she needed. She was *not* going to ask him.

Laughter peeled through the kitchen and Victoria spun. Seeing Mitchell throwing back his head, she stood. He'd laughed at her portmanteau, and now was laughing at her.

"What's so funny now?"

"You. You took notes, no doubt watching a servant make a fire and now you think you can do it."

"I can, oh, ye of little faith. I'm here to help you and the children."

His laughter died. Then, keeping his focus on her, he took the few steps needed to stand far too close to her. His voice dropped. "I know you want to help, Victoria. And, yes, I shouldn't laugh. This is serious."

Her chin wrinkled. "You obviously don't believe that."

"I do. I just didn't want you here because I thought you'd most likely take one look around you and turn tail back to your uncle's house."

"I would like to think that I am made of sturdier stock than that," Victoria answered with arched brows.

"Are you? You needed to write down how to make a fire."

"Ignorance isn't the measure of a sturdy character, Mitchell. It's what you do with your circumstances." She tilted up her head to study his face. "Please let me try this."

He shook his head gently. "And when you realize that

you can't do it and dash away home? Where will that leave my children?"

"I won't go. But I can't prove that to you because you refuse to swallow your pride and let me help."

Mitchell stiffened. "I allowed you to come here, didn't I? Isn't that proof enough that I have swallowed my pride?"

She clicked her tongue. "Your consent wasn't founded on conquered pride, Mitchell MacLeod. It was part urgent need and part expecting me to fail. *Hoping* I would fail." Foolish tears stung her eyes. "I don't think you've let go of an ounce of the pride in your heart."

"Like you have?" he answered softly.

She lifted her chin. "Yes. I've learned a lot about myself these past few days."

"And the pride and snobbery I saw on the train? I'd say it's been replaced by pride in your accomplishments." He flicked his head to indicate her notebook on the plain, planked floor. "But, Victoria, it's still pride."

Her throat tightened, a sure sign those ridiculous tears were going to spill out and run down her cheeks, making a mess of her face and dissolving her struggling courage.

No, she would not allow any failure. She wanted to help. He needed help. That was enough.

With an unladylike snort, she marched past him toward the kitchen door.

Outside, Victoria glanced around, her focus falling on a stack of firewood and the scraps of kindling raked beside it. She marched over to it, stooped and began to load up her arms. It was awkward and heavy. As she struggled to her feet, she felt the wood lifted from her.

Mitchell was taking her share. "Why, Victoria?"

"Why what?"

"Why come here and help me? You owe me nothing. In fact, I have yet to pay you the remaining salary I owe *you* because I didn't want to leave the money with a servant and, frankly, I was too mad at you at the recording office. So, why try to learn things you will never need to know?"

Again, the heat of embarrassment rose in her, no doubt cementing Mitchell's belief that she still had far too much pride. She wouldn't stand there with her hand open, expecting him to pay her now. Still, she heard her stiff reply. "You know my situation."

He shook his head. "I can presume some things, but I don't know as much as you think I do."

On the train, she had been sure that he had told her that he knew her plan. But now she wasn't sure what he'd meant. What plan was he thinking of?

Did it matter? They stood there in the warmth of a fall sun. This morning had been brisk, with the hint of a light frost. The nice weather was ending. But in that moment, Mitchell's gentle manner, his care for his children coaxed her to trust him with her deepest shame. Victoria could think of nothing but spilling out all her misfortune.

"My stepfather gambled away my entire inheritance. My mother had allowed him free access to my money because she felt it was unladylike to deal with it." She blinked back fresh tears that threatened to water her view of Mitchell's handsome face. "And when his debts became too large, he committed suicide. My mother was horrified, not because she'd lost a loved one, but because of the social stain it left on our family. She had been hoping that I would marry into one of the wealthy Brahmin families in Boston."

"She actually abandoned you? Left you to deal with all of her husband's mess?"

Victoria bit her lip. Suddenly, it felt important for Mitchell to understand the situation. She didn't hold any malice toward her mother. Abigail was who she was, a woman who'd been taught to aim high on the social scale. In a way, Uncle Walter did the same here, vying to have the best home, the nicest things, to keep the money in the family by trying at first to marry his daughter, then his niece, to his business partner.

No, she wouldn't focus on that.

She continued her story. "She couldn't take me to her sister's house in the Carolinas because my aunt is trying to marry off her unruly daughters."

Understanding dawned on Mitchell's face. "And you would be competition. I can see that."

Her cheeks pinkened further. He thought she was beautiful enough to be competition? "My mother arranged to have the remaining assets, the house and summer home, liquidated to quietly pay off Charles's debts so we didn't become the scandal of the season. Mr. Lacewood had suggested that, I think in part because of my mother's desire to keep the disgrace private. It was the only way out for her. She sent a telegram to her brother, Uncle Walter, and he agreed to take me in."

"In return for what?"

Surprised he'd pegged Walter Smith so easily, she gave a vague shrug. "He'd hoped to pay for my train ticket so that I could repay his generosity by marrying his business partner."

"Clyde Abernathy." The name was spat forth in a disgusted tone.

"Yes." She took back a few sticks of wood. "Mitchell, my mother also thought that Clyde would be suitable."

"Is he?"

"Absolutely not! I want to live my own life and be responsible for it and not be owing to anyone. I don't want to have to go to someone else just for a coin or two!" Feeling suddenly angry, she hauled back even more firewood and marched into the house. Having left the door and the window in the front room open, Victoria could already smell an improvement in the air. She dumped the firewood beside the stove and then peeked into the front room. Matthew and John were sleeping, while Mary and Ralph sat on the far tick, playing with some small wooden toys. Craning her head, Victoria peeked into the basket. Emily remained asleep.

She returned to the stove just as Mitchell entered. As they stooped in front of the fire, Victoria consulted her notebook again. She found the smallest scraps of wood and grass and made a bed of them inside the firebox. Then she carefully stacked the smallest kindling around it. Now she needed a match—

"Here, I use a fire piston." Mitchell reached up and took down a small cylindrical metal and glass tube. "I don't always have matches, but I have plenty of fine tinder to use for fire cloth."

He pulled a metal box from behind the stove and opened it. It held torn pieces of rope. "I'll show you." He removed the piston and stuffed its small hollow end with a tiny piece of rope. Then, after reattaching the lid, he shoved the piston down hard. Immediately, the glass cylinder glowed, and just as quickly, Mitchell pulled out the piston. Then, while holding it in one hand, he freed his knife from the small scabbard on his belt, and picked out the burning ember and dropped it onto her bed of fine tinder. He leaned forward and gently blew until smoke trailed up.

Victoria started when a flame burst forth. Leaning back, Mitchell smiled at her.

"What a wonderful invention! I was just going to use a match."

"Matches are a great invention, too, but they run out and are expensive. I keep this handy instead."

Victoria glanced into the firebox, happy to see her bigger kindling already burning on the bed of old coals. She beamed back at Mitchell.

"Here is the stove's damper. You can control the burning by opening it or shutting it." He stood, showed her the handle, and then stooped again. He was still smiling at her, just inches from her face. "Thank you for coming, Victoria. I do appreciate it."

Her own hesitant smile widened. "You're welcome. It's my pleasure."

"Exactly what you want, then. To make your own decisions about what you want to do."

"Yes!"

"What would your mother say?"

"I don't plan to tell her."

"You must be upset with her."

She shook her head. "I'm not. She can't help being who she is. And in a way, she believes she's looking after me. Mother didn't make the best decision, but I haven't sometimes, either. I accepted your offer of employment to spite her. Oh, and to not be beholden to my uncle."

Mitchell lifted his eyebrows and smiled. "No, really?"

The moment of companionable silence lingered. Victoria felt her heart thudding in her throat, but the doubt her aunt had seeded in her head sprouted again. Behind her, she could hear Emily cry out softly in her sleep.

"Mitchell, I need to know something. No, I mean I really need to know this."

His guard rose. "Know what?"

"Why did you bring Emily here? You must have realized how difficult it would be for you to care for her and the other children and ranch at the same time. It's just that Aunt Louise—"

"Your aunt may be a faithful supporter of our church, but she's really not, how shall I say it? The most prudent woman."

Victoria reluctantly agreed. What Mitchell was trying not to say was Aunt Louise liked to gossip. "But she raised a good point. One that has been unwittingly cultivated in her by my uncle's behavior. She asked what your motive might be for bringing Emily here. Then when I discovered, quite accidentally, I assure you, even though you may not agree, that Emily has inherited her mother's share of your ranch, I couldn't help but wonder if that was the reason."

"As opposed to what? Bringing her here out of the goodness of my heart? You can't find that possible?"

Her watery smile dissolved. "You have a great deal of goodness in your heart. But was that the reason, or was it so you would have full control of the ranch? I know it means a lot to you."

Mitchell didn't say anything for a long time. Finally, as the heat in the stove grew, he said, "You're right. I do care about this ranch, but I'd already decided I wouldn't abandon Emily long before I read Lacewood's letter saying Emily was half owner."

Relief washed through Victoria. "So why did you bring her out here?"

"My family needs to stay together, now more than ever. It's hardly the child's fault that her mother—" He paused. "I've heard about children getting fostered out, only to die mysteriously. I couldn't take that chance."

He sighed. "Agnes and I didn't love each other. Not like a husband and wife should love each other. Ours was a marriage meant to help Agnes out of dire poverty and help me settle down. You see, my parents wanted to leave me their farm, but I was a restless teenager. I wanted my own land, to build my own life, not to take over my father's dream. In fact, that's the last thing I wanted.

"When my mother traveled to Boston once, she met Agnes's family. My parents then arranged my marriage to Agnes because her family was desperate and my mother knew that marriage shouldn't be about the money, but about God's will for us. My wife's family had too many daughters. At first, we tried to make a normal life for ourselves, outside of Boston, with me working at a stable, but it wasn't enough for me, and I think Agnes knew she wasn't, either."

"So you left?"

"It was only temporary. I came here to build this place. I even hoped for a while it would help our marriage. But it was doomed long before I moved out here. I don't know who she met, or if that relationship meant anything to her, but when I returned, I discovered she'd died in childbirth and I knew I wasn't the father. It still feels so strange. She did all that, and yet still took our children to church. It goes to show you that I don't understand women, especially her."

"Perhaps you feel responsible for Emily because you

made mistakes where Agnes was concerned?" Victoria paused. "Have you forgiven her?"

His mouth thinned. She'd hit a nerve. A proud, tattered nerve.

"Do you forgive your mother for abandoning you?" he snapped back.

Her heart faltered a little but she knew the answer. "Yes. How can I call myself a Christian if I don't? How can I think that her sins are worse than mine?"

"You can't."

Victoria shrugged. "No. Besides, she is still my mother. She hurt me because I care for her. I have to decide what is more important. My love for her, or her mistakes. It's my love that's more important. Do you understand? I have to learn to forgive those I care for."

Mitch stilled, then stood abruptly, Victoria's words ringing in his ears like the church bell on a crisp morning. He'd cared for Agnes. He hadn't *loved* her, but he had respected her. Then she'd torn apart that respect and shamed him. It was different than what Victoria had experienced. The shame was more on her stepfather than on her mother. He'd been trying to explain how he felt to Victoria and she'd posed an unanswerable question.

Much more slowly, Victoria rose. "What is it?" she asked.

"Nothing."

"No, it's something. I'm here to help you, not just around the house, but in other matters, too. Is it about someone you loved? Or your late wife?"

"I don't want to talk about it anymore." He hastily closed the wood stove's door. "You've got your fire. Now you can do all those things you've learned. I have other things that need tending. My dog has been injured."

"Your dog? What happened?"

"He was attacked by the neighbor's dogs. They were set loose in my pasture to disrupt my herd. In fact, they caused a stampede that killed several of the heifers that I had sold but not yet delivered. I have to decide which of the others I should offer as replacements. But the heifers that died had been hand-picked, so I don't know what the other ranchers will want to do."

Victoria gasped. "I'm so sorry. And your poor dog. Will he recover?"

He walked to the door. "He'll be fine soon enough, but I need to see to the herd."

"Those men, especially the brothers, will they accept your other heifers? They were reluctant to buy from you in the first place. They wanted older, good stock heifers that had been bred early."

At the door now, he turned back, sharply. "How do you know all that? I only mentioned heifers to you, not that they were older and from good stock."

Victoria clamped shut her mouth as her eyes widened. She finally asked, "Didn't Jake tell you?"

"Tell me what?"

She bit her bottom lip.

"Victoria," he warned. "What did you do?"

Victoria swallowed and smoothed her dress. "I arranged for the sale of your heifers. Jake told me those ranchers were too intimidated to buy them directly from you, so I worked as an intermediary."

His brows shot up. "You know how to do that?"

"Of course. A good marriage arrangement is often facilitated by a third party who knows both sides, usually after a courtship to see if the couple is compatible. You said your marriage was arranged, so didn't you know the intermediaries?"

"Yes, they were my parents and Agnes's parents. But I hadn't realized that you would know so much."

"I've watched my mother and stepfather act as the third party several times." Her expression saddened. "Selling a bride isn't much different than selling heifers. And sometimes, like when I sold your heifers, it's done quietly because the bride's reputation has been compromised."

"Too bad you lost your fortune. You could have arranged a suitable marriage for yourself." Despite knowing his pride had been pricked, Mitch cringed. He hadn't meant for his comment to make it sound as if Victoria was some conniving old woman. Or a heifer.

Victoria, to her credit, blushed and appeared to take his accidental insult with a grain of salt. "I had started a courtship with a young Brahmin man, but even Boston's elite prefer wealth over anything else. I should have read the writing on the wall when Mother told me she was sending me here. She told me she couldn't arrange a hasty marriage. I know now that if the wedding had gone ahead, there would have been a terrible disgrace once the family discovered I had no fortune and yet if they'd learned beforehand of my dire financial straits, they'd have backed out and there would have been an embarrassing situation the likes of which we hadn't seen before."

"There is more to a decision to marry than just wealth." He frowned and stared pointedly at her. "But let us stick to the point, Victoria. This isn't about marriage. It's about my herd. You sold my heifers?"

* * *

Victoria couldn't believe her ears. Was he still on about that? "I only acted as intermediary. I convinced the ranchers your livestock was well worth the money, and no one was going to threaten them because they couldn't prove the heifers came from you. I actually bought them using Rachel's money, sold them to those ranchers, and then returned the money to Rachel. So technically, Rachel bought and sold them."

"She knows about it?" He gaped at Victoria.

"I trust her completely." A small gasp slipped from her lips. "But you don't? Oh, it's because of her reputation, isn't it?"

Mitchell frowned. "What reputation?"

"Of going out at night to meet men and frittering her life away at saloons with disreputable characters." Her fingertips touched her lips. "Oh, no! Is that how you two met?"

He bristled. "No, it's not! We met in church. Rachel hasn't told you what she does?"

"Not outright, but she's apparently unashamed of it." She gasped again and placed her hand to her throat. "That's why my uncle stopped trying to marry her off. She is like I was to my mother—no longer suitable. But Uncle Walter thinks I am, as broke as I may be."

Mitchell shook his head, as if baffled by her swift thoughts. "Your uncle wants to keep his business in the family, that's all. You're not damaged goods," he growled. "Clyde Abernathy wants a beautiful young woman as a bride because he's a filthy old man."

Despite the subject of their conversation, she beamed. "You think I'm beautiful?"

"Yes, but we're getting off topic here." He pointed

his finger at her sternly. "You should have stayed out of my business."

"Why?" She heard the defiant tone to her voice and was pleasantly surprised by it.

"Because it's my business, not yours."

"You're too proud."

"Pride has nothing to do with this. You're too nosy. You don't know what you're dealing with, Victoria. We're talking about ranchers. We're not sweet little Brahmin boys from Beacon Hill. Meeting men with large sums of money in your purse can be dangerous. And you're getting yourself mixed up in your uncle's business. That's even more dangerous."

"Why?"

"Because your uncle hired my neighbor to spook my herd and make them stampede."

Victoria's eyes widened further. Despite Mitchell's ire, their conversation made her feel amazingly alive. "Can dogs be trained to do that?"

"It's more like it's in their nature. Especially that litter. But even a man can spook his own herd just by striking a match, especially if the heifers are already stressed. A cough or any sudden noise can startle a herd. Walter Smith knows a stampede could easily kill some of the young heifers or at least cause them to lose their young. He knew I planned to sell them."

Victoria gasped. "Why would he do that?"

"He wants my mineral rights. I refused to sell them to him, so now he's trying to ruin my ranch. He wants to force me to sell him those rights when I can't make my next mortgage payment."

"And with those heifers dead, you won't be able to?"

"That's right."

"But you have the money already."

Mitchell shook his head. "Yes. I have the cash, but unless I can replace those heifers that hadn't been delivered yet with ones that those ranchers will accept, I will have to return the money."

"I can help!"

The mood around him hardened sharply. "No! I don't care if you can talk a dog off a meat wagon, which I am beginning to think that you can. You're not going to do a thing about this." He pointed to the kettle sitting on the stove. "You have enough work to do." And then he stormed out.

Mitch couldn't believe how he'd been manipulated by Victoria. Women! If it wasn't them sneaking out behind your back, it was them trying to take over your life.

He fumed all the way into the barn. Glancing around, he noticed that Jake's horse was gone, so he assumed the man had hightailed it out to the far pasture where he'd managed to corral the herd, probably as soon as he saw Mitch and Victoria return from church. He must have figured that Mitch would learn the truth about that sale and decided not to be around when that happened.

The afternoon had turned breezy and warm, allowing the last of the year's wild roses to bloom on the south side of the barn, where Jake often tossed the cleanings from the stalls. Mitch stopped to savor the sun-warmed scents as the rays shone obliquely in the open door at the far end. At the sound of a soft whine, he glanced over at the pile of hay. Growler lay on a horse blanket, his leash chained to a nearby hook to stop him from following Jake. Beside him sat a bowl of water and another empty bowl that looked as though it had been licked clean of its contents.

Mitch walked over. "It's okay, boy. How are you feeling?" He scratched behind the dog's ears, noting that Jake had salved the puncture wounds, then sprinkled on them bright yellow iodoform to prevent Growler from licking them. No one, not even dogs, liked the smell or taste of that bitter powder.

Satisfied that the dog was healing well, Mitch stood. Behind the strong scent of the iodoform was something smoky. Had Victoria decided to cook? Mitch hurried out of the barn. The wind, now gusty and still warm for the season, was coming from the west. The chimney smoke was trailing away from him.

Mitch sniffed the air again. It *was* smoke. He walked around the barn and peered up at the mountain vista that he could call his own.

His upper pasture was on fire!

Chapter Nineteen

Mitch tore into the house. "Victoria, the upper pasture is on fire!"

She stood at the dry sink, stacking dishes. "Where is Jake? Is he up there? What about the herd?"

"I don't know. I have to ride up."

"Ride up?"

"My herd is up there."

"Are they worth your life?"

"Jake is up there, too. I need you to get the children ready to leave. If these winds pick up, it won't be long before the fire races down here."

She hurried to the stove and shut the damper. "Is there anything else I can do?"

"Pray."

"I shall." She rushed up to him, laying a hand on his forearm. He still wore his Sunday best, but it was too late to change. "I'll take care of the children. But you must be careful, too. Please."

He nodded, staring for that moment into her eyes. After she searched his face with anxious eyes, Victoria grabbed his jacket front and hauled his face down to hers. Their noses bumped while their close gazes locked. Then she did the unthinkable.

She kissed him soundly. He was stunned only for a moment. Then he wrapped his arms around her and returned her kiss with equal vigor. His heart, already pounding since he spotted the fire, raced ever more quickly.

The fire!

Mitch released her. "I have to go. Remember what I said. Get the children ready and in the wagon. And don't forget Growler."

He wanted to watch her stir into action but couldn't. He still needed to saddle up his horse. Mitch spun and left her in the kitchen, knowing she followed him to the doorway.

Don't look back. Don't let your heart start giving you bad advice. After this fire is out, then you can deal with her.

His gut twisted and it was all he could do to keep facing the barn. He needed a clear head right now and her kiss had done the opposite.

A scant few minutes later, he galloped out of the barn, racing up toward the pasture. He'd grabbed a spare horse blanket, knowing it was good for pounding out errant flames or wrapping around a person who had caught fire.

Lord in heaven, keep Jake safe.

Repeating the prayer several times, Mitch pushed his horse farther up the hill. The animal shouldn't have gone from standing in his stall to a full gallop so quickly, but God willing, there would be time enough later to rub down Bruiser's sore muscles.

Victoria hurried back into the kitchen, panic swelling over her in a way she'd never before experienced.

She stood for a moment in front of the stove, its warmth adding to her flush of fear. No one liked a wildfire. Although she'd lived all her life in Boston, she knew how dangerous they could be. Why, she could still remember the deadly fire of '72, a decade ago.

"Is everything all right?"

With a start, Victoria turned to the front room. Matthew stood in the doorway. The simple cotton curtains were fluttering at the window she'd recently opened and the door to her left was open, both allowing the smoke-scented wind to barrel through.

"There's a fire in a pasture. Your father has gone up there to get Jake and see what can be done." Although she tried to keep her voice calm, she heard panic make it squeak.

No! She would not frighten the children. She ushered Matthew back into the front room and modulated her voice. "All right, children. Listen. We need to get dressed. Mary, gather together all the clean diapers for Emily. John, help Ralph get into his clothes. You may all take one toy. We're going to load up the wagon." She began to gather up the blankets. Who knew where they would be sleeping tonight?

"What can I do?" Matthew asked.

She looked up at him. *Thank you, Lord, for this young boy's sensibility.* "Get some things together for your father and for Jake."

"Jake sleeps in the barn."

The barn. It stood between them and the fire. She didn't want Matthew in there.

But Growler was in there.

"I'll be right back. Get your father's things and put them in a bag and into the wagon." She hefted up the bedding and hurried out to the wagon where it still sat beside the house. She dumped the bedclothes into the back. Then, hurrying over to the barn, she unhooked Growler, who'd sensed the excitement and had begun to howl. Shushing him, Victoria led him out to the wagon, pulling down on the back to make it easier for the dog to get in.

"Come on, boy, jump up." She patted the bedclothes. Thankfully, the dog obeyed immediately. Giving him one last pat, she looked up at the front of the wagon.

No horse.

Victoria spun. Was there another horse in the barn? In her haste she hadn't noticed. Even a sturdy pony would do right now.

Matthew was herding his younger brothers out of the house toward her. The sky above was filling with smoke, and its scent stung her nostrils. "Matthew," she cried out, "we need to hitch up a horse. But I don't know how."

"I do, Miss Templeton." He ran to the barn, and Victoria helped John and Ralph into the wagon. When she looked up again, Mary was carrying Emily out of the house. She raced over to her and took the baby from her. "Go get her things and her basket." The girl ran back.

A minute later, Matthew was leading a pony out of the barn, dragging along beside him the bridle and reins and harness. While he attached the harness, Victoria slipped the bridle into place. Neither of them could pull the wagon up behind the patient animal, so Victoria led him to the front, and after careful coaxing, managed to get him to step back. Then, anxiously, she watched Matthew hook the traces that secured the wagon to the pony. "How do you know how to do this?" she asked.

"I've helped Papa a few times. He's shown me."

Victoria smiled at him and the boy returned it readily.

Victoria prayed they'd hooked everything up correctly, but a quick test assured her they had.

"Are we going to leave Papa up there?" Matthew asked with a deepening frown.

Victoria shook her head. "No. I just wanted us ready to go at a moment's notice." She bit her lip and glanced back at the younger children, all wide-eyed and worried. "Everything is going to be fine," she reassured them. "Wrap up in the blankets." It wasn't that cold, but they were only just recovering from an illness. She didn't need for them to get sick again.

"What else can we do?" Matthew asked.

Victoria bit her lip. Between the house and the barn sat a small well. An idea blossomed in her mind. "Come, Matthew. You, too, John. I need your help."

With their help, Victoria set up a relay, with John pumping water into buckets and Matthew carrying them around to the back of the barn. Once Victoria had soaked the ground behind the building, she noticed that the water ran in rivulets into the barn. She hurried inside and found a tool, its name unknown to her, with which to carve out a long, narrow trough around the barn. Matthew caught on quickly, and began to pour the buckets of water into the trough. She had no idea if this action would make a good enough firebreak, but it was something to do while waiting for Mitchell to return.

Lord, keep him and Jake safe.

Puffing now as her anxiety wore off, Victoria paused and scanned the hillside. She felt her heart leap. Not only was the wind turning, but coming close to her was a herd of cattle, and two tall figures on horseback.

She sagged. But, realizing where the herd was headed,

she dropped the tool and called to the boys. "Into the wagon, now!"

They rushed around the barn and scrambled up into the wagon, Victoria unceremoniously yanking up her skirt and petticoat in order to climb quickly aboard. She snatched up the reins and moved the horse and wagon down the lane.

Twisting in her seat, she sagged with relief. The herd stopped behind the barn. And around the darker side rode Mitchell. He was never a better sight to see!

Thank you, Lord!

He trotted up to the wagon, dirt and sweat covering his face. She knew she looked a sight herself. Sweat and dust matted her hair, also. She ran one hand over the top to smooth it, but she knew it was pointless. Her forearms, too, were smudged, having been exposed when she pushed up her sleeves. "You brought the herd back!"

Mitchell shook his head, his expression grim. "Not all of it. Most of the younger ones are in a ravine. They panicked. Those that weren't killed tumbling down the side will have to be coaxed out later. We're just thankful the wind turned, driving the fire back onto itself. We managed to beat down the fire line, and the blaze extinguished itself. We drove what was left of the herd off the pasture." With a firm rein, he circled the still-anxious horse in an attempt to distract him. "I have one steer who leads the herd, and thankfully he guided them through it."

Victoria couldn't take her eyes off him, even more so when he walked his horse in close to the wagon to peer down at the basket that held Emily. "We can help water them," she offered. "We've been soaking down the ground behind the barn to act as a firebreak."

Mitchell lifted his eyebrows. "Really?" Then he shook his head. "Thank you, but Jake and I will manage the cattle. They're used to us."

"Can I take the children back into the house?"

"No." Mitchell shook his head. "I want you to take them to the parsonage in Proud Bend. Ask the pastor for directions to Jake's house."

"I thought Jake lived in your barn?"

"His parents live in town. Take the children there. I'll meet you after I see the sheriff."

Victoria gasped. "Why the sheriff?"

"This fire was deliberately set." He held up a battered and charred hat. "I think whoever set the blaze was surprised it caught so quickly and ran off without his hat."

Victoria took the hat from him and flipped it. The inside tag was covered with fine gray soot, but she smeared it clean. "I know this label. It's from a high end milliner in New York. They're quite reputable."

"Are you sure? The hat is pretty scruffy."

"That's because it's a dated style, at least a couple of years old. Look at this stain. It's been there for a while." She handed it back to him.

"I'm taking it to the sheriff. If we can find the owner, we'll find our firebug." He leaned forward, and her heart jumped. "Thank you so much for being here."

All she could think of was that bold kiss she'd given him. She swallowed hard. When this was all over, and he thought back on it, would he continue her silly attempt at courting?

She gasped. Was it courting? No. Only the excitement of the moment had caused her to kiss him.

"Mitchell—" she began.

He looked away. "I have to go. As soon as you settle the children at Jake's house, I want you to go home. And stay there."

She sat back. "Why?"

Mitchell's expression darkened. "Because you shouldn't be involved. This is my problem, not yours. I'm grateful for all you have done, but I can't have you around anymore."

He flicked his reins and the horse trotted back to the barn. Over the sound of her pounding heart, she could hear the restless calls of the cattle he'd driven in. Her eyes watered and by the time he rounded the back corner of the barn, she could no longer see clearly.

She blinked several times. What had she expected? A declaration of love, a promise of courtship? After a wildfire and impromptu cattle drive that followed her silly kiss? What a foolish girl she was.

Victoria turned in her seat and picked up the reins again. Her hands were filthy and blistered from digging that narrow trench. For a moment, she wondered where her gloves were. Had she left them in Mitchell's bedroom? Most likely. Surely if Aunt Louise saw her now, she'd fall into a dead faint, Victoria half-dressed and ready to finish ruining her hands by using reins without gloves. And adding to her misery, sweat stung in several of her broken blisters.

Mitchell was right, she thought dejectedly. She wasn't made of the stern stuff needed up here. Of course, she'd been sensible enough to gather together blankets and clothing, but she had to be honest with herself. She couldn't handle this life on a day-to-day basis.

Swallowing down the lump in her throat that usually preceded tears, Victoria twisted about to ensure all the children were snug in the back. They all stared at her like they had that first day she'd met them. Poor mites! She turned away, hating to see their anxiety. She could never erase that look, no more than she could fit into Mitchell's hardworking life. She ached all over, too. Her corset bit into her sweat-drenched frame, and she wanted only to wash away the grime of the afternoon and fall into her feather bed.

Proof positive of Mitchell's belief.

Victoria flicked the reins and moved the pony forward, down the trail toward Proud Bend.

She was halfway there when her mind, having idled as they bumped over the trail that led to town, hit upon the truth of what she'd seen today.

A truth that was as dangerous as it was obvious. She flicked the reins to push the sturdy pony from his plodding walk into a decent trot.

Chapter Twenty

Victoria closed the door and turned to face the sheriff. It had been only this morning that she'd first seen the man in church and she was glad he was still in his office this late in the day. He stood, and she realized then how tall and stern he appeared.

Smoothing her dress, Victoria walked up to the man's desk. "Has Mitchell MacLeod been in yet?"

"No, ma'am. Is there a problem?"

Victoria glanced back at the door. Had something happened to Mitchell? Perhaps she should have gone to the doctor's house first and sent the man to Proud Ranch as a precaution. After all, she'd left Mitchell to deal with a herd of anxious cattle.

Or was another rancher a better choice?

"Ma'am?"

She looked back at the sheriff and the desk behind which he stood. The small placard said Alexander Zane Robinson. "Sheriff Robinson, there was a fire up at one of his pastures."

"I know. I sent a deputy to investigate. He isn't back yet."

Lost for words, Victoria wet her lips. The sheriff stared at her. Oh, she must look a fright! At Jake's home a short while ago, Mrs. Turcot, his mother, after learning Victoria was headed here, had helped Victoria smooth her hair and fix her dress. She'd handed Victoria a warm shawl to fight the cool, clear night that was falling fast. But none of that could erase the fearful afternoon she'd had, and she was sure Sheriff Robinson could see it clearly on her face. Just as she was about to open her mouth, the door swung open. Into the sheriff's office walked a young, thin man, who held the door open for—

Mitchell! Praise the Lord!

She took a step forward, but stopped when Mitchell's scowl intensified. He moved the battered hat he'd found from one hand to the other. "Didn't I tell you to go home?" he growled.

"Yes, but you need me here."

"How do you figure that?"

"I can help with that hat." She pointed to his left hand. "You didn't even know what kind of hat that was. Well, I can tell you exactly when it was bought. My mother purchased two of those hats two years ago as gifts. One was for my stepfather and one for my uncle. Unless you know of some other wealthy man in Proud Bend who shops at that particular milliner in New York City?" She lifted her chin.

His expression darkened. "All the more reason for you to go home."

"To the house of an arsonist?"

"Yes. The less he connects you with me, the safer you'll be." He worked his jaw. "He's not going to hurt you. He wants you safe and sound at his house because

he wants to marry you off to his business partner, remember?"

Victoria's mouth fell open. That last part spewed from
his mouth as if it was that vile coffee train depots sell to
only the most desperate of travelers.

So why say it? Did he not want to save her from that
terrible fate? Had he somehow decided to placate Uncle
Walter? Give in to his demands? She searched his face
but couldn't find the answer. Before she could stop herself, she blurted out, "You said I was unsuitable for ranch
life and I shouldn't be helping you. Now you're saying
I'm to be preserved to placate my uncle. Well, you may
be ready to accept those excuses, but not me. I'm here
to prove both of them wrong."

Mitch clamped shut his mouth. Then finally, as he
passed her, he muttered, "This isn't the place for that
discussion, Victoria."

"But I have an idea that will help!"

Tearing his gaze from her, Mitch thrust the hat at the
sheriff. "This was found near where the fire was started.
Now, if you'll excuse me, I need to have a word with Miss
Templeton." He caught Victoria's arm and steered her toward the door. With a surprised expression, the deputy
hastily opened it for them.

Outside, no moon hung in the clear sky of early evening. The only decent light came from the outside lamp
that the sheriff had lit. Mitch led Victoria around the
corner into a sheltered nook between the sheriff's office and the jail. Good. It was dark here. She could no
more see his hesitant expression than he could see the
hurt in her eyes.

"Victoria, you have to go home."

"But I have an idea!" She grabbed him as he shook his head. "Listen, Mitchell. We both know that my uncle wants your mineral rights. If he can stop you from making your mortgage payment, you'll be in default and be forced to sell those rights. When do you have to make that payment?"

Just over a full day. "By midnight tomorrow."

"You have the money from the sale of the heifers. You can do it."

The heifers. Oh, yes, the ones she sneakily sold for him. "Besides that being the subject of another discussion," Mitch said, "I can't give that money to the bank. I don't have the heifers to give to the men who bought them."

"All your heifers are gone?"

"No, but the ones they looked at and agreed to purchase have been injured or killed. Even if they bought my stock, the cows could lose their young because of the stress, and I promised that they would calve at the end of the coming winter." He pulled in a deep breath and continued. "And I won't put those men into financial hardship just so I can pay one of my own bills. So if you think about it, Victoria, that money isn't mine." He shook his head. "You don't understand about financial hardships."

"Excuse me?"

Mitch didn't need a lantern to tell him she was glaring at him.

Her spine as straight as a lodgepole pine, Victoria snapped. "I climbed aboard that train in Boston with less than a dollar to my name. I couldn't even afford the food we brought back from the general store. Ninety-two cents! That was all the money I had in the world. After tipping the porter, I had less. There isn't one red cent coming after it's gone. And I don't have any way to earn more."

"I still owe you your salary."

"I don't want it. You said yourself that I foisted my role of caretaker onto a strange woman. What was the word you used? *Reneged?*"

"Is that why you came to my house? Were you feeling guilty that you hadn't properly earned your salary?"

"I came to help you out, Mitchell. Your children were sick. You said yourself that ranch life is hard work, and you can't be a mother and father to those children and a rancher at the same time." She folded her arms. "Besides, by your logic, if I was feeling guilty about taking a salary, then I am honest and trustworthy, so therefore you should be listening to my idea of how to trap Uncle Walter."

He rubbed his face. He'd been tired first thing this morning after a night up with the children. He felt worse now. When Jake had offered to take care of them so he could go to church, Mitch had jumped at the offer. Then, sitting in that pew, surrounded by warm, quiet bodies, he'd very nearly fallen asleep. The afternoon had turned wild and dangerous, and riding hard out to the fire, back again with the herd and then here had thoroughly drained him.

He didn't need this confrontation with Victoria, especially after she'd hauled him down for a kiss before he'd ridden off toward the fire, a kiss that he remembered clearly. What he needed was for her to go home. He could handle it from here. That's what his kind did. They shouldn't have to worry about women like Victoria who seemed oblivious to the danger around them.

But he couldn't blame her, not after his talk with his

pastor about how she'd never learned how to care for children. Here, she'd never had to deal with this life before, so how could she be as wary as she should be?

What she also didn't realize was that the longer she hung around him, the more his children became attached to her. When she finally left—and she would leave—it would break their hearts. First their mother, then Victoria? *No, thank you very much.*

But he was having a hard time finding a decent woman to look after them.

What about Victoria? You want her around.

No, he told himself sternly. And he wasn't going to tell her again how unsuitable she was. He'd already hurt her feelings, he was sure, and the last time he'd sent her packing, she'd returned, armed with a notebook on how to do things and an attitude he hadn't felt like battling.

What had she been saying? Oh, yes, something about trapping her uncle. "I won't have my words twisted around, Victoria. It's unfair. You wouldn't like that to happen to you." What he needed to do was to somehow get Victoria to think staying away from him was her own good idea. She'd more likely do it that way.

"Where do you think you should be?" he asked her.

"Helping you."

"Because if something happened to me, you can help with the children, correct?"

"Absolutely."

"So your safety is as important as mine. Maybe more so because you're my backup plan, right?"

There was a pause, and Mitch held his breath. As his eyes adjusted to the light, he could make out her slight frown. He could see she didn't know how to answer, so he gently filled in the right words. "You need to go home and be prepared to help me at a moment's notice."

She looked dubious.

"Perhaps you can study that map you obviously consulted in order to find my ranch." He tried to keep his words gentle. "You will need to know the area better."

Victoria's shoulders stiffened. She opened her mouth, but shut it again.

A sharp, deep voice answered instead of her. "And I need to know the facts about this fire, if you two don't mind tearing yourselves away from each other."

Mitch turned to the source. The sheriff stood akimbo at the corner, his right side bathed in the thin light that glowed from his office's outside lamp. He would not be intimidated by this man. He'd do exactly as he was supposed to do. He might not completely trust the way things worked in Proud Bend, especially where Walter Smith was concerned, but he did trust his Savior. The Lord was with him. Teaching him.

Teaching him what?

Never mind, he told himself. "Are you prepared to hear my complaint?" Mitch asked the man.

"Of course. But not out here in the dark," the sheriff answered.

As Mitch took Victoria's arm, she held back. "We're not here just to complain about an arson attempt," she said. "I came here because I have an idea."

"We will listen to it inside," Mitch said, feeling confident that his suggestions to her were sinking into that beautiful head of hers.

Inside, they found that the deputy had lit several large lamps. Gaslight might be the choice of lighting out east, but here, the oil lamps filled the rooms with warm, oil-scented light.

Victoria immediately turned to Mitch. "You say I should go home, but first listen to my idea. I should go home and tell Uncle Walter that your herd is safe and sound and closer to the house, and that you are going to be able to deliver the heifers to the men who purchased them."

"But the herd isn't completely safe. I managed to get the injured ones back to the barn after you left, but I wouldn't call them safe. I don't want you lying."

Victoria shook her head. "I won't argue with you on what constitutes a lie, but really, Mitchell, the herd *is* safe from the fire but right now it's in a *tinder-dry* barn. That should be enough to spark an idea in Uncle Walter's head, if you'll excuse the unintended pun."

She looked hopefully at Mitch, ignoring the two other men in the room. Her eyes, wide and innocent, yet knowing, spoke so much. He looked her up and down. She'd cleaned up at some point, and again, he was struck by her beauty. The woman could wear a feed sack and a pound of dust and still look stunning, he was sure.

Mitchell shoved the attraction away. Her suggestion would put his herd at too much risk. It would put everything he owned at too much risk. Not to mention his family. If he was alone, he might consider it, but not now that he had five children.

"Mitchell, we both know Uncle Walter is responsible for all that has happened." She pointed across the room to where the dusty, sooty hat lay on a desk. "That hat belongs to him, a gift from my mother. It would be up in the pasture only if he was there lighting that fire."

"He's not the sort to get his hands dirty."

"But I heard him arguing before church this morning with that man you called Donner, who said he won't do my uncle's dirty work anymore. Donner said something that didn't make any sense to me at the time, but it makes perfect sense now. He said that whatever my uncle wanted him to do would jeopardize his land and herd. Uncle Walter must have wanted him to set your pasture alight, but Donner knew he'd be risking his own land, as well. My uncle said something sinister sounding, about how Donner would regret not doing as he was told."

"You're suggesting that next Walter Smith will try to burn down my barn and kill my cattle?"

Victoria nodded vigorously. "Yes. It's brutal and horrible, but in his mind, he needs to stop you from making that bank payment. With one wildfire already started, it's not a stretch to think another may start close to your herd. He's probably thinking that could be his defense."

The sheriff spoke. "Or he'll break in and steal the money."

"He has to know where it is in order to steal it," Mitch answered absently. Thinking of the hiding spot he was sure even Walter Smith would not find, Mitch felt his mouth thin.

Victoria stepped closer to him. Mitch wanted to back off, for surely he smelled of horseflesh and smoke and sweat. But she didn't seem to care. Her face was slightly smudged, a small spot that her hasty grooming this evening had missed. He flexed his arm to prevent himself from reaching up and brushing it away.

"My idea will work, Mitchell. You'll see. Uncle Walter will not want to sit idle, knowing his plan has failed. He's already told Donner he will do it all himself. Nighttime is the best time to finish off what he started, and you, along with the sheriff here, can catch him in the act. My uncle won't take a chance that you will be able to make your mortgage payment."

Still, pride prickled him. *Her* idea. Shameful, wasn't it that he couldn't think of a single idea to help himself? All he could think about was getting her safely away.

For her own good? Or so she couldn't hurt his children when she left, as she was surely going to do?

Or was there some other reason?

When pride cometh, then cometh shame.

Was his pastor right? Was he too proud? Was he upset that the idea wasn't his, instead of thinking of the very real danger if they didn't stop Walter Smith? Because Smith's evil behavior would surely escalate.

He stared straight into her eyes. Pride or not, he could keep her safe. "Will you stay home if we do what you suggest? Promise me you will."

She didn't answer right away. He could see hurt in her eyes, multiplying the shame he felt.

Victoria would have thought that satisfaction tasted better, but it didn't. No, it was bitter and hollow, like an overripe cucumber that some kitchen maid had tried to cover with too many herbs before making into a sandwich. Bitter it should be. There was so much danger about them, so much risk. To the herd, to human life. To Jake, to the sheriff.

To Mitchell.

The plan was dangerous. They had to catch Uncle Walter in the act of sabotage, before he could set alight the barn or the house or do something more dangerous.

She looked between Mitchell and the sheriff and caught the knowing expression they exchanged.

"She'll go home and do nothing. We will deal with Smith should he decide to prevent MacLeod from making his payment," the sheriff announced, as if he fully expected Victoria to roll over and obey. Shocked, she whirled back to stare into Mitchell's face, silently pleading with him to intervene. She wanted to help. Couldn't he see that she had already been helpful? She could even ride out after Uncle Walter. She was an excellent horsewoman.

Oh, to be useful, and not just for suggestions. Certainly not just to be a pawn, either, in a game of trying to keep banking wealth in the family, so that Walter could control it. If she married Clyde, Walter knew that she'd probably outlive the old man, and that would secure Walter's plans of controlling the whole business, because surely as Clyde's widow, she would need Walter to continue managing her inherited share. If she refused to marry, she'd be tossed out. If she couldn't handle ranch life, she certainly couldn't handle being truly homeless.

Oh, Mitchell, don't leave me to that world.

But what was the point? Mitchell would still not allow her into his life. His pride had already stopped him, and her pride in thinking she could do so much more was just lunacy.

What a pair of fools they were.

Still, she said, "What will it be, Mitchell? I do nothing and Uncle Walter slowly takes over this town, or you let me help?"

With a controlled sigh, he answered, "Go home, Victoria. Tell your Uncle Walter *only* that the herd is safe and close to the house and barn." His expression hardened. "And then clean up and go to bed. Get some rest. That would be the best help of all."

Her eyes burned. Why was she upset? He was accepting her plan. But that was all. Tears rolled down her cheeks. Victory was indeed hollow.

Chapter Twenty-One

"I'm taking you home." Mitchell's words sounded grittier than a swallow of that dust that blew constantly in everyone's faces.

"Whatever you wish," Victoria answered with a calm smile she did not feel. She may have snapped out her share of their testy banter outside, but now the situation was sinking in.

Mitchell was clearly exhausted. He wore the strain of the day like a heavy woolen overcoat on a hot day. It wasn't fair to twist his words, ignoring the spirit in which they'd been said. He wanted her safely away from danger. Although that was all he wanted, shouldn't that be enough?

With shoulders so stiff they ached, Victoria allowed Mitchell to open the door for her. She had to admit, she was exhausted herself, and even though Jake's mother helped to make her presentable, her dress was desperately in need of a thorough scrubbing and she would do anything for a bath and a solid night's sleep. All in good time, she told herself.

The deputy had already left to watch her uncle's

house, and in minutes Mitch would be riding out to his place, as soon as he walked her home. Her plan was getting under way.

When they stepped outside, the night was deep with nothing to light their way. The only street worth mentioning in this small town was also the only one lit with lamps in spots, not at all like Boston with its modern gaslights throughout the city. Why, she'd heard that Scollay Square, a delightful spot in downtown Boston, had an electric light now. So different was Proud Bend with a slower style and dry air that parched the lips and skin.

She glanced down at the saloon. It continued its raucous activities, as if epitomizing the life out here. The society in which she'd grown up would have turned up its nose to such an establishment, but times had been changing, even in Boston, with the influx of new people and ideas.

Victoria swallowed hard. She and her mother had left at the right time, she suddenly realized. Both of them had been living a delusion. She would not have married into a fine, Brahmin family. Those families were looking to augment their dwindling wealth with more than what she'd had.

She'd been a fool to believe she could fit in.

Money was moving West. Those old families were filtering away, investing in the inevitable expansion.

A night breeze pressed against her skirt and chilled her arms. Or was that chill the realization that life was turning out differently than she'd envisioned? She'd always wanted to follow God's leading and for a while she'd assumed it would be to stay in Boston. It wasn't. But where was He taking her?

Some distant animal answered with a lonely howl.

Beside Mitchell, Victoria quickened her pace. Her uncle's house loomed in the night, most of the windows lit as if to tell the town they could afford the expensive oil.

Victoria hesitated. As she'd raced past Rachel after church today, she'd asked her cousin to tell her aunt she was going to help Mitchell. All she could do now was hope that Rachel had done as she'd promised, and that her aunt wasn't worried for her missing niece.

Victoria felt her mouth twist wryly. Aunt Louise might be concerned, but Victoria couldn't see the woman worried.

At the whitewashed fence, Mitchell stopped. Victoria's nerves danced. He'd said nothing all the way across the small town, only guiding her off the wooden sidewalk and through the dusty hardpan that was the street.

Nervousness danced through her like a butterfly on a hot summer's day. There was no reason for this, she told herself sternly. Mitchell was hardly courting her. He'd made it abundantly clear she was unsuitable for his lifestyle.

He was so right.

They walked closer to the door. "Go inside, Victoria, and stay there."

She looked at Mitchell, hating that her tears were starting again. "I'll find Uncle Walter. I see a lamp lit in his study."

"I don't like it. I don't trust him."

"You said yourself that he won't do anything to me." *Except try to force me to marry Clyde*, she added to herself. "I am more valuable to him if I remain unharmed."

Mitchell said nothing.

She reached out and touched his arm. "It will be fine.

We need to do this if that sheriff is to catch him in the act."

"Let's hope so. The sheriff is new, so I don't know him. But I know his deputy is a layabout, and probably in your uncle's pocket."

Victoria clamped shut her mouth. Another reason for Mitchell to want to stay far away from her. Walter Smith may be her mother's brother, but any relationship was purely an accident. Abigail had been proud of her brother's success over the years, but Victoria could never be. How odd that a man who stirred pride in one woman would inspire shame and humility in her daughter.

"I don't know what to say," she whispered.

"Say that you'll only do what we decided and nothing more." He leaned closer. "Will you? Like it or not, I see that you're important to my children."

"Like it or not?" she echoed.

Mitchell folded his arms. "Yes. Exactly that. We both know you aren't going to be in my children's lives for very long. Even if you master the art of running a household, this life you are currently living isn't your choice. And it will be less of a choice if everything goes according to plan."

"You mean when you catch Uncle Walter in the act?"

"Or I find myself completely penniless, without even a ranch to support my family. That's probably what will happen. I'll be worse off and I don't want you to be a part of that."

He stepped closer before she could think of a suitable answer. "All I'm asking is that you stay safe. Then, after the dust settles, you gently extricate yourself from my family's life. They've been hurt enough. They need stability, not someone who is still learning how to live like the rest of us."

She lowered her gaze.

"You know that if we're successful, your uncle will be facing serious charges and his family decimated, you included. You will have no choice but to marry Clyde or return east."

She looked back up at him. "There's nothing for me in Boston. My mother and I were deluding ourselves, thinking that today's society would carry on forever. In fact, I saw the change coming years ago but didn't believe it. I don't have a place in it, anyway."

"Then you'll go to the Carolinas where your mother is and find someone more suitable there."

An odd hitch sounded in his voice and Victoria peered through the dark to seek out the reason. But sadly, even though the lamplight from within the house lit upon his face, Victoria could not discern his emotions. Her eyes were filling with too many tears.

"Mitchell, I don't want that," she whispered. But if her family here was destroyed, what would be her choices? Mitchell didn't want her in his children's lives.

He didn't answer with words. Instead he stepped forward and his lips found hers.

In that moment, her heart, which had already pounded with the pain of realizing her life wasn't ever going to be happy, suddenly leaped in her chest. All of her being spiked with an emotion she could only describe as brilliant as lightning. She felt totally blinded by it.

Only when a distant thump sounded from within the house did Mitchell step away. "Remember, go inside and stay there."

Before she could speak, Mitchell turned and disappeared into the darkness.

Behind Victoria, the front door opened. Her aunt hurried toward her. "Victoria, thank goodness you're safe! I've been worried for you."

Victoria turned. "Didn't Rachel tell you I would be out?"

"Rachel told me you were going to visit a friend. But it's getting late." Louise drew her into the house. "Was it your friend Clare?"

"No, another."

Louise shut the door behind them. When her gaze fell upon Victoria, she gasped. "You look like you've been dragged behind a horse! What happened to the dress you wore to church?"

Victoria had forgotten that. Matthew had collected her things from the ranch house, but she'd left everything at Jake's parents' house, including the pony and wagon. "I got a bit dusty today, that's all."

The older woman leaned forward and sniffed. "It smells like you've been in a fire! And look at your hair!" She smoothed it down. Apparently, Mrs. Turcot hadn't been successful enough with her styling to fool Aunt Louise.

"Never mind that, Aunt Louise." Victoria caught her aunt's hand. "I need to speak with Uncle Walter."

"Not looking like that you won't. He's busy in his study and will expect you to be better dressed. We've delayed supper for you, so you had best go upstairs and change and fix your hair. I know I am quite hungry and I am sure Walter is, too." She shoved Victoria toward the stairs.

"I'll help her, Mother."

Victoria looked up. At the top landing stood Rachel, dressed as if she was leaving. Victoria glanced back at her aunt, finding the older woman's mouth set in a tight line. She turned once again to her cousin. Rachel stood calmly as Victoria hurried up the stairs. Inside her bedroom, Victoria locked the door and spun. "What did you tell your mother?"

"I said you were going to visit a friend." Rachel walked over to her wardrobe and pulled out several dresses, eyeing each one until she chose a simple but warm dress, the rose dress Victoria had worn on the train. "Let's get you washed and changed. We'll see if we can't get rid of that smoky smell while we're at it. I'm guessing you won't want my father to know you've been fighting a certain grass fire."

"You know about that?"

"I just returned from the saloon. I'd forgotten something. It's all they're talking about there."

Victoria stopped her work of changing for her hand shook too much. Oh, she couldn't do this quickly! "Rachel, you went to the saloon? Is that wise?"

"I had an escort. I always have one. Even Mitchell MacLeod on several occasions." She returned to her work, but Victoria stepped away from her.

"A variety of men! That's even worse!" Victoria threw up her hands, then shook her head. "Never mind my troubles. Rachel, you can't go on like this! Imagine what your reputation is like! Not to mention your personal safety! You could get hurt, or worse. Your escort could—"

"My escort is always trustworthy." Hurrying up to her, Rachel spun Victoria and began to assist her in undressing. They worked in strained silence for several minutes. Victoria could only think of several fast prayers, but they jumbled all together and she hoped that the good Lord made sense of it all.

After a few more minutes of silent work, Rachel finally said, "I'm fine. Really, I am. I've been going to the back of the saloon most evenings for a long time." She caught her cousin's shoulders, stopping Victoria's protest before it could start. They both stared into the cheval mirror across the room. "It's not what you think," Rachel added.

"How could it not be?"

Rachel pulled out of her skirt's pocket a small printed piece of paper. Thrusting it toward Victoria, she said, "This is what I am delivering. Among other things. It's these papers I forgot tonight."

Only halfway through her dressing, Victoria stopped and took the paper and read it. There were several verses from Psalms, and a small, simply written sentence about hope, with a sketch of Jesus and the fallen woman. She looked up again, totally baffled. "A Bible tract? I don't understand. You're giving this to people at the saloon?"

"I'm giving the women who work there hope. I haven't been going to carouse and shame my family." A shadow crossed over her features. "I go to minister to the women. And girls, for some are younger than you."

"It's so dangerous. Why do you do it?"

Rachel wet her lips. "I didn't like what I found out. One woman, Rosa's mother was—" Rachel cut off her words. "I'll tell you all about it someday. Tonight's not the best time."

Victoria had to agree with that part, but still, she asked, "Do your parents know?"

Rachel glanced toward the door, as if the words she was to speak were a secret. "Mother knows. Her only stipulation is that I attend church and Bible study. Even the pastor knows. He's the one who wrote the tracts I deliver. But he insisted I take a man from the church to ensure my safety. Mitchell was asked to do it on several occasions, but I have to tell you, he was more uncomfortable in there than I was."

"What do you do when you're ministering to them?"

"Everything. I've baked bread, cooked meals, washed laundry, bandaged wounds and especially prayed for these women."

Victoria's brows shot up. So that's why Rachel knew so much about how to do the menial tasks. And why her hands looked a fright.

Forgive me, Lord, for thinking the worst of Rachel.

Rachel turned Victoria around again and continued to assist her into a fresh gown. They worked in silence for a bit longer until Rachel spoke again. "Now, not another word on this. We'll talk about it another day. Whatever you want to say to my father, you had better be looking your best for it. He's in a foul mood tonight, and having supper delayed hasn't helped it."

Fear spiked in her. For a moment, she didn't know what to do. Then, hurrying over to her dressing table, she quickly undid her hair and ran her brush through it vigorously. Her mind whirred like a windup toy. Then she hastily sprayed a light cologne to mask the smell of smoke. She doubted it would be successful, though.

But she couldn't back down now. This was her idea and she wanted Mitchell to know he could count on her for everything.

Hastily wrapping her hair back into a French knot, she suddenly realized that if she followed through with her part in the plan, Rachel's life would radically change.

Her family would be torn apart, and she and her mother might lose their home, their fortune, everything. If he got caught, her uncle would need a very good solicitor. Was it fair to save Mitchell's home and property at the expense of another's?

But Walter was breaking the law, she argued with herself.

Shoving the last pin in her hair, she straightened her shoulders. *Lord, be with me. Give me the right words and the courage I need to do what's right.*

She didn't stop praying until she heard her uncle answer her knock on his study door a few minutes later.

Smoothing her hair, this time for courage, she stepped inside. She hadn't even rehearsed what she wanted to say. Perhaps this was for the best. It forced her to stick to the truth, as she should.

"Uncle Walter, I want to say I'm so sorry for being such a poor guest. I dashed off right away after church and the time got away from me."

At his desk, Uncle Walter looked up then, his expression pensive. She wished she knew what he was thinking. "It's quite all right, Victoria. As soon as we noticed you'd come home, I sent word to Clyde. He will be joining us in a few minutes."

She couldn't stop the gasp. Clyde Abernathy was coming this late? That meant that Uncle Walter would stay, not leave for any reason. He'd be anxious to see his plans for Victoria realized.

"Mr. Abernathy is coming here? It's so late. I just assumed we'd have a quick meal before retiring."

"It's not that late and Clyde lives alone. He wants to come." He cocked his head. "I hear his coupe pulling into the yard right now."

Panic surged over her. She stepped forward, feeling the sudden press of time. "But don't both of you have to work in the morning?"

Walter batted his hand. "You needn't worry about that, Victoria." Abruptly, he sniffed the air. "You should spray on a bit more cologne, though. Clyde has a discriminating nose. While you're at it, I suggest a light cream for those hands. And clean your nails."

Victoria curled her fingers but said nothing. She'd given her hands a good washing at Mrs. Turcot's but that had been all she'd had time to do.

Walter set down the cigar he'd been smoking and walked around his desk. Flicking his gaze up and down her frame, he frowned. "So where were you this afternoon?"

Only now he wanted to know where she'd been? She was still only twenty and under her uncle's care. Surely he should have asked as soon as she walked in. Even Aunt Louise had asked.

Like the windup toy finally being released, she began to speak, hardly believing her own calmness. "I have a confession. I went up to Mitchell MacLeod's house after church."

His face seemed to drain of color. "Why?"

"His children are sick. I wanted to help."

"What could you have done?"

Honestly, Victoria thought to herself, did everyone think she couldn't do a single thing?

You can't. She folded her arms, ignoring her own doubt. "Not as much as I first thought. And then a grass fire started. Mitchell rode up to save his cattle." She held out her hand. "Don't worry, he managed to extinguish the fire."

"And the cattle?" By now, Walter's eyes had widened to saucers.

"They're all safe, but I'm worried about the barn. It's a tinder-dry building and there has already been one fire close by. If they hadn't managed to put the fire out completely, I don't know what might have happened."

Abruptly, Walter's eyes narrowed to near slits. From outside the room, Victoria could hear Clyde being let in the house.

Walter's expression then eased back into a calmness that made the fine hairs at her nape stand on end. "So, tell me, Victoria, what does MacLeod say about your being here?"

Chills rose on her flesh, despite the warm room, for some servant had kindled a fire in the small, enameled stove in the corner.

"What do you mean?"

"He didn't want you to return to his ranch?"

Victoria stiffened. "No. Why do you ask?"

He picked up his lit cigar again. "So he's not courting you?"

"No."

"And he doesn't care what happens to you?"

"He cares, but in a Christian way."

"Then why did I see you two kissing before you came in?"

Blood rushed to her cheeks. For a moment, they stared at each other, horror burning across Victoria's features while Walter continued to smoke his cigar with unruffled smugness. Then he walked back to his desk, where he extinguished it with great precision. He picked up an envelope and an ornate silver cigar case, the kind with the matches tucked into the top. Her father had had one, which her mother now retained as a keepsake.

Finally, Victoria found her voice. "Mitchell's kiss meant nothing."

"Hmm." Walter opened a drawer and pulled out a gun.

Victoria's eyes widened as he aimed the barrel at her. "We shall see how little he cares for you."

Chapter Twenty-Two

Victoria considered screaming, but if such an act caused others to race into the room, Uncle Walter might panic and shoot them all.

With surprising swiftness, he grabbed her arm. Beyond the room, the voices had died away, and Victoria guessed that her Aunt Louise had taken Clyde into the parlor to await the others. Walter opened his study door a crack, then a bit more as he flicked a fast look one way and then the other. Victoria caught a glimpse of the quiet hallway.

His grip tightening on her, Walter yanked at her as he hurried into the hall and out the front door. The night was quiet, colder than before. Victoria heard the horse in the drive dead ahead snort quietly. The coupe that had brought Clyde here was similar to the one Walter owned, but while the Smith family's was black and ornate, this one was deep burgundy with even more delicate filigree designs on it.

Walter threw open the small door and shoved Victoria in. She cried out in pain when her shin smacked against the step.

"Shut up, girl," he growled. "If someone comes out here, I'll shoot them. Have that on your conscience."

"It won't be my fault."

"It will. Get in, now." He twisted her arm back to hasten her compliance.

Relenting to the pain at her shin and in her arm, Victoria bustled inside. Walter jumped up with a heavy wheeze and sat in the driver's spot. The light coupe lurched downward under his weight. Victoria stared in horror as he flicked the reins hard, urging the pair of horses to a full, immediate trot.

Victoria gripped the upholstery to keep herself secure. While the coupe's sitting area was enclosed in glass and steel, she could still feel the speed at which Walter drove it.

She looked out the small window behind her. Wasn't the deputy supposed to be watching the house? She couldn't see anyone. No one hurried after them on horseback.

She swallowed down her fear. Should she try to open the door and jump out? Walter had a gun. He could easily turn the horses and reach her again, where she'd be an easy target. If she survived the fall.

Or he could abandon her and head out to the ranch. With a gun. It had taken her nearly an hour to clean herself up, before going down to speak with Uncle Walter. By now, Mitchell would have returned to his home. Victoria was sure that he owned a rifle, but rarely did a man, armed or not, survive an ambush.

The coupe hit a bump and she fell forward, banging against the glass that separated her from Walter. He turned. "Stay still, girl. Or else." He twisted back to his driving.

Or else what? Again, they hit a bump and she grabbed the bar in front of her to steady herself.

She looked behind her again. Proud Bend had become a small collection of black, awkward boxes of various sizes, some showing off lit squares of windows that did nothing to dispel the sudden loneliness she felt. There wasn't even a moon to cast a thin, yet comforting light upon the town.

She faced forward, and, steadying herself against the bumps on the trail, she gaped as Walter raced past where the trail split. Mitchell's ranch was to the right. Where was Walter taking her?

After what seemed an age later, Walter reined in the horses and drew them to a halt. Victoria lurched forward, wondering if this was her time to escape. Her hand on the handle, she was ready to throw open the door and leap out.

Before she could, Walter jumped down and yanked it open instead. He leaned in and grabbed her hand. "Get out."

Victoria stumbled out, her shoe catching on her hem as she struggled to find the small step. Impatient, Walter tugged harder and for his efforts she toppled forward onto the dusty, dry grass.

"Stand up, girl. I can't believe how useless you are."

She flew to her feet. "I am not useless! How dare you treat me like this!"

"Fool woman! I'll treat you as I please. Oh, you're all alike. My wife doesn't care, my daughter refuses to obey me and now there's you, another female defying me." He leaned in close. "It's bad enough to deal with Clyde, but not you, too. Don't you think I know that you have no intention of marrying him? At least this way, I will get something out of you." He shoved her forward, around the back of the small carriage and into the dark night.

"Where are we going?"

"Keep your voice down." He jabbed her in the back with what she could only assume was the barrel of the small revolver.

They trudged up a short crest. Panting, Victoria struggled to not trip on her gown, for she'd torn the front of the skirt and it drooped down. Beside her, she could hear Walter wheezing. She expected to feel the altitude, but Walter? Perhaps he wasn't the fittest man in Proud Bend.

At the top of the hill, she paused to catch her breath and try to still her pounding fear. Below and to the right lay several buildings, two of them lit with lanterns.

Mitchell's ranch!

Behind her, she heard Walter let out a short, sneering chuckle. He grabbed her arm and twisted it back. "Stay quiet, or you'll both end up dead. Now pick up the pace. I don't have all night."

Mitch bent to tuck in a stray wire end, which finished off the makeshift fence. He'd sent Jake down to the drive in case Smith decided to fall for Victoria's plan. The sheriff had put his deputy at the Smith house, but in all honesty, Mitch didn't trust either lawman, not with Victoria's or the children's lives. And he knew of the deputy's reputation. Mitch had seen the man frequent the saloon on the occasions the pastor had asked him to escort Rachel Smith. He wouldn't be surprised to learn that the deputy had abandoned his post. Mitch hadn't even seen the lawman when he'd taken Victoria home earlier.

He straightened, feeling the strain and fatigue that followed a day of hard work. A part of him wanted this to end tonight, one way or the other, and he hated that he could actually consider relinquishing his hold on the mineral rights or, for that matter, the ranch. Anything to stop the hardship and the uncertainty for his family.

At least his children were safe in town, as was Victoria. Her willingness to help was commendable, but they had to face facts. They were too different in too many ways to be anything but acquaintances.

Satisfied he'd done all he could with this corral at the back end of the barn, he picked up his lantern. He hated that his herd was crowded, some pressing against the wire he'd strung across the open end that faced his home. But it would have to do tonight. All he could hope for was that the sheriff would catch Smith before the man did any damage. But the man had yet to arrive, which was worrisome. If they weren't successful in stopping a fire, Mitch had rigged the barbed wire so one flick would release it and the animals would be able to escape.

He walked around the barn. The cattle were restless. As he slowed his pace, he crooned out a soft song. Last summer, when he would be up at the pasture at dusk, he'd often eased their tension with his singing. Now the older cows ended their restless grunts and shifting. One larger animal deep within the herd snorted loudly, and several of them shifted back, but Mitch continued his singing as he rounded the front of the barn.

"MacLeod."

At the sound Mitch looked up to see Walter Smith in front of him. With Victoria. They stood in the circle of light flowing from a lantern he'd hung up above the barn's front door. The animals within shifted away.

The night stilled. Did he not tell Victoria to stay put?

Why was she here? Setting down his tools, Mitch stepped forward, his attention nailed to her.

Her dress was that same rose one into which she'd changed that day on the train when she'd traded her fine dark green suit for milk for Emily. It was badly torn as if she'd stepped on the front hem. He could see dust smeared on her cheek and her hair had fallen out of its usually perfect coif, rolling in long waves down one side of her head.

In that moment, he realized something. She'd paid for his child's milk, simply because she couldn't bear to see the child suffer. It had cost her a lot. It had not been a selfish act at all. The clothes she'd brought were all she owned. She had nothing else. And this one dress looked torn beyond repair.

She wet her lips. Her worried stare was wide, shifting as she swallowed. Walter Smith stood close to her, but slightly behind. The man shifted and Victoria arched her side away from him.

The hairs rose on Mitch's neck. Around the lantern buzzed a few late-season insects, drawn close by the warmth and light, their drone suddenly loud.

Victoria let out a hitching gasp. "Mitchell—"

"Shut up, girl," Smith spat.

"What's going on?" Mitch demanded.

"You know very well what's going on, MacLeod. Shame on you, sending a girl in to do your work. Why did you want me here? To set fire to your barn? Did you think you could set me up so easily? I bet you have a man down at your gate." Smith shook his head. "We didn't come that way. I took the left road instead of the right one that goes up past your gate."

Mitch felt his jaw clench. "Let Victoria go. She's got nothing to do with this."

"You're right. She has nothing to do with this." Smith shifted slightly away from Victoria, and the lamplight glinted off a small revolver whose barrel was pressed into Victoria's side. "But she is a valuable tool to me. A way of ensuring your compliance."

His heart pounding, Mitch gritted out, "In what?"

"In signing this." With his free hand, Smith drew from his jacket pocket a long, battered envelope.

Mitch went cold. When Smith had first approached him to purchase the mineral rights, he'd held out a similar envelope.

Now the same envelope, albeit battered, stretched toward him. Mitch wanted to decline again. This was his land, his rights, his pride of ownership.

Pride? The stuff didn't equal to a mound of beans when a life was at risk. It had been easy for Mitch to rely on pride to see him through the bumps and curious heartaches Victoria was causing in him, but not now, not as long as she was in danger.

She'd relinquished her own foolish pride by trying to learn simple domestic tasks.

Look what his pride had done to him. It had ruined him.

When pride cometh, then cometh shame.

He was truly shamed now. He'd put his ranch above all else, and now, like the insects buzzing around the lantern, the shame had returned.

Smith tossed the envelope on the ground between them. Then, after digging in his pocket again, he tossed down a fine fountain pen. "Sign it. If you don't, Victoria will find herself in an unfortunate accident."

Mitch shook his head, partly in disbelief. "And when this night is over and I report you to the sheriff?"

Walter laughed. For a moment, Mitch expected the older man to tell him he had the sheriff in his back pocket. The cattle within the barn's open doorway shifted restlessly. In the morning, Mitch needed to recheck the makeshift fencing he'd set up.

"You can report me all you want, but it'll be my word against yours. And Victoria will still be missing. She'll be found on your land, by the way, and you'll be responsible. I'll simply say that she raced out of my house as soon as I mentioned that Clyde was coming here for supper. I will say that when I realized she'd taken Clyde's carriage, I took off after her, knowing she would come here. I'll say that I took one of my horses and brought it back tied to the coupe. No one is going to question me, the owner of all the mortgages in this town. I will say that I'd seen you two kissing on my front doorstep. I'm sure the deputy would back me up. Oh, don't think I don't know he was sent to watch my house. I saw him arrive just before you, but I knew he wouldn't last on any guard post. We both know he prefers other activities to work, so he won't incriminate himself by saying he doesn't know what happened."

Walter snorted in a self-satisfied way. "If you don't sign, I would add that you probably spurned her and she fled. They'll eventually find her body somewhere. But if you sign, I'll let her go and simply say she would rather choose you than marry a wealthy man who can properly care for her. Her word will mean nothing to the judge, who'll think she's only a fool woman." He shrugged. "It's not like the other women in my family aren't foolish, either."

Mitch worked his jaw. There was no way he would allow Walter Smith to win at this.

But unless he came up with a decent and immediate plan, Smith would win everything.

Without such a plan, Mitch had only one choice.

Chapter Twenty-Three

Mitch stepped forward.

Walter leaned close. "That's it, MacLeod, do what your conscience tells you to do."

"I will. And, Smith, you may think you're winning, but when you put worldly things over human life, you don't win. It's a false security." With that, Mitch picked up the pen and envelope. Not letting his eyes leave the pair standing near the barn doorway, he opened the envelope and pulled out the papers.

A quick scan told him they were indeed the mineral rights papers he'd seen at the beginning of this mess.

And that was what his land was going to be after this. A mess. If he'd considered Smith's offer earlier, he could have negotiated the preservation of the land, but now all he could do was negotiate Victoria's release.

"Let her go, Smith."

"Just as soon as you sign the papers and return them to me."

He looked down again. The price had been changed, reduced to a mere pittance. Smith had expected that Mitch would not be able to make his mortgage payment.

In lieu of calling in the loan, he would have offered this agreement. But this amount wouldn't cover his mortgage payment, leaving Mitch still in default. This ranch and the rights would go to Walter.

Jaw tight, Mitch removed the ornate cap from the pen and signed the last line. Then, while waiting for the ink to dry, and with great precision, he screwed the cap back on the pen. Satisfied that the ink was now dry, Mitch folded the papers and returned them to the envelope.

As he stepped forward and handed them over, he heard Victoria sniffle.

"It's all right, Victoria. I did what was best." Then to Smith, he growled out, "You have my rights. Let her go."

After tucking his revolver into a pocket and grabbing the envelope, Smith pushed Victoria forward into Mitch's arms. "Fill your boots with her. Women are nothing but trouble."

Mitch hauled Victoria closer to him. He looked down at her as she shut her eyes and leaned her cheek against his chest for one long moment. Smith pulled out his cigar case. "It was good doing business with you, MacLeod."

"Get off my land," Mitch spat out.

Smith tapped out a thin cigar and flicked open the matchbox at the top of his case. "If you had read that agreement closely, you would have noticed that I have added a right of way clause. I'm allowed here as many times as I want. For as long as I want. Of course, that assumes that you keep ownership of the land, which we both know won't happen."

Smith gripped a match. After snapping closed the box, he scraped the match head quickly against the striker.

It flared to life, complete with a shot like a small firework rocket, streaming into the doorway beside him.

The burning match head flew into the dark depths of the barn. Straight toward one of the already agitated animals.

It bellowed, and kicked back at another cow before bolting forward to break through the fencing. Suddenly panicking, the others followed suit.

The stampede started so quickly, Mitch had barely enough time to slam Victoria against the barn wall beside the open door. He pressed against her, pinning her so close she could not move a muscle.

Victoria had never heard such a roar as the powerful hooves of frightened animals. She could feel Mitchell's tall frame press her hard against the roughhewn logs of the barn. His hands encircled her head, pinning her so snugly, her cheek scraped against the harsh wood of the barn. The rush of air, thick with bovine fear, brushed past both their faces.

She had no idea where the animals went. They all rushed through the bottleneck toward the open area where her uncle had held a gun on her. At such a speed, it was as if the stampede was a pyrotechnic in itself. And amid the noise of pounding hooves there was a cry and a terrible, sharp crack. Bones breaking? A shot fired? She didn't dare guess. No wonder some heifers had been hurt when the animals had stampeded that afternoon. Now all Mitchell could do was protect her and let the herd run free around his house, through his garden, and down the lane. They would eventually run themselves out.

The herd finally gone, Mitchell eased away from her. Victoria turned to face him, but he spun back, directing her attention away from the barn door. "Don't look!"

She gasped. "Uncle Walter? Did he survive the trampling?"

"Stay back, Victoria."

She did, but turned in time to see Mitchell leaning over Walter's body to check him. Glancing back at Victoria, he shook his head. She bit her lip.

Something fluttered out of the circle of light to land at her feet. She stooped to snatch it. It was the tattered remains of the agreement to sell the mineral rights. Mitch hadn't closed the envelope and somehow the hooves had ripped it to shreds, so much so that the evening breeze spread it like fine seed. All Victoria had now was the envelope and the first page, both barely recognizable.

A growing noise from beyond the house caught their attention. Mitchell grabbed her and shoved her into the barn, pulling the door closed. He pressed her once again against the wall.

When the pounding hooves ended, it was Jake who called out, "Are you all right?"

Mitchell opened the door. "Victoria and I are fine. And you? The herd headed your way."

"I'm fine," Jake answered as he dismounted. "The herd took a sharp left and disappeared toward Proud Bend. The town will stop them. We'll round them up in the morning when they've worn themselves out."

Seeing the body, Jake bent over Walter, his expression as grim as Mitchell's.

"Arson wasn't in his plans tonight after all," Mitch explained, "but murder and blackmail were. He came around the back way so that's why you missed him." He paused. "He came to get me to sign the rights over to him."

Jake flipped open Walter's tattered jacket, revealing

the revolver the older man had tucked in his pocket as well as a wound in his side. He checked the gun. "He'd loaded all the chambers, but I can see that one has accidentally discharged. It shot him in the side, probably when he fell."

"Get a blanket for him," Mitchell ordered Jake. His words were quiet, filled with compassion for the man who'd just threatened to murder and extort.

Victoria glanced over at him. Tears burned her eyes, but they were not for her uncle. They were for everything but him.

"We need to get into Proud Bend," Victoria finally said with equal gentleness. "I should be there for Aunt Louise."

Mitchell nodded. "I'll take you home."

"Thank you."

"Don't look at him." Mitchell paused. "If nothing else, your uncle confirmed what we both suspected."

"What's that?"

His shoulders stiff, he answered, "That I would never be able to give you anything."

"How do you figure that?"

"If he had survived, I would have lost everything because the amount I sold the rights for wasn't enough to cover my mortgage payment. And now I have probably lost more heifers. Some were no doubt injured and whichever ones weren't branded will be claimed by other ranchers. Plus the expense of whatever damages this stampede caused. Either way, I've lost the ranch. I don't even have anything for my children this winter. They came here with nothing."

Victoria bit her lip. Mitchell looked away. He was so wrong, but she found she couldn't speak.

"Where are your horses?" he asked her.

She stifled a sob, swallowing it too quickly for it to bubble to the surface again. "Uncle Walter took Clyde's carriage." With a shaking hand, she pointed to the hill to the south of the house. "It's on the other side of that rise."

He was frowning at her. "Are you up for a walk? I can carry you if you wish."

Victoria shook her head tightly. "No, I don't wish to be carried. I'm perfectly fine." She plucked at her skirt, realizing as she bent that one of the stays of her corset had torn through the soft cotton to jab her in the side. "Although I can't say the same for my clothing. But it's just clothing." With her head high, she lifted her hem and marched away from him.

At the edge of the barn, she turned in time to see Jake covering Uncle Walter. She looked back at Mitchell. His face was a mask of anger and pain. So much tragedy for him. Though he was released from that terrible blackmail, he had nothing, not a thing for his family. His herd had killed a man, and now his ranch faced foreclosure. When he glanced back at her with a hollow expression, she added another tragedy.

They could never find happiness together.

She swallowed hard. It was too late, or perhaps it was never meant to be.

It wasn't about any money, though, or the size of a house. Mitchell was simply too proud. And that pride had been ripped from him, along with a stampeding herd.

Victoria frowned. Wouldn't those mineral rights Uncle Walter had purchased have belonged to him, anyway, after the foreclosure? Why go through with the blackmail? Yes, he'd have had to share them with Clyde, but their value could have made both men rich, for iron and gold and rhyolite were valuable products. Why make Mitch sign over the rights when he just had to wait a day or two?

Victoria trudged along, her mind trying desperately to find the answers she sought. Ahead of her, Mitchell walked so stiffly proud, it must have hurt him. She knew how he thought. He had nothing to give her, so he would not offer even a word of comfort.

The trip into town with Mitchell driving was punctuated by only one short stop. The sheriff met them on the road, his horse as edgy as he himself appeared to be. Mitchell explained all that had happened, keeping his tone tight and clipped.

"I saw the stampede," the sheriff answered. "I was delayed because of my deputy, and when I saw the herd headed into town, I tried to divert it. My concern is mostly for the train. It had been delayed in Denver and has only just arrived. It doesn't have a cow catcher on the front and if any wandered onto the track, they could have derailed the train."

"What happened to the deputy?" Mitchell looked even fouler than before. "Can you get him to find some men to round them up?"

"My deputy is in the drunk tank. He is no longer employed in that capacity." At their bewildered expressions, for Victoria had opened the coupe door to listen, the sheriff explained, "I had asked him to watch the Smith house, but he stayed only a few minutes. When someone reported a fight at the saloon with guns drawn, I went down there and found him unfit to work. This is why I didn't leave for your ranch right away."

Victoria pursed her lips. So that was why no one had followed Uncle Walter when they left. At the thought of him, she turned toward Mitchell. "We had best be going. I need to see my aunt and cousin."

Mitchell eyed her, his frown deepening. She didn't want to linger on what he might be thinking. All she knew was her aunt needed to hear the truth about tonight and Victoria was the best person to gently break it to her.

Fatigue rolled over her but she fought it back. She needed to be strong, for if Aunt Louise decided to blame Mitchell for this, he needed an ally whether or not his pride wanted one.

But as soon as Mitchell helped her out of the coupe and Victoria was standing in the Smith driveway, she felt all nerve, all strength and all courage drain from her as if someone had pulled the plug from the washbasin she'd used the day Rachel taught her how to wash clothes.

Victoria's knees then buckled and she collapsed to the ground.

Dim lamplight greeted Victoria as she opened her eyes. She was in her bed.

In bed? She'd been tucked in her bed, her hair carefully braided and set to one side, her bedclothes snug around her. Blinking, she sat up, and seeing that she was alone, she eased back onto the well-fluffed pillows. Now she remembered. It had happened as soon as she'd stepped from Clyde's coupe. The day had been long and she'd eaten nothing. With that and the broken stay in her corset constantly digging into her side, she'd collapsed. She vaguely recalled being given a draught to help her sleep, and feminine arms preparing her for bed.

It must be the very early hours of Monday, before sunrise. With her lamp still lit, someone must have been sitting up all night with her. Mitchell? Her heart leaped at the thought, but whoever it had been was gone.

After a few moments, when it became clear that her guardian wasn't returning, Victoria slipped from her bed. She felt remarkably refreshed despite all that had happened. It was a new day, a chance to tell Mitchell how she felt, how she was willing to stand by him, even if he had nothing. She quickly set about completing her toilet. As she reached for her dark blue dress, her stomach growled in strong protest, but she had to ignore it. Food must wait.

The choice of attire needed to be somber. Strange that last week, she'd hated somber clothing due to Charles's death, and now the reaction was repeating itself with Walter's.

Victoria wondered who had broken the news to Aunt Louise and Rachel. She should be downstairs with them. But surely, it would be too early, especially if her aunt had been given a draught like she had been.

Satisfied with her dress, she stepped into the hallway. Only one sconce at the end of the hall was lit, and Victoria returned to her room for her lamp. The mood of the house weighed heavy on her like the Boston weather in late summer when a humid afternoon pressed against the bones to warn of an impending thunderstorm. Scents of roasted meat and vegetables, of bread and something sweet snaked up to her, and Victoria was shamed by her empty stomach's reaction to the fact that someone else was up early, cooking and baking.

The tall grandfather clock in the hall downstairs struck the hour as Victoria stepped from the staircase. Pausing, she held her breath and counted. Eleven? How could it be eleven at night? She slowly stepped forward, trying to fathom how long she'd slept. It had been long past eleven when she and Mitchell had returned to the house, so it must be Monday night. Had she slept around the clock?

Light squeezed out from under the closed door of her uncle's study. A flickering light, with a shadow passing in front of it. Her aunt, searching for something? She should see her. Victoria pushed open the door.

Clyde was rifling through some paperwork and lifted his head at the interruption.

"You're up."

Victoria felt her mouth thin. "What are you doing here?"

"With Walter dead, I need to see to his business affairs. His will and such."

The hairs on her neck rose. "This late in the evening? Can it not wait until morning?"

"No. It needs to be done by midnight."

That made no sense. "What needs to be done?"

Clyde paused his search. "Where is the agreement?"

"What agreement?"

"The papers to conclude the sale of MacLeod's mineral rights."

Bristling at Clyde's sharp tone, Victoria stepped in toward the center of the room. "They were destroyed in the stampede. Whatever was left of them blew away."

"So MacLeod did sign the rights over to Walter?"

Don't answer. The two words sparked in her head. She stiffened her shoulders. "Whatever belonged to Walter, be it in this room or in any personal contracts, would be willed to Aunt Louise or Rachel."

Victoria paused. She was sure Mitchell had sold the rights to Uncle Walter, not to the bank. The reason had nagged at Victoria. Had it been done to stop Uncle Walter from having to share the rewards with Clyde? Why was Uncle Walter conspiring behind Clyde's back?

"I know what an honest man MacLeod is," he said. "He won't renege on an agreement, even if the paperwork has been destroyed."

Her thoughts raced. She was running on instinct alone and that instinct reminded her to stay silent. But what if Walter had willed the bank to Clyde? It was unlikely, as Walter hadn't appeared to like his business partner enough to will everything to him.

But Walter had been frustrated by his family's disrespect of him. Had he planned to punish them after his death?

Clyde returned to his search.

"What are you looking for?"

"Walter took our copy of the mortgage MacLeod had taken out on his ranch. I know he brought it home. He would need it in case MacLeod didn't sign those sale papers." Clyde looked up. "MacLeod has less than an hour to make his mortgage payment or else he's in default."

Victoria raced forward. "You can't be serious! After all that happened, you don't have the decency to stop work for a day?"

"Ha! If you only knew. Do you think I'd risk losing this valuable opportunity?"

"What valuable opportunity? The ranch? His herd is who knows where, and his best pasture nothing but a burned-out field." She gasped. "You want the mineral rights, don't you? You're as bad as Uncle Walter."

Clyde chuckled.

Victoria gasped as she suddenly realized something. "Uncle Walter was doing your bidding? He was your puppet. You're the one who has been pulling the strings all along, yet Uncle Walter was trying to double-cross you."

Spying a set of papers, Clyde grabbed them before lifting his gaze to her. "Very astute. Oh, I'm not after just mineral rights. If MacLeod signed them once, he'll sign them again. There is much more at stake than them."

"Such as?"

"My bank holds the mortgages on most of the land and businesses here. Of course, some are thriving and will pay off what they owe in due time. The bank will get its share. But I will get the bank and eventually, I'll own most of Proud Bend."

Victoria frowned. What about Aunt Louise and Rachel? Had Walter willed everything to Clyde?

No. Something else was amiss.

Clyde stopped rifling through the papers he'd found. "But back to the issue at hand. I have a proposition for you, Victoria. Do you want MacLeod to stay on his land, free of debt?"

"Of course."

Clyde consulted his pocket watch. His expression showed mock worry. "He has only forty minutes to make his payment."

She rushed forward a few steps. "You can't expect that, not after what has happened! Do you even know where Mitchell is? He's probably seeing to his herd, even this late. They stampeded."

Clyde shook his head. "Ha! Rather, being relieved of the burden of your presence, he's probably celebrating down at the saloon. He's been there before, you know."

Victoria felt her face heat. "Only to escort Rachel as she did ministry work with the women."

"Rachel is a fool." His gaze turned cunning, licentious. "You on the other hand, are quite a prize. I'm more than willing to relinquish my right to call in the loan on one small ranch. You see, you represent something far more valuable, whereas others, like Louise, are a waste." He looked thoughtful. "Although, I was always surprised at how much she knew of Walter's business dealings. She is quite intelligent. It's too bad really that…"

"That what? What are you saying?"

Tucking the papers he'd found into his jacket, Clyde smiled. It was wide enough to see the gaps where his teeth were missing.

"In about half an hour, I will go to MacLeod's ranch and begin foreclosure proceedings on it." Clyde shook his head. "He'll have to move away. I heard that one large ranch in Texas is looking for good, reliable ranch hands."

"And the children?"

"He'll soon learn that he can't keep them." Clyde shrugged. "The boys can be shipped to various farms. The girls shoved into an orphanage, even the illegitimate brat. Oh, yes, I know about her. It doesn't take a doctor to figure out that MacLeod isn't her father. Ironic, really. The brat's mother had hoped that by willing her share of the ranch to the baby, she'd be cared for, but now, the exact opposite will happen." He laughed again, then sobered. "Of course, all this could be avoided if you marry me, Victoria. I'll forgive the mortgage on MacLeod's ranch."

He sounded so calm, as if this was a simple business transaction.

"I'm not that valuable."

"Don't pretend to be modest. It doesn't become you. You're too much like your uncle, too proud."

Victoria stepped back. She didn't understand, nor did

she care. All she could think about was Mitchell. Losing everything he'd worked for, and worse than that, losing his children. Even Emily.

Please, Lord, let it not be!

She had the answer. Suddenly she understood, in a small way, true sacrifice. How the evil of pride was stripped away and that in Jesus there was only sacrificial love.

She knew, oh, so humbly, that her sacrifice would never compare to her Lord's, but if it kept the family she loved together, she would do it.

"If I agree to marry you, will you give me those mortgage papers and fully forgive his loan? Right away?"

"Well, not quite that quickly. You see, I don't trust you. We will marry first thing in the morning."

"But I want my mother here."

"That's not possible. Besides, if she cares about her brother, she'll be in mourning and so shocked that you're marrying so soon after a death, she'll have to be medicated, too."

Victoria didn't understand. Who else would have to be medicated? Clyde's words made no sense.

He continued. "I'll make the arrangements and you will tell your pastor you are more than happy to marry me with no coercion on anyone's part. Once we're married, I'll give you the papers."

Victoria had witnessed enough arranged marriages to know that while Brahmin men valued honor, that didn't always extend to others. She knew how her mother had handled those arrangements. Victoria's expression was as cool as Clyde's was false when she said, "In that case, we will have a neutral party hold the papers until the wedding is over. And I also reserve the right to examine the papers before they are handed over to said neutral party. That person will then be one of our witnesses. He will be instructed to hand those papers over to me as soon as the ceremony is completed."

Clyde shook his head in awe, obviously pleased. "You're going to make me a fine wife, Victoria."

"I doubt that." She continued her cool look. "I also demand that you leave my family alone. And Mitchell's."

Clyde lifted his bushy brows, the effect lining his forehead with half a dozen wrinkles. "Acceptable."

"Now, who to trust?" Victoria's stale smile broadened. "The sheriff, of course."

Clyde's smug expression fell. Then grew again. "A cunning woman, a refreshing change from my first wife." He walked closer. "Fine. We have a deal, then. We should find the sheriff and, in the morning, the pastor. Victoria, I'm thrilled beyond words that you have agreed to become my bride. You'll never know how thrilled."

He leaned forward to steal a kiss, but Victoria turned her head away in time. Then, from the corner of her eye, she spied movement in the open doorway.

Her heart dropped. Mitchell was standing there, and his hurt expression stabbed like a knife into her heart.

Chapter Twenty-Four

$\sim\!\!\sim$

Mitch had found the front door open. When he'd called out to the silence, he'd heard nothing and simply walked in.

Late last night, when Victoria had collapsed as soon as her feet touched the broken slag and gravel beneath her, he'd carried her up to her room. A young maid took over. He'd sent for the doctor before meeting briefly with Louise and Rachel. Abernathy had been there in that front parlor, the excuse of his missing coupe had kept him lingering, no doubt.

The excuse didn't hold water anymore, but still the old man had stuck around.

Mitch had given the ladies the briefest of explanations of Walter's death. While Louise had remained stoic, Rachel had shed tears. And Abernathy... Well, Mitch didn't care how he reacted.

After the doctor had arrived, Mitch had headed to the pastor's house. Rachel would want the spiritual comforts the pastor and his wife could offer. His actions had been wooden, done by rote, as if he was in some terrible dream.

He'd spent all day Monday rounding up his cattle and dealing with the sheriff. He'd taken several breaks to go to the bank to ask for an extension, only to find the place each time in an uproar with Abernathy missing and Walter dead. Adding to the mess were the men who'd purchased his heifers. With his best dead or lame, all they'd wanted was their money back.

Now, late Monday night, Mitch had returned to the Smith house to check on Victoria. Surely, she would be up, unable to sleep.

She'd been up, all right, up and accepting a proposal that no decent man would have offered at such a time as this. But Victoria succumbed to the desperation instead of trying to figure things out. The idea wrenched his heart.

He'd also come to the Smith house to tell her that he was going to fight to keep his ranch and that he was going to ask her to stay in Proud Bend for a while, in case she felt the need to dash away now that her benefactor had died. Her aunt and cousin would need her, he'd been prepared to argue.

He needed her.

Well, all that was draining from him, like a heavy rain on the hard pan of a dry summer, rolling away between the stalks of parched grass on the high pasture, on its way to the Proud River.

Now Mitch couldn't believe the scene he'd just witnessed. All he could do was stalk away. If Victoria had called out his name as he stormed away, he hadn't heard it.

His heart squeezed. She'd been accepting Clyde's proposal of marriage. She didn't love the man, Mitch knew that, but she loved her lifestyle and had been too desperate to see any other option. If the only way she could deal with it was to marry a gap-toothed old man whose scruples were on par with her uncle's, then so be it.

He shouldn't blame her. Frontier life was rough, even living at the Smith house would be considered difficult for someone used to Boston with all its finery and access to whatever new inventions that made life easier.

Forget her. He wasn't going to fight anymore. He would return to his family home in Michigan to help his aging father on the farm, to introduce his children to their grandparents and to ask them to help him raise his family. This was his only choice now. His parents were good, loving people, but their farm had been their dream. He'd always wanted his own life, something he could say he'd built all by himself.

"Mitchell!"

He stopped at the open front door, torn between wanting to turn and allowing his pride to fuel his flight from this house. In that moment, he hated himself. If he turned, he was sure he would acquiesce to whatever she said. His pride railed against it. Pride was trying to stop him from turning.

He shoved that pride away and spun on his heel.

Victoria rushed up to him. She seemed breathless. "What did you hear?"

"I heard you accepting Abernathy's proposal. What do you think I heard?"

"Allow me to explain."

"There isn't any need. I'm not an idiot."

She grabbed his arm, propelled him out the front door and shut it behind them. Mitch wondered if she would have ever done that back in Boston. How she had changed.

The truth dawned on him—he knew she'd changed. He'd known it for a while. So why accept Abernathy's proposal if that was so?

For a long moment, they just stared at each other. Finally, she said, quietly, "Why are you here?"

He pulled in a deep breath. Should he say "I came here to see you"?

"I just woke up. Let me ask you something. What are you going to do about the ranch? You've missed your payment."

"Only by a day because the bank was in an uproar. But that doesn't make any difference. I don't have the money. If the bank wants my ranch, it can have it." He shrugged. "I'll start again. I've done it before, and I can do it again."

"And the children? Would you give them up?"

He frowned and shook his head. "Of course not! Why should I?"

"Who will take care of them?"

"I'll go back east to my parents' farm. My mother would like to have a crack at educating them, I'm sure."

Mitch watched Victoria swallow. Then she whispered, "You'll keep the ranch, Mitch. You'll see."

How would she know that? "Maybe, but I've already lost some good heifers and I may lose more livestock in the coming days. The herd has been spooked and there is a good chance that the heifers I'm left with will lose their calves. It can happen when they're under stress. They will be more so because the best pasture I had is now burned."

"Is there any other place you can let them graze?"

"No. The neighboring ranchers are angry that I fenced in my pasture land. But I did it because it's my land and because I didn't want your uncle trying to sneak on it and start some kind of illegal mining operation." He sagged. "It's over for me, but at least you get what you want. All the wealth and comforts of Boston, without the humidity in the summer and the dampness in winter."

She stepped closer and for that moment, he was tempted to reach out for her. But she belonged to another now, even though he couldn't deny the temptation. But it wasn't right to want what belonged to another man.

In the dull light from the lamp above them, Victoria's eyes glistened. "Neither of us is getting what we want."

As Mitch opened his mouth to contradict her, furious footfalls tore up the driveway toward them. They both turned.

Mitch recognized Rosa Carrera from the saloon. The young woman from down south rushed up to them, her heavy shawl blowing in the wind. Mitch had met her when he'd escorted Rachel to minister to the women a while back.

"Mitch! I'm glad I found you. Where's Rachel?"

Victoria stared at the woman. She knew Rachel was doing ministry at the saloon, but to hear a young, unfortunate woman speak of her cousin as though she were a *confidante*… How was that possible?

It was because Rachel would cultivate a relationship of trust.

"She must be inside," Mitchell said after introducing the women. "There has been a death in the family."

Victoria glanced at him for a moment, forgetting about Uncle Walter. She had been trying to tell him that his ranch was safe, that he could continue on, but with what? A compromised herd? It would take years to rebuild it.

At least he had the ranch and the herd to rebuild.

The young woman was shaking her head. "I know. She sent a message saying what had happened, and that she would still come tonight."

"I'm sure the doctor has given her a sleeping draught." Victoria took the woman's arm. "Let us walk you back."

Rosa wrenched her arm free. "No! Rachel said she would never take a draught! She said she would come! We were going to talk about that man Mark who knew Jesus. I wanted to tell her that—" The girl faltered a moment, her accent increasing. "Well, I remember learning about Jesus as a child, but I understand now and well, I wanted to tell Rachel I was ready."

Mitchell asked, "For what?"

Victoria knew. Rosa wanted to give her life to the Lord.

She then gasped as yet another realization dawned. "Mitchell, something *is* wrong! I remember Rachel telling me that nothing would take her away from her evening activities."

"Surely not tonight!"

"But, yes, Mitch," Rosa cried. "I have her note." She pulled from a small pocket a crinkled sheet of paper. "She said she would come."

Victoria gripped Mitchell's arm tighter. "We have to find her. I have a terrible feeling that Clyde has done something." She spun and threw open the door, yelling behind her, "Rosa, go get the doctor."

With Mitchell in tow, Victoria raced to Walter's study, but found it empty. Where was Clyde?

"He's gone. I didn't realize what Clyde was saying to me tonight, but now I know." She pushed off from the doorjamb and tore upstairs to her aunt's room, the first on the right. She could hear Mitchell behind her. Once inside the fussy and crowded bedroom, Victoria raced to the bed. In her night clothes, Louise lay still, on her stomach, her face turned into her pillow.

Yanking hard to put her aunt on her back, she pulled the woman free of the smothering effects of the soft pillow. Her aunt drew in a deep breath, but didn't stir. She seemed deeply unconscious. Drugged, even.

"Rachel!" Victoria rushed out and down the hall to her cousin's room. Mitchell pushed past her and barreled inside. Rachel was face down on the bed, fully dressed, her head pressed into the pillow.

Mitch rolled her over to face the door. He leaned over and smelled her breath. "She's had a sleeping draught. I bet it had laudanum in it. They mix it with honey and whiskey." He looked up, his face a mask of worry. "Look at the bruising around her neck. I think it's been forced into her. Rachel would never willingly take laudanum. She told me once that it's an insidious drug and that she has seen several women brought to ruin with it. And the way both your aunt and cousin were turned into their pillows, it's as if they were meant to suffocate."

Victoria began to cry. "They would have, too. I wonder if it was Clyde's movements upstairs here that awoke me. He could have waited until the draughts took hold before he moved them onto their stomachs. Is there anything we can do for them now?"

"I don't think it was too long ago that they took it. What made you suspicious?"

"Clyde said something curious. He called Rachel a fool and Aunt Louise a waste. It was very odd. He talked about drugging my mother if she came." She swallowed hard as she sought to figure out what he meant. "Clyde was searching for your deed tonight. I think I understand what he was saying. He only wanted me because if Aunt Louise and Rachel die, Walter's share of the bank would fall to my mother."

Victoria put her hand to her mouth. "If my mother chose not to come out here, Clyde would have control. If she came out here, he could easily end her life as he was trying to end Rachel's and Aunt Louise's. A laudanum overdose wouldn't be unheard of when a woman has suffered a tragedy, and he hinted that my mother might suffer the same fate as Aunt Louise and Rachel. I didn't realize what he meant until now."

Mitchell took Victoria into his arms and held her there. "It's all right," he finally said. "The doctor will be here soon."

A commotion started downstairs. Both Mitchell and Victoria hurried out into the hall. The housekeeper, now roused, had stopped Rosa from bolting up the stairs, but Victoria could see a middle-aged man push past them.

Mitchell tugged her to one side. "That's the doctor." He gave the man a brief explanation.

"If it hasn't been too long, I will be able to revive them," he said. "Charcoal does well in the stomach, but I'll need some water and a large basin first. This will be very messy." He barked out a few instructions to the housekeeper before looking over at Victoria. "You're pale. You had best lie down."

Mitchell took her into her room, directed there by Victoria. As she lay down, she grabbed Mitchell. "We have to stop Clyde!"

"I will. He won't get far."

She clung to him. "Mitchell, I am so sorry for all I've done. But you must understand. Clyde was planning to go to your ranch and begin foreclosure proceedings and I was afraid you'd be forced to give up your children. The boys would be sent to farms and the girls to an orphanage. But Clyde promised me he'd forgive your mortgage if I married him. You can rebuild your herd, Mitchell. I wanted what was best for you, and to keep your family together. But now, it's overshadowed by all of this and Clyde still has the mortgage papers. He'll follow through with his threat."

Mitchell's mouth fell open. "You were going to marry him to save my family? I came here tonight to see if you were all right, but also to ask you if you would stay. If you like, we could start again someplace. I can't give you all you deserve, but I can give you my love. And my name."

"Deserve? I deserve nothing! Oh, Mitchell, what a fool I've been with my pride. Even my pride in my foolish and simple accomplishments. To think, I believed I knew everything about running a house after one lesson." She leaned forward, a watery smile forming. "Are you proposing to me?"

He nodded as a smile took over his face. "I love you, Victoria. I want to marry you."

Her smile echoed his. "I love you, too."

"It won't be an easy life, but I can tell you that my pride would be a far worse companion. It was a sin against God and you, and I am glad to say I'm rid of it. It was my love for you that conquered it. Just now, I knew I needed to let it go to turn around and face you."

He paused, and Victoria's expression fell. "What about Clyde?"

"No need to worry. The sheriff will stop him. He'll have to pay for what he's done." He pulled her close. "And I can tell you for certain that Pastor Wyseman would not have performed the ceremony if he thought for a moment that you were being blackmailed."

She smiled through her tears. Mitchell loved her! Suddenly, that love gave her the strength and courage to look to the future. A future that included all her family. *Lord, save Rachel and Aunt Louise. Keep them safe.*

She repeated that same prayer often as the night wore away and morning finally came. Victoria waited impatiently for the doctor to stop rushing back and forth between the two other bedrooms.

Finally, he closed Rachel's door and walked into Victoria's bedroom. "They're both going to be fine."

Victoria sagged and offered a new prayer, a silent one of thanks. Mitchell took her in his arms as the doctor explained his care.

"I administered an emetic and then gave them charcoal. Miss Smith is awake and talking, but Mrs. Smith is still groggy. They had been given large doses of laudanum, far more than I prescribed." His expression sobered. "I'm told it was Clyde Abernathy who prepared their doses. I sent a note to the sheriff that Abernathy be found to answer to the charges of attempted murder, for he then turned them on their stomachs and their faces into their pillows. If the laudanum hadn't killed them, they would have smothered."

Victoria shivered, and Mitchell held her tight.

The day drifted by slowly as she spent her time checking on her aunt and cousin, so much so that Rachel ordered her from her room. Downstairs, and trying not to be miffed by her cousin, Victoria met Mitchell in the front room. He'd disappeared for some time and had returned.

"Did the sheriff find Clyde?" she asked.

"He was caught boarding the train for Denver. Clyde would have been gone but the train had hit some of my heifers and had been delayed. He had a ticket to San Francisco. He knew he had been caught and was running." Mitchell led her to the settee, where they sat beside each other. "I also went to the bank today. They will extend my payment date, but it comes with a hefty penalty that has to be paid first. It's going to be rough for a while, Victoria."

"Yes," she answered practically. "But after all we've endured, and nearly losing Rachel and Aunt Louise, I've learned I can handle anything. As long as you help me start the occasional fire in the stove."

Mitchell laughed just as the maid entered with a silver server. On it was a letter that had arrived with the train.

"For me?" Victoria asked as she took it. Who would be writing her? Her mother? She opened it and read quickly. Then gasped. "It's from Mr. Lacewood. He sold my house and the summer home. They belonged to me, not my mother, but were to be in my mother's care."

She read further. "It sold for more than anticipated. Francis bought the property only one day after I left. He's engaged now."

After reading more, she looked up in wonder, holding out a check she'd pulled from beneath the letter. "All of Charles's debts have been paid and Lacewood has sent me the balance." Victoria bit her lip. "After all I've learned these past few days, it feels as though I don't deserve this money. I'll send this check back."

"No." Mitchell's hand stilled hers as she began to slip it back into the envelope. She could feel the warmth of his palm press comfortingly against her knuckles. "Your father left you his estate because he wanted you to have it.

This is what's left of it. Don't send it back just to absolve any guilt you might have. This money is yours, Victoria. It's neither a source of pride nor contempt. It's just money. Give it away to charity if you must, but don't make any rash decisions because you've learned a hard lesson."

"But—"

"No buts. You have a lot to consider. We both do. I have my mineral rights, and plan to lease them. It's the only way to rebuild my ranch. I know of several men starting new mining companies who are interested in them. It's good to diversify, but I won't decide anything quickly, and nor should you."

Mitchell was right, Victoria thought, her heart swelling with love for him. She should be neither proud nor in contempt of the money she now had. She smiled suddenly. "I know what I should do with this money. I want to invest it first thing in the morning."

"That soon?" Mitchell lifted his eyebrows and a small smile hovered over his lips. "Were you paying any mind to what I just said?"

"Of course I was. I'm taking it to the bank." As Mitchell began to speak, she lifted up her hand to stop him. "Even though I will follow you anywhere, Mitchell, and I will live anywhere you live, I'm going to pay off your mortgage here and now. I'm going to invest in your ranch. Maybe we can also raise sheep or grow more vegetables for the church to distribute." She boldly leaned over and kissed Mitchell on the lips. "But most important, I want to invest in our future, as husband and wife. I expect to get a good return."

He laughed out loud and pulled her close. "Yes, ma'am. You will get the best return. I promise."

Epilogue

Five months later

Just inside the church vestry, Victoria completed one last check of her wedding gown. It was white, even though white wasn't the current choice for brides. Victoria didn't care. She'd seen it in a shop window in Proud Bend, where it had apparently been for several years, and she loved it.

"You look perfect."

Victoria looked over her shoulder at Rachel, her maid of honor. Behind her stood Clare, her only bridesmaid, who straightened her own pale green gown with nervous fingers. Thankfulness swelled in her for the friendship of these two women, not to mention gratitude that Rachel and Aunt Louise were all right.

Rachel turned and took hold of Mary's hand. The little girl held a basket of early flower petals in her other hand.

"Aunt Rachel, I want to throw the petals on the floor like Miss Walsh promised. I can't do that if you hold my hand."

Victoria looked up to Clare, who shrugged. "I read in a recent periodical that it's all the rage."

From deep in the church, Emily wailed, her tiny voice reaching through the closed door. She was sitting up on her own now and grabbing everything in sight. Aunt Louise held her, no doubt having removed her fine feather hat so it would not be torn to shreds. Mother had arrived last week, having moved here and the two older women were sharing the responsibility of caring for the active baby.

"Let's go. We're late as it is," Rachel announced with her usual briskness.

On her signal, Matthew, having been waiting patiently, opened the door into the sanctuary just moments after Victoria stepped out of the way so she would not be seen until it was appropriate. Mary slipped free of Rachel to walk first, tenderly, up the aisle, just as she'd been instructed. With a cheeky smile, she left a trail of early spring rose petals in her wake as she passed her siblings and the townspeople in attendance.

Clare stepped out next. Victoria saw Mr. Livingstone from the recording office offer his arm to her. The young woman smiled up at him, but his solemn manner refused anything but the most sober of expressions.

Rachel leaned over and kissed Victoria on the cheek as she passed her cousin to enter next. "This is your special day. Take your time walking up the aisle." She slipped out to allow Jake to take her hand and place it on his forearm.

Then, finally, it was Victoria's turn. A year ago, she had been dreaming of a perfect Boston wedding at the height of the season in Boston's finest cathedral, a wedding to rival any in New England.

Now she was in a tiny Western church on an early spring day, the only flowers in her bouquet those that bloomed on the south side of Mitchell's barn. And her home would be a three-room house up in the mountains.

It was going to be perfect.

Matthew opened the door wider to allow her gown a full, worthy entrance. Victoria smiled to herself. *Worthy.* She wasn't worthy of the happiness she felt but was grateful to God for it just the same.

And grateful for the man standing tall at the altar. Her husband. He turned, and with his loving gaze, he drew her closer.

Closer to a life full of love and learning, a life in which pride was kept only for their faith and for the children, all of them and any more that might come.

Her heart swelled.

* * * * *

If you loved this story, don't miss these other heartwarming books by Barbara Phinney

**BOUND TO THE WARRIOR
PROTECTED BY THE WARRIOR
SHELTERED BY THE WARRIOR**

Find more great reads at www.LoveInspired.com

Dear Reader,

Thank you so much for taking the time to read my book. *The Nanny Solution* certainly laid out what pride can do to us, and what the Bible thinks of it.

Have you ever allowed pride to prevent you from doing what is right? I think we all have to some degree. I think that's why my book's theme rang so clearly for me. We all have pride, and for some, it will be their downfall.

At one point, Victoria learns that her love for her mother is more important than pride and that's a valuable lesson.

If you're struggling with some matter of pride, especially when dealing with a loved one who's hurt you, ask yourself this: What is worth more in the long run—your love for this person or feeding your stubborn pride? I can tell you one thing. Pride is never satisfied. It's a terribly hungry beast. Don't feed it.

I hope you enjoyed this book and I hope you will check out other Love Inspired titles. These books are filled with warmth, encouragement and, of course, love!

Blessings today and always,

Barbara Phinney

REQUEST YOUR FREE BOOKS!

2 FREE INSPIRATIONAL NOVELS
PLUS 2 FREE MYSTERY GIFTS

Love Inspired® HISTORICAL

YES! Please send me 2 FREE Love Inspired® Historical novels and my 2 FREE mystery gifts (gifts are worth about $10). After receiving them, if I don't wish to receive any more books, I can return the shipping statement marked "cancel." If I don't cancel, I will receive 4 brand-new novels every month and be billed just $4.99 per book in the U.S. or $5.49 per book in Canada. That's a saving of at least 17% off the cover price. It's quite a bargain! Shipping and handling is just 50¢ per book in the U.S. and 75¢ per book in Canada.* I understand that accepting the 2 free books and gifts places me under no obligation to buy anything. I can always return a shipment and cancel at any time. Even if I never buy another book, the two free books and gifts are mine to keep forever.

102/302 IDN GH6Z

Name _____ (PLEASE PRINT) _____

Address _____ Apt. # _____

City _____ State/Prov. _____ Zip/Postal Code _____

Signature (if under 18, a parent or guardian must sign)

Mail to the **Reader Service:**
IN U.S.A.: P.O. Box 1867, Buffalo, NY 14240-1867
IN CANADA: P.O. Box 609, Fort Erie, Ontario L2A 5X3

Want to try two free books from another series?
Call 1-800-873-8635 or visit www.ReaderService.com.

* Terms and prices subject to change without notice. Prices do not include applicable taxes. Sales tax applicable in N.Y. Canadian residents will be charged applicable taxes. Offer not valid in Quebec. This offer is limited to one order per household. Not valid for current subscribers to Love Inspired Historical books. All orders subject to credit approval. Credit or debit balances in a customer's account(s) may be offset by any other outstanding balance owed by or to the customer. Please allow 4 to 6 weeks for delivery. Offer available while quantities last.

Your Privacy—The Reader Service is committed to protecting your privacy. Our Privacy Policy is available online at www.ReaderService.com or upon request from the Reader Service.

We make a portion of our mailing list available to reputable third parties that offer products we believe may interest you. If you prefer that we not exchange your name with third parties, or if you wish to clarify or modify your communication preferences, please visit us at www.ReaderService.com/consumerschoice or write to us at Reader Service Preference Service, P.O. Box 9062, Buffalo, NY 14240-9062. Include your complete name and address.

LIHI5

"Just wanted to return your book."

Book?

Lula May saw her children slinking out of the barn,
guilty looks on their faces. So that's why they'd made such
nuisances of themselves out at the pasture. They'd wanted
her to send them off to play so they could take the book to
Edmund. And she knew exactly why. Those little rascals
were full-out matchmaking! Casting a look at Edmund,
she faced the inevitable, which wasn't really all that bad.
"Will you come in for coffee?"

He tilted his hat back to reveal his broad forehead, where
dark blond curls clustered and made him look younger
than his thirty-three years. "Coffee would be good."

Lula May led him in through the back door. To her
horror, Uncle sat at the kitchen table hungrily eyeing
the cake she'd made for Edmund…and almost forgotten
about. Now she'd have no excuse for not introducing them
before she figured out how to get rid of Floyd.

"Edmund, this is Floyd Jones." She forced herself to add,
"My uncle. Floyd, this is my neighbor, Edmund McKay."

As the children had noted last week when Edmund first

stepped into her kitchen, he took up a good portion of the room. Even Uncle seemed a bit unsettled by his presence. While the men chatted about the weather, however, Lula May could see the old wiliness and false charm creeping into Uncle's words and facial expressions. She recognized the old man's attempt to figure Edmund out so he could control him.

Pauline and Daniel worked at the sink, urgent whispers going back and forth. Why had they become so bold in their matchmaking? Was it possible they sensed the danger of Uncle's presence and wanted to lure Edmund over here to protect her? She wouldn't have any of that. She'd find a solution without any help from anybody, especially not her neighbor. Her only regret was that she hadn't been able to protect the children from realizing Uncle wasn't a good man. If she could have found a way to be nicer to him… No, that wasn't possible. Not when he'd come here for the distinct purpose of seizing everything she owned.

The men enjoyed their coffee and cake, after which Edmund suggested they take a walk around the property to build up an appetite for supper.

"We'd like to go for a walk with you, Mr. McKay," Pauline said. "May we, Mama?"

Lula May hesitated. Let them continue their matchmaking or make them spend time with Uncle? Neither option pleased her. When had she lost control of her household? About a week before Uncle arrived, that was when, the day when Edmund had walked into her kitchen and invited himself into her…or rather, her eldest son's life.

"You may go, but don't pester Mr. McKay." She gave the children a narrow-eyed look of warning.

Their innocent blinks did nothing to reassure her.

Don't miss
A FAMILY FOR THE RANCHER
by Louise M. Gouge, available August 2016 wherever
Love Inspired® Historical books and ebooks are sold.

www.LoveInspired.com

LIHEXP0716